CIRCLE OF CHANCE

CIRCLE OF CHANCE

MICHAEL DION

ITI Music Corporation

ITI Music Corporation Publishing

16057 Tampa Palms Bl West

Tampa, FL 33543

Registered with Library of Congress October 2017

ISBN: 978-0-9995684-0-8

Printed and bound in the United States

Cover: RoxC LLC/www.roxc.graphics/Roxanne Clapp

Author Photo: Gigante Productions Inc.

Model: Gabrielle Oosterling

To My Wife Laura, sometimes it's been a long road, but we are still here and experiencing life together. Much Love to you as we continue down this path.

To My Daughter, you have been our shining star and we love you dearly.

To My Mom, because without giving birth to me, I couldn't have written anything.

I wish to thank my family and friends for listening to me for years about this book. For listening to me about my next endeavor, including my dreams and bucket list, which seems to grow on a regular basis. I want to thank my music partner for his own efforts, both in writing his own novels and for his music that continues to express thoughts and emotions.

Writing has been an almost life long journey, whether in poetry, birthday and Christmas cards or drafts of potential books. Hopefully those who do read my penned works will enjoy them as much as I have in creating them.

CIRCLE OF CHANCE

CHAPTER 1

My name is Jack Riley. I'm a private detective, living in the desert community of Palm Springs California amongst the rich and the array of locales. Some are movie stars from Hollywood, some are artists with galleries and such and then there are the "family members from Chicago" and other major cities of the East Coast. Likewise, and a bit strange living amongst and amid all this grandeur is the Army Cavalry and Navy Pilot Officers training for war, cattlemen and "Latinos", who do much of the "busy" work in our fair community by mowing and caring for the lawns, being busboys and cooks in the many fine restaurants and of course picking the California crops.

It's Tuesday, April 7, 1942. It was another one of those bright sun lit days, but I am unaware that it's a day that will take me into the depths of the war and the people and organizations that control the outcome.

After a tough year of losing the men in my life, my Dad, Captain John Riley, and then my fiancé, Lieutenant James O'Sullivan at Pearl Harbor, I decided that I needed a change of pace, life style and residence. So, I packed up my belongings and decided to move from San Diego to Palm Springs in the middle of January. And while most of the women in America, whose husbands or boyfriends were now in the service, and who found work as one of the thousands, "Rosie The Riveter", in the factory and shops across the United States, I turned to an occupation that was unheard of for any woman, being a Private Investigator.

Growing up, my daddy always told me that I had an inquisitive mind. As he always reminded me, "Jacqueline, you have a head like a rock, work and think like a man and will do as you damn well please", so after settling into the community, I applied for my license with the help of family and friends and received my certification in late February.

Even though I receive a monthly allotment from the Navy and my Dad and the remainder of his estate, I try to live a pretty normal life except for clothes, which I love being "dressed to the nines", even in the desert weather. And though my income afforded me the luxury that most other women and or men did not have particularly in the environment today, I still wanted to work and found the lifestyle in The Springs my cup of tea.

As I gazed into my drink I thought, "Somewhere on foreign lands, our "boys" were fighting for the sake of freedom and humanity. In Europe, they were fighting the "Gerrys'". And in the Pacific, the Navy and the Marines were slugging it out with the ever shrewd "Japs".

Me, I was at my favorite restaurant, Pasquale's, trying to forget about the "PI" business of finding lost purses and dogs, the war and how hot it was in the desert, even in April. Pasquale's was also a favorite of both locals and the "families", and since arriving here I had met several of them through my "PI" business of tracking down missing things. Funny, most of them respected me once they got to know that I was a no-nonsense woman, loyal and good at what I did. So, I was pretty much employed by at least one of the "family members" most of the time, as they knew that I could be trusted. And they always paid, which didn't hurt my pocket book.

Listening to Joey B., I relaxed sitting at the mahogany bar, having my normal gin & tonic, while the trio played an

Irving Berlin tune, "A Pretty Girl is like A Melody".
Minding my business, I was lamenting my lost lover and a
great Dad when appearing in the front door was one of the
local L.A. boys, Nicky the Leg. A nickname presented to
him during his stint in Chicago. Apparently, some of the
boys cut Nicky alongside his family jewels, where the leg
and the abdomen were joined together, so I am told.
Fortunately for Nicky, they were only giving him a
message for his mistakes, otherwise he would have become
a soprano. This story was told to me repeatedly, when
some of the boys had too much to drink.

I had first met Nicky back in February after I had moved to
the Springs. He was at the restaurant and doing his Mario
Lanza imitation, singing to his colleagues. He made fun of
me that night when he found out I was a P.I. He kept
calling me Sam, after the movie "The Maltese Falcon".

Anyway, Nicky dressed in an Italian light weight black
shark-skin suit, but rumpled shirt, approached the bar
where I was sitting and plunked his heavy body down next
to me and said, "Good evening Sam or should I say Jack!
As usual you are looking rather well, or should I say
beautiful. It's kind of funny, I've never known a woman
who could wear a man's suit and look so damn much like a
lady. And by the way, did I mention that blue pin stripe
looks great on you. I'll have to get your tailor's name the
next time I decide to buy a suit. Did the blue sapphire
buttons cost extra?"

I looked at him and chuckled. I said, "Nicky, you're full of
it". He didn't know how to respond to me but forced a
smile and then told me that his boss, who had come to Los
Angeles from New York, needed my help. I looked at him
again and smiled and said, "Is this any way for a woman of

my stature to get a date." He laughed with that big goofy smile of his said, "No Jack, he needs for you to find someone, here in the area." Looking back at him after taking a sip of my drink I said, "What for, you're here along with half a dozen or more of your buds that could do the job. Can't you guys locate this someone?"

Nicky thought for a second then leaned forward and said, "It's not family business, its personal business that only a P.I. should handle. So, he asked me to ask you if you could handle it for him, since you are a dame and all!"

After some minor chit-chat and thinking that I was bored looking for dogs, I said to Nicky, "OK, I'll see your boss in a couple of days, as I have to go to San Diego tomorrow on my own personal business."

Nicky smiled and said, "Thanks Jack, I knew we could count on you." Then Nicky turned to Eddie behind the bar and asked for a beer and smiled at me again as he walked to a nearby table where other known "family associates" were eating dinner.

As I continued to sip my drink and watch Nicky as he sat down, I turned to Eddie and asked him to bring me a medium size plate of Bolognese, with rolls and a salad. Eddie knew that it was my way of saying I need some food, so I don't have to crawl out of the restaurant again this evening. Unfortunately for me, since arriving here in the desert four months ago, I seemed to have gotten into a habit of being tipsy on an occasion or two, but I also knew that I was secure and protected amongst these "guys", because no one had ever taken advantage of me, because of my occupation.

On Wednesday, I found myself winding my way through the canyons and cow pastures, driving BIG RED. It was a real beauty, my 1941 Buick Roadmaster, 2 door convertible with 8 cylinders and painted red with red interior. Like most American cars, it was a heavy car, not like a foreign made Ferrari or Porsche, but I loved it just the same. Though normally this region was mostly dusted in ground fog, driving from The Springs to San Diego, it was one of those clear and cloudless days.

Though I would have normally just driven the speed limit, I decided to hasten my way to the port city that was now in a complete chaotic state due to the war. It became a man-made machine to crank out ships, sailors and ammunition. With so many young boot camp sailors now being placed on ships that were not destroyed at Pearl Harbor and on newly built ships, the city of San Diego had become a well-oiled war machine. It was christening ships as fast as they could be built and loading troops and bombs on them almost weekly. This once sleepy seaside community was now caught up on the news of the war and if their loved ones were still alive. Everything that was made was now a war commodity.

My closest friend, Commander Derek Kent, who helped me through the past year's calamities, was my fiancés best friend and shipmate. He had asked me to come down to San Diego to look over a case that he was handling and see if I could lend a hand in a little investigative work. Derek was now the staff jag officer for the Task Force of the Seventh Fleet. However, during the bombing of Pearl Harbor, he and James were stationed on board the USS Tennessee. James was on duty when the attack came and was killed instantly from the torpedoes that initially hit the ship. At least that was the report given to me. Derek was ashore at the time of the bombing, visiting with Admiral

Needham, the Commander in Chief, Pacific Fleet Forces (CINCPAC). Derek was a Lieutenant Commander then serving under Captain Redman, skipper of the Tennessee. They had visited with the Admiral the night before regarding the possibility of the Japanese bombing Pearl Harbor. They were still deciphering the interrupted message decoded on December 6 that instructed the Japanese embassy in DC to burn all codes and destroy their cipher machines. The Admiral thought it was necessary for them to stay the night and work as late as possible, so they could send a message back to DC as to what they had uncovered. And as we all know the next morning on December 7, 1941 at 0730 all hell broke loose. By the time that Derek and Captain Redman had gotten back to the submarine base, they were hastened to a shelter where Admiral Needham was being housed. There was nothing that anyone could do except to wait out the bombing and watch the ships around the harbor burn and sink. When the attack was over, it was around 0945 and almost the entire Pacific fleet of the American fighting ships were all but destroyed. As Roosevelt said, "A day of Infamy…"

On the phone, Derek told me that an important message was found in a pocket of one of the sailor's attached to a cruiser, the USS Raleigh. He had become drunk and disorderly at some local bar two nights back and after they searched the sailor, the shore patrol had found an encrypted secret document.

I had become close with Derek since Pearl Harbor, so I thought it was only my duty to go and help him sort out this message if he thought I could help and that it would assist our cause in the war.

When I had swung the big Buick into the 32nd St. Main gate of the Navy Base I was greeted by the armed sailor guard who looked at me as I handed him my Navy identification card. He said, "Good morning Miss Riley. Commander Kent is waiting for you at the Command Headquarters, down on Perry Street." So, I smiled and winked as the sailor lifted the gate and said to him, "Have a Good Navy Day," and I drove from the gate to where the street of the HQ building was located. Standing there in the morning haze of fog mixed with sun I thought, how appropriate that two very large white granite spiraling pillars appeared as though they were holding up the building by themselves. This Roman architectural building somehow represented our strength today and the fortitude for this war. These columns extended from the top of the steps to the roof. It was like a monolith. Scary looking outside, yet once inside you felt unbelievably secure.

As usual, coming to the base brought a smile to my face and fond memories, as I remember it well from all the days I played in the streets as a young girl. My Dad was after all, the first Commanding Officer of the Naval Base, so I did know my way around. As I recalled, once upon a time my picture adorned as many walls in many buildings as my Dad's own picture. I was the base mascot, no doubt about it.

The base was built in 1921 under President Harding. He and my Dad had officially cut the ribbon for the grand opening of the base and when the picture was taken, it came to pass that I was in the corner, pigtails and all smiling and eating a Baby Ruth candy bar. Those days I was all legs and "a ham". How things change in one's life as you get older and lose people close to you and life becomes terribly serious.

As I got out of my car, two young lieutenants walked on by and said, "Good Morning, Mam." Perhaps they thought, "Is that the Commander's wife, or girlfriend," as I was dressed in my red and white pinstripe dress, with small round white buttons adorning the neck line to the waist line. The dress of course was set off with a pair of shiny red shoes, as if I had just gotten back from seeing the movie, 'The Wizard of Oz"!

Anyway, I climbed the long steps to the double wooden doors with brass handles that appeared as though some seaman sailor had just polished and buffed them. It was always amazing the way the Navy kept everything so tidy. Passing through the doors, I was greeted by the Chief Petty Officer of the Quarterdeck. I told him who I was and he looked at me titling his head ever slightly and I expressed to him that I was here to see Commander Kent. He smiled and stood erect and then proceeded to escort me to Derek's office, which was three doors down the hallway on the right. As usual, I was extremely polite and thanked the Chief, and walked into Derek's office. I did notice however that the Chief looked back at me as I went through the doorway. Maybe he remembered my Dad?

Entering his office, his administrative assistant, LT. Elizabeth Yardley looked up from her desk and papers and smiled at me and said, "What a pleasant surprise Jacqueline to see you again. I hope everything in the private investigative world is good these days. I know it must be filled with fun and all that. I am sure that is why the Commander has called you in. We have this whopper of a puzzle here, and I know that he wants to keep the Navy Investigative Service out of this until he has something more substantial to tell them. Especially due to all the rumblings about Pearl Harbor these days and who knew what, when and where and why it happened."

Just as I was about to answer Elizabeth out stepped Derek from his office. As usual he was as handsome and charming as you might imagine. All dressed up in his "Blues," with all those ribbons and gold, he was the purest image of what a NAVY officer should be. He could have been the picture in a recruiting poster, plus he was very good looking and fit.

Derek, the ever so funny guy that he was when not being a lawyer said to me, "Jack, you don't look like anyone I know who comes from Kansas, but then I have heard that they have some really beautiful women there just like you."

To which I replied, "And you sir, well, you can make a grown woman blush." With that, I walked through his door as we both smiled at one another realizing that there has always been a bit of a spark between us and had it been another time, another place...

Derek motioned for me to sit, so I sat down in the left chair facing his desk, so that the sun would not be shining directly into my face. Trying to be the professional, Derek then went around and sat down and opened a tan manila folder that had large capital letters in black stamped on it, "DEPARTMENT OF THE NAVY TOP SECRET."

He said to me, "Jack, what I'm about to tell you is to stay in this room. I know that you can be trusted. More importantly, I know that you wouldn't want the United States to be destroyed or crippled in this war, if you could help the Navy and America in anyway." Then he began to tell me what he knew. "The Japs original war plan was to set up a perimeter to protect their newly conquered empire.

And since then they have taken over Wake[1], the Midway Islands, Guam, The Philippines, Java, and Singapore. And when the Japanese surprised most everyone at Pearl, except for several higher ups in D.C., it seemed like we were caught with our pants down. And believe me, we were. It seemed that the Japanese espionage agents had informed Tokyo that only two of our U.S. ships were at sea. And they also knew where all the ships were, where they were heading and when they were due to return. Furthermore, they have continued to surprise us with their knowledge of almost every plan, every move we are thinking about, even before we write it down. Sure, we all use spies. Yes, we have broken their Japanese diplomatic and naval codes through "Magic," which is our own decoder, but when the Mafia got into the middle of this war, the whole thing of using them in our efforts seemed to be a little absurd, particularly when some of the Italian families seemed to be playing on both sides. Hence, we all know the Japanese are going to attack our allies and our territories, but we don't or didn't know when?"

As Derek continued his story, he also told me, "By March of this year, the Japanese had controlled almost all the Pacific Ocean, some 4300 miles. He stressed that we had wanted to maintain Java, because it had a considerable amount of oil deposits, but we lost it because we didn't keep it supported with our own troops. And as America had been regrouping its military for any short-term battles it could win, it was also trying to rebuild itself for the defeat of Japan at the same time."

---

[1] Wake Island is a coral atoll, shaped like a "U". It was a stopping point enroute to Japan. It was also the site of the Pan Air Airways station and hotel.

He told me that we had only most recently set up ourselves at Bora Bora in Tahiti as a refueling base. This was our way to help Admiral Halsey on the Enterprise, along with the Northampton and the Salt Lake City, bomb the hell out of the Japs at Marcus Island during March. And just a week or so ago, the President placed General Douglas MacArthur in charge as the Supreme Commander of the Pacific Theater.

Derek went on. "Now we believe that this second-class engineman, by the name of Peter D'Angelo was in fact somehow tied into this mayhem that has been going on in the Pacific. And we also believe that Peter is tied to one of the Mafia families that has been helping the Navy or at least we thought, based on our information gathered by Naval Intelligence. Furthermore, this Mafia family, whom ever it may be, has been in fact hand in hand with the Japs for some time. So, we are convinced that all our fleet's information, whether shipbuilding, supplies, air ops or whatever, has been flowing like water back to the Land of The Rising Sun. Jack, we know that this sailor was not working alone. We also do not know who his contact or contacts might have been. But we do know that we must plug this hole up fast, so that we can get on at winning this war, without any more lives being lost than is necessary. This is where you come in Jack!"

Well here I am thinking that it was some little job to help Derek resolve some minor problem and then we could have dinner and get to know one another more! But no, I am staring at Derek, replaying what he has just told me and find myself kind of "shell shocked". Little did I know or even imagine that I might be involved in helping the Navy change the course of the war. Finally, I say to Derek, "Are you sure that I can help you? I'm not in the Navy, so how can I possibly..."

Derek cut me off and said, "Jack, just be you. Look around. See what you can find out and Uncle Sam will pick up the tab, just as if you were a civilian working for the Navy."

I stared at Derek for a few minutes and extended my hand for the folder and Derek held onto my hand as he handed me the papers and said, "Jack, just be careful, this is extremely serious business and could only get worse before it gets better."

I smiled and thanked him and told him that he owed me a dinner over the weekend and he nodded his head as I got up and left his office. After leaving, I drove out to the old piers where all the ships used to be. Now there were only a few, a destroyer, cruiser and an oiler, busily being serviced with food, bombs and fuel. Sailors everywhere, running up and down gangplanks.

I turned my head, my heart sank as I sat there staring out to sea, remembering James and thinking of all the men that we had sent overseas, and those who would never return home. Ironically, many Soldiers, Marines and Sailors would return one day as beaten human beings, seeing things that they would never forget.

Looking back at those ships, I thought, "Life would change forever. Life was changing daily for us all, caught up in this crazy war of nerves and steel. After centuries of fighting, the human race was still at it. It never had changed, nor will it!"

Coming back to the present, I placed my hands on the steering wheel. Sitting still for a few minutes in the Buick, I glanced down at the folder on the passenger seat. I reached over, grabbed it and opened the top and looked over the information that supplied all the data on Peter D'Angelo, the drunken sailor. The message that was found in his pockets was in both Italian and Japanese. Translated, it was all the current ship information, deployment of ships and personnel, primarily for the Navy and the Marine Corps for the Pacific. The dates and ships noted on the schedule were, December 1, 1941 through March 31, 1942. How in the hell, could this "Turk" get this information, I thought to myself? I glanced over the other documents that Derek included. The war reports from the Navy Intelligence, Secretary of The Navy and the local Admiral who Derek reported to, as well as Peter's personnel records. Born 1918, in Palermo, Italy, he then migrated to America with his parents in 1925. Who were his parents? And what was he involved with, and why?

After spending almost an hour at the pier, reading and thinking about the war and the contents of the folder, I placed it in its lock proof case, which was provided to me by Elizabeth. My mind wondered about her. To me she was a funny creature. She had been with Derek as his civilian secretary for a few years and when the Navy offered her this new position that had just become available to women, she gladly became a Navy WAVE.[2] Like most secretaries and nurses who were already serving in the Navy Department, they were already taking up their new positions as Officers in areas of administration. I had known very little about her, as we never did chat about anything other than what Derek was talking to me about. It was always about Navy business. Even during this past year when I was spending a lot of time with Derek, it was

---

[2] The Navy officially established the WAVES, Women Accepted for Volunteer Emergency Service, on 30 July 1942, but the Navy had implanted this right after 7 December 1941.

always about The Navy. Strange I thought, and then my mind moved on to the matters at hand.

On my way back to Palm Springs, I decided to stop in El Cajon alongside the road at a farm with a fruit stand to pick up some fresh items. After all, it was spring and the vegetables and fruits for sale at the local market sometimes were mostly rotten by the time they hit the shelves. No doubt it had to do with the war, but nevertheless, I did like my cantaloupe orange, not brown.

As I was crossing the road to get back to my car, with my bag of fruits and vegetables eating a banana, I looked up and there was a truck barreling down the road, heading directly for my car and me. I looked at the driver to see if he could see me and I thought I recognized his face. However, I knew that he was not going to slow down, so I quickly jumped into the pasture, only to roll down an embankment, just as the truck sideswiped my car. I couldn't catch the name on the side or even a license number as it shoved the big Buick like it was made of tin on four wheels forward and into the embankment. I looked at the Buick as it came to rest, halfway up the small hill. I then glanced back over my shoulder where my groceries now covered the field of freshly plowed dirt. "Damn it", I yelled!

By the time the truck had disappeared down the road, the grocer had come running out of the barn to see what had happen. I got up, a little dumbfounded, but alert and quickly took off my high heels and trudged back up the hill to where my car was now sitting. Fortunately, there was nobody around the car, when this happened, otherwise they would have been injured, as my car was now about fifteen feet from where I had originally parked it.

14

I noticed that the entire left side of the car looked like it had been mowed over by one of those farm vehicles cutting down wheat. The grocer tried to smile and asked me if I was all right and I told him yes. Then I asked him if he had a phone and if I could borrow it? He told me that there was one around the back of the shed, in the house. He asked if he should call the sheriff. I told him no, but that I would inform the proper authorities of what had just happened and that I was attached to the Navy Department. He looked a little bewildered, but walked me back to the house. As the farmer walked me up the steps to his house, his wife tried to smile as she opened the door to let me in. She looked at me and gasped and asked me, "Miss, are you OK?" I answered. "Yes, thanks, but can I have a glass of water and where is your phone?"

The farmer's wife pointed to the corner of the hallway that separated the kitchen and the living room. As I dialed Derek's number, the farmer began to tell his wife the story of what had just happened.

When the Base finally put me through to Derek's office, Elizabeth answered the phone and seemed a little surprise to hear from me. She said, "Oh Jacqueline, I didn't think that I would hear from you so soon." I ignored her comment and asked her tersely, "May I please speak with Derek?" She said that she was sorry and that Derek was out. Then asked me, "Was there anything that I can do for you"? I hesitated and then said, "No, just tell him I called and could he call me tonight at home around eight." She said she would give him the message.

I thanked the farmer and his wife and went out to look at Big Red. But as I was walking back to the car, the farmer ran up to me and said, "Miss, here are some items for your trouble." I smiled and told him "Thanks, but he needn't have troubled himself", whereby he just smiled and bowed slightly to me.

I smiled back at the farmer and nodded to say thanks as I walked across the road, still in my stocking feet and placed the bag of veggies in the back of the Buick. I then hiked up my skirt and climbed into the front, since the door was stuck and couldn't open.

Starting the car, I could depress the clutch and release the handbrake and Big Red rolled backwards off the hill. Fortunately for me the Buick was still able to drive, even if it didn't want to drive any faster than 45 miles an hour. Most of been something bent around the left tire or maybe it was the rim. So, the ride home was a slow drive and painful one since the ache in my shoulder began to settle in, due to the tumble I took alongside the road. When I finally got back to the Springs, I immediately took the car to my service station, The Desert Inn Garage. It was about five fifteen and I was in no mood for jokes, but Melvin, the owner, looked at the car and said, "How bad does the other guy look?" I said, "Very funny, just fix it and how about getting me something else to drive while you are repairing it?" He said, "O.K. Jack, there's a green Ford out on the lot that you can use while I patch up your baby."

With my grocery bag in one arm and my shoes in my other hand, I said thanks and walked out into the lot to find it. After getting in I drove back to my place and took a hot and cold shower. I then got into my green kimono with blue cranes on it and took some aspirins for mending my shoulder. Looking at the grocery bag on the kitchen counter, I wanted to eat some of those fresh veggies and fruit, but decided to start with some gin over ice instead. Later I thought, I'd slice up something to eat later. Right now, I needed to get my thoughts together on what had happened over the last twenty-four hours.

That evening, sitting on the couch, I listened to the radio more intently regarding the war. Not since Pearl Harbor and the loss of James had I been interested enough in listening to and reading about the war and the efforts of the U.S. and its Allies. All of that now seemed to change for me.

Standing up and looking into the mirror I said to myself, "Jack, all of a sudden, you're in the thick of something based on the information that you now know. That truck was not an accident. It was made to send a message no doubt about it. Someone wanted me to know that they were watching me, but who?"

Gee I thought, you haven't even started to look for trouble, but it seems that it has found you. Remembering a quote, I mouthed, "Time and Distance are to reckon with when at War." So, I told myself, "Now is the time to keep my distance from whoever was trying to take me out of this investigation."

After eating a nice chicken and veggie dinner, I settled into my sofa, having turned on my radio to listen to Sinatra and the Tommy Dorsey Band, "Somewhere a Voice is Calling" and drank my two very cold glasses of Bombay gin.

Later I curled up in my bed and said to myself, "Tomorrow, I go to work!"

CHAPTER 2

Thursday, I awoke early to a quiet morning which was good considering what I went through yesterday. My shoulder still hurt, but I think my ego was more bruised than anything.

I thought to myself, "It was a type of day in which you sensed that there was a lot in-store for you, no matter how good you felt and no matter how much better you wanted to make it."

I walked out my front door to fetch the weekly Desert Sun, which had been lying in my rose bushes since last Friday. As I was now getting involved with the Navy again, it was a good time to get caught up with the War and what else was going on in my own local news.

After fixing a pot of coffee I sat down at the kitchen table. Though the paper was one week old, it had both Roosevelt & Churchill and their respected political colleagues orally fighting with the "evil leaders" of the AXIS POWERS. Comments included Churchill telling his advisors that back in August of '41, Roosevelt had promised to wage war against Germany and do everything to force an incident. However, Roosevelt stated that he made no such agreement. Funny, while men from both our countries were rotting in their graves on the beaches, fields and roads of far off places, here they were, two of the world's largest economic countries along with their famous politicians lying and denying about who said what.

"Who cares" I said to myself, "What's important now is, when would this war be over and would my involvement help to change the course?"

Deciding to read or browse through every page and story, I noticed that since January of '42, our government had rounded up some 110,000 Japanese Americans and interned them in various locations throughout the U.S. The nearest one to the Springs was in Blythe California, some 120 miles away, almost on the Arizona border. The next closest intern camp was at Manzanar California, which was up on the eastern side of the Sierra Mountains and just west of Desert Valley. Business men, students, nurses, it didn't matter who you were, they just took you from your home and then took all your belongings, be it a home, a store, money or whatever. To me this was a crime during the war that no one else thought much about. But then again, how did you know who was on your side and who was not? No matter, it was still a sad tale of woe for the thousands treated like criminals who did nothing but try to have a better life in America.

Trying to validate the internment, I noted a reprinted article by the Editor on the Blackout of Los Angeles which took place on February 25, when two days earlier a Japanese submarine surfaced near Santa Barbara and pumped thirteen rounds of five and a half inch shells into an oil installation. Not only did Santa Barbara go crazy, but Los Angeles, San Francisco and of course the Navy. They had had their own problems since Pearl Harbor. The Japs had sent "phantom" planes from carriers and buzzed both San Francisco and Los Angeles during December 1941. Also, a Jap sub sank the tanker Emidio off Eureka, California in late December. So, the Navy had another black eye for not shielding the United States and its citizens and its soil. I could now understand why Derek was so concerned about the Petty Officer with the "Secret Messages" in his pocket.

There was also a move by our own city council to have any dual citizenship Japanese placed under arrest and sent to an internment camp. The council furthermore had discussed putting the entire city on a curfew. However, based on the ruckus it caused with the local money people, movie stars and celebrities, the city fathers decided that it was not a very good idea now. I agree I thought, "What a stupid idea, it's Palm Springs! What could possibly be going on here that we needed to shield ourselves from, gambling, prostitution? The Family would not allow that I was sure of it!"

Page two included a statement by several senators regarding the Battle of the Java Sea, which occurred on February 27th. Apparently neither the Japs nor the Allies won the battle. And both sides lost ships and planes but that was it.

Right below this was the ever present "Relief Drive for China" which was well under way since March. The Japs were kicking their butts, so some way I guess it was our place to get food and clothing to the good Chinese people. Besides we had a retired U.S. Army Air Corps Captain, now Colonel Claire Chennault and his American Volunteer Group, The Flying Tigers, heavily engaged in the war with the Japanese in China. He had been able to employ over 300 pilots from all branches of the service to assist him in this endeavor and according to the latest news was making an impact.

Ernie Pyle, the war time correspondent, who had visited our fair city in March, had written a commentary about the war and his thanks to Palm Springs for his few days of R&R.

On page 3 were two articles. One noted that the March Field Bombardment Squadron would be in town for the week as part of the Cavalry Ball, sponsored and presented by the Desert Inn on Saturday night, April 18th. And the other article was that the Marines had taken over the local airport for training purposes. I thought, "Why not let the Japs know what we were doing. Is our government nuts? Why should these items be advertised?"

The Draft which had been started in 1940, was accepting ages 18 to 64 years of age for enlistment into all branches of the service.

There was a recap of the British fortress in Singapore surrendered back in February. And now Burma had surrendered as well.

The Bataan Death March by Japanese forces in the Philippines, was also illustrated. Thousands of the POWs had already died. Filipino and United States soldiers who were commanded by Major General Edward "Ned" P. King were scheduled to formally surrender to the Japanese, under General Masaharu Homma. The report noted that the prisoners marched on a three-day journey to Camp O'Donnell, which was an unfinished Filipino camp. Japanese photos showed them marching with a brief paragraph that said, "They marched most of the way, but were also transported via railroad cars."

Meanwhile Allied forces elsewhere in the Philippines were fighting on.

An article that really caught my attention was that in 1942, months after the attack on Pearl Harbor, the Army decided to place the Buffalo Soldiers from the 9th and 10th

Mounted Cavalries at Camp Lockett, located east of San Diego and north of the Mexican border. They were charged with protecting the water supply for San Diego, safeguarding the railroad and keeping an eye on the US-Mexico border. Their areas were from the American borders in the rural areas of San Diego to Arizona. The Campo Valley was 60 miles east of San Diego, about half way between San Diego and El Centro. It was also about 180 miles from Los Angeles to Campo. San Diego had become particularly important due to location, military bases, and the war-related industries, that cranked out the ships and planes 24 hours a day.

The Army determined that they needed support in this area in case of an invasion from the Japanese who might come up from Baja, since Campo was just a mile from the border. The railroads were of major importance because of movement of supplies and personnel and connecting San Diego to the rest of the country. A plausible physical attack required stationing of the Buffalo Soldiers throughout the area, including tunnels that were built and watch towers along the border. The Horse Soldiers also protected electric transformers and the dams which provided the drinking water for San Diego.

Shaking my head, I finally chuckled on page 4. It noted that 93% of all unmarried women had gotten married so far in 1942 and it was just April. I was shocked. Had to be because of the war! I thought, "Happily I certainly wasn't one of them. Nor did I have any intention of becoming a new suburban wife... Life was too good to be tied down and cooking over a hot stove. I was a modern woman, with modern needs, thank you."

Page 5 said that some 1800 people had attended the Sunrise Service on Easter Sunday last week. Thinking to myself, I thought, "That must have been almost all of the locals, apart from me and the Mafia kingpins and their bodyguards".

Paragraph two stated that the Army took over the El Mirador Hotel and turned it into a hospital. I'm sure this didn't win any favors with the locals who were living there. I wondered where the city put the hotel guests up?

It seemed to me that there was an awful lot of military activity here in the desert, and that everyone was so blatant about spelling it out. I guess the U.S., even with the disaster of Pearl Harbor, still felt that we were invincible and that the Japs and the Gerrys wouldn't have the guts to try and march over here and fight us on our turf! "Perhaps" I thought.

Just as I was going to butter my toast, my phone rang. It was Derek. He said, "Good Morning Jack. I can only think how you might look in your white silk robe, drinking your coffee, with your hair all ruffled and...." I interrupted him and said, "Just like the last time you saw me, DK." I then chatted with him about the happenings in the Desert and asked him, if he knew about the Marines and the airport and was he returning my call. He said no to both, but that he would try and get the lowdown on what was going on in the Springs. He also told me that he didn't know that I had called him. He said that he was going to Pearl Harbor for a couple of days, but could be reached through Elizabeth, if I needed him. I said to him, that I had left a message last night with Elizabeth. And he replied, "Perhaps she just forgot and what was it about anyway?" I told him that I would much prefer to tell him in person when he returned from his trip. Derek then said, "Speak to you soon Bright Eyes" and hung up.

I placed the phone in the cradle and just stared into the room, seeing nothing, but thinking about Elizabeth and how odd it would be for someone of her position to just forget about relaying a message to the Commander. I thought weird, very weird. I need to be extra careful in my conversations with Derek. I probably can't be too careful, even if Elizabeth is wearing a uniform.

After taking a shower, I put on one of my favorite three-piece suits with matching colored shoes and then I looked into the mirror and thought, "Not bad."

At high noon, I decided that I would go downtown to my office and wait for Nicky the Leg or his boss, as I did promise to help him, if I could. I jumped into the Ford that was loaned to me by Melvin and headed for my two-room office. When I got there, I was concerned that the door was ajar. As I peeked into my office, I noticed cigarette smoke drifting from behind one of the two black leather chairs, in front of my desk.

I reached into my soft black suede briefcase and pulled out my Colt revolver just in case, and walked directly to my desk.

The gentleman sitting there was a little startled at the sight and sound of me in the room. He stood up, taking the cigarette out of his mouth and said in broken English with a heavy Italian accent, "I am a very sorry Miss, I was waiting for Jack Riley!" I smiled, put the gun back in my bag and stuck out my hand to shake his hand and said, "I'm Jack Riley."

He reached for my hand, looking into my eyes and brought it to his lips and gently kissed the top of the back of my hand lightly and smiled. He then said, "My name is a

Carmine Ialucci and I was expecting a ruffled man, perhaps about fifty, unkempt and in need of a shave. Instead, I find a beautiful woman with red raven hair, very long for an American woman these days and cat like green eyes. Plus, a woman in a man's three-piece gray pin-stripe suit, probably American made, with no shirt and gray suede shoes. I am a little surprised, yes."

I laughed a bit and told Carmine to sit down. I then sat down behind the desk, so I could study this captivating and gracious, yet untrustworthy looking gentleman. I could feel his heartless attitude, as if to say, "I will harm you if you try to offend me." I could feel that this was a man not to miscalculate your intentions with, so I told myself to remember this feeling.

I informed Carmine that not too many women were P.I.'s. He laughed and said, "Jack, you may be the only women in this line of business."

Carmine then said, without much hesitation, "I would like to hire you to find my girlfriend." I replied, "How come you don't have Nicky do that for you." He said, "He's busy with other pressing matters, besides Chloe knows Nicky and if she saw him, she would probably run away to another hideout spot."

I said to Carmine, "Why did Chloe leave you?" He said, "We had a how do you say, 'A Lovers' spat', and I wish to make up with her, but she is so stubborn and that is why I need your help."

I looked at Carmine knowing damn well that he was hiding something from me, and yet, I was almost taken in by his charm and the sweet scent of garlic and cologne that I had never smelled before. But as I did tell Nicky that I would help, even though I was now more suspicious of Carmine than before, I told him that I would look for Chloe. However, he had to give me some more information about her, so I could at least have a lead or two on where she might be.

He told me that her name was Chloe Chung, a French Chinese girl, about five feet three inches. Compared with Carmine, who was my height, about five feet nine, I thought she was probably like a rag doll in this guy's hands, or would be if she crossed him. As he continued, he told me that she was born in Shanghai to a French girl, who was the daughter of the consulate at the time, and to a young man who was a local Chinese politician. Of course, it was hush-hush for years, but when the Japanese began to invade China, the girl's family, took Chloe and headed for France, to live with the consulate in Paris. This didn't last too long and soon the family had moved to Trieste, which was right past the main Italian border, but still located in a part of the Italian state. However, it also had a relationship with the Slovenians of Yugoslavia. So, the area was a bit neutral, because both countries controlled it. During one summer, Carmine's family had met Chloe and her family and they became sort of boyfriend and girlfriend. They spent a great deal of time together in Milan. And then one evening on a trip back from a nearby restaurant, Chloe's parents died in an automobile accident, driving from Lake Cuomo. Chloe then spent the rest of her teen years living under the same roof as Carmine in Italy, before moving with him to New York in 1939.

When Carmine was finished, he stared out the window and took a puff of his cigarette. I wanted to believe the whole story, but thought otherwise. I didn't know what parts were fact or fiction so I looked at Carmine and said, "Where do I contact you if I come up with anything?" He said that he was staying at the Stardust and did I know the telephone number? I said "Yes. "

Then Carmine smiled and said, "You can reach me at my Los Angeles number as well", and proceeded to give me his business card.

He stood up, brushing the ashes from his black, almost satin suit and clicked his heels and bowed to me and said, "Until we meet again, Jack. I will expect a call in a day or two regarding this matter."

He turned and walked out the door and I just slumped down into my chair and opened the folder to look at the photos of Chloe and the other information about her that he had left, which was what Carmine had told me, almost word for word.

I walked over to my wet bar area and got out a couple of ice cube trays. I throw them into the shaker that was on top of the bar and poured in about three fingers of gin. After shaking it for about ten seconds, I poured the drink into a martini glass and walked back to my desk and sat down. Swirling the gin in the glass I thought to myself, what on God's green earth am I getting myself into? I was overwhelmed suddenly. I could feel the sweat dripping from my underarms down onto the vest. There seemed to be some weirdness going on in my laid-back karma with Derek's drunken sailor, my car being crashed into, and Elizabeth's actions and now Carmine's story.

I decided that I would spend the afternoon making calls to several of my L.A. contacts trying to track down Chloe. To no avail, no one had seen this girl, nor could anyone remember seeing her around. By 5 o'clock I was about to go out for a little early dinner, when a newspaper friend of mine, Brad Davis, based at the L.A Chronicle called to tell me that Chloe Chung had been seen in Chinatown just a few days ago. He then said that he would call me back when he heard more on her current whereabouts.

I told Brad thanks. He said, "Jack, if you're coming to the city, maybe we can have dinner." I replied, "Maybe", and then told him to stay in touch, this was important. Brad replied, "OK Jack. Can I reach you at this number or at home later if I find out anything?"

I told Brad, "Yes, anything and at any time."

I hung up the phone and thought, "Maybe the day was progressing nicely after all, with some of those little pieces of the puzzle turning up, it was very encouraging."

Looking out my window and seeing dusk settling over the desert, I thought now I must concentrate on Peter D'Angelo, the wayward sailor and perhaps if I have the time, maybe even Elizabeth. My gut was telling me that something was funny with her, maybe even connected. What was the sailor's story, and did it connect to Elizabeth and or vice versa?

I called another friend of mine, Lieutenant Maggie Fletcher at the Navy Base in San Diego, who was in the personnel and records department. Fortunately, she was still there at 5:15. I asked her if she could look up Elizabeth's file and send me a copy of everything and anything about her, as I was investigating the incident regarding the sailor that the Chief of NIS wanted me to look into. I told her that I was looking at everyone connected in case of a possible national security leak. I knew that Derek would clear this for me if Maggie had any problems. Maggie said, "Jack, I can do this, besides it's been a little too quiet lately" and

that she would get the papers together during the next
couple of days and have a military courier bring them out
to me. As usual as girls sometimes do, we continued to
chat about who was with whom and what was new in San
Diego etc.

Approaching six o'clock, I realized that I hadn't eaten
anything since the morning and that after such an intense
day of playing Sherlock Holmes, I decided that I deserved a
very good dinner at my favorite restaurant. Before leaving,
I wrote down a note to call Melvin in the AM, to see how
Big Red was?

When I arrived at the restaurant, I noticed an inordinate
number of automobiles. Strange, I thought, "it was early
and a Thursday night." So, I dropped off my car with the
valet and headed into Pasquale's, looking around the room
in amazement. I think every single crime syndicate boss
was in town. If not, they appeared to be well represented in
force, as I would have to say that the evening was a
convention of family powers. Something had to be going
on, but I figured that I already had my plate full enough.
With so much activity going on inside, I thought about
leaving and just as I turned to walk back out the door, I
heard that charming voice of Carmine's, "Jack, what a
surprise! What are you doing here, I did not think that you
would be dining here tonight, otherwise I would have
invited you to this celebration?"

I said to Carmine, "What is going on anyway, someone hit
the big one at the races?" He chuckled and said,
"Something like that. Will you join me and my friends this
evening for dinner?"

Hungry, but not stupid, I quickly said to him, "No thanks
Carmine, I am a little tired tonight and don't think I would

be much fun in your company. So, I just came in for a plate to go. May I ask for a rain check, for the next time?" He smiled, took my hand, did his bow and kissed it, just like he did this afternoon and then said, "I understand, Ciao, another time." He turned around and walked back into the crowd and was lost in a second in the heavy smoke, the laughter and the massive array of bodies that had filled the room.

I told Max to get a bowl of linguine with cream sauce and chicken together so I could take it home. He nodded and went to the kitchen. He was only gone a couple of minutes, which gave me some more time to take note of some of the members in the room. When Max came back with my "to go" package, I told him to put it on my tab and he just smiled and wrote down the amount in his ledger. I then stepped back outside to retrieve my car and while the valet went to look for it, I took out my compact case from my purse and retrieved my pen and note pad that I kept there. I then jotted down the 22 license plates of the limos and four door sedans that were parked in the lot. I had to find out what was going on in town with all these "meatballs" here. They just didn't show up for the weather.

Still hungry, I went downtown to a small whole in the wall Chinese restaurant called the Red Moon and picked up some won ton soup and chow mien to take home. Now I had choices when I got home.

Once I got home I started to strip down and went to my bedroom to fetch my terry robe that always made me feel comfy. It was something that I needed at this very moment.

Passing on the Italian dish I decided to eat the Chinese faire instead. Full stomach, now I had a chance to think straight, so I added some more notes next to the information about the cars in the parking lot. I really needed to find out who was in town and whether this was a party for something more important than winning a race.

About 10:30, the phone rang. It was Derek. He said, "Didn't want you to get too lonely Jack, since I'm not in town, so I thought I would give you a call." I laughed and said, "How did you know that I would be home, I could have been out dancing or just having a good time, doing who knows what." Derek laughed and said, "I know you Jack! You have been working on the case all day and now you are home trying to match the pieces. Am I right?"

I laughed and responded very shyly, "Yes, you're right once again, DK."

Derek chuckled and then told me that he would be back over the weekend, probably Saturday, but wanted to meet with me in San Diego on Sunday or Monday to follow up on D'Angelo and some of the things that he had found out in Pearl.

I told him great, and that I would see him then. But before I hung up I said, "Derek, what do you really know about Elizabeth? Could she be involved with D'Angelo somehow? Maybe is me or it's just a woman's intuition, but I believe that she's involved way up to the top of her bloomers."

Derek made one of those manly moans, when the other person is right about something and then said, "You might be correct, Jack, but then again you just might be jealous or something." I replied, "You know I am right and I'll explain it to you next week."

Derek said, "Ok, stay well and be very, very careful, see you next week" and then hung up the phone.

As I drifted off to sleep, I was thinking that I was in the middle of a herd of buffalo. They were circling around me, either trying to keep me penned in or getting ready to trample me to death...

CHAPTER 3

The next morning was Friday and I was at my office early, 9AM sharp calling my uncle, Detective Michael O'Keefe of the Los Angeles police department. He was not only my uncle from my Mom's side of the family, but also was one of the best coppers on the force and of course being Irish, it didn't hurt either. He had come to this country with my Mom, who was his twin, when they were only ten years of age. They both grew up first in Boston and then later in Los Angeles. After my Mother passed away, my Dad made him make a promise to look after me, if anything ever happened to my Dad. And like a second Father he had.

I told him about all the cars parked at the restaurant and that I needed information on who owned these automobiles.

Sensing I might be onto something, my uncle said to me, "Jacqueline, you haven't been troubling these bad guys, have you? They are nothing to be messed with. And by the way, what are you getting yourself into? I tell you girl, sometimes I wish your Dad were still alive to make you see that you are in the wrong business. You should have joined the Navy Department and became a WAVE. You would have made your old' Dad proud. Instead, you're out stomping' around in people's back yards and such, just like your Mom and I used to do when we were kids."

Just then, I butted in and said, "Please Uncle Mike, can you just get me the information?"

He said, "OK me lassie", but only if you promise to come next week for dinner?"

I said I would and told him to call me with the information as quickly as possible.

No sooner than I hung up with my uncle, Brad Davis my newspaper contact from LA, called to tell me that his contacts had located Chloe. He gave me an address and asked me if he should look in on her or if I wanted to do it myself.

I told Brad that I would come up in the morning and visit with her, but I asked Brad to stay vigilante to make sure she didn't disappear again.

Then Brad told me that Chloe was in Chinatown, staying in a hotel on Broadway, called the Mandarin, which was run by the TONG.[3] He was afraid to dig any deeper about why and who and I told him that it was OK, as I would do that.

I told Brad that I would call him in the morning and hung up. Were the pieces coming together? Maybe I did not know the why or what but I did know that Chloe was being protected by the TONG. But why? Was it from Carmine? Or was there something or someone else that hadn't risen into the spotlight? "Jack" I thought to myself, "You will have to wait till I meet with Chloe tomorrow to quell your curiosity."

The rest of the day I spent trying to connect the dots of the puzzle, but it was still missing many points and connecting lines, so I decided that I would go home and change into my swimsuit and lounge by my pool. However, timing in life is everything and Melvin called to tell me that BIG RED was ready for another smashing. I told him that

---

[3] The TONG were called TONG BAO which means compatriot. Primarily heads of families, they took care of their own. Throughout the U.S. the Tongs established themselves in the Chinatowns to deal with all problems. Some were good, while others were like gangs, raiding their own and demanding payment for protection.

wasn't very funny and "not if I can help it", and that I would be over after lunch to pick it up.

So much for lounging I thought...

Daydreaming again, sitting in my office, twirling my letter opener, I wrestled with some ideas about the possible connection of all these different players, knowing damn well that I hadn't even gotten close yet and that I needed to pick up the pace a bit, to see who was going to bite first.

Deciding to forgo my lounge time in the afternoon I picked up my car and went to the library to check on some things about our local Desert community, regarding people, places and the past. My hunch paid off, I found out that during the late 30's many Italians came to the desert, as part of the rich and famous Hollywood party crowd. A lot of companies, mergers and deals took place here and sometimes, even movie careers were started and ended here. This was not the sleepy little resort town, that some people in LA or elsewhere thought it was. This was the land of power and money.

Places like the Racquet Club had members that included singer/actor Rudy Vallee, director Dick Taylor, singer/actress Carmen Miranda, band leader Kay Keyser and my new best friend, Carmine Ialucci. Other frequented haunts like the La Valencia Hotel and the La Mirada were the hangouts for actors and actresses alike. There was George Brent, Frances Neal, Joel McCrea and Giuseppe (Tio) Mancini. Who was this guy I thought? He looked like a mafia member to me. The headlines from the past newspapers and society pages was a who's who, with all kinds of dignitaries and guests listed in every issue. It always included the noted families from Boston, New York, Philadelphia, Miami, San Francisco, Chicago,

Detroit and Cleveland. Me, being the new kid in town was getting my head full of the real deal in the Desert!

The newspapers also told me what movie stars had been in town and where they ate and who's house party they attended. There was Errol Flynn, William Randolph Hearst and Marion Davies of course, Charlie Chaplain and a host of others.

Previously Brad thought that I should know some of these facts, but when I told him no, he supplied me with key information that helped me look for it in our own local papers. It was all there in the open for anyone to see. The Families and Stars didn't hide anything.

As it turned out, Carmine and Nicky were connected to a family in Boston, by the name of Mancini, which was the same Tio Mancini, who frequented Palm Springs. The family came from Milan, which unlike the families from southern Italy, befriended Benito Mussolini and helped him come to power. Carmine Ialucci was based in New York, where he ran the "shoe business", for the family. As I found out, most of the families that were connected in Palm Springs turned out to be from Milan.

I thought to myself, these families must be connected to the war in Italy. And more than likely, they are probably moving guns and ammunition back and forth, to be used against the Americans and their own European Allies. If this is true, no wonder the Sicilians hate these guys.

Another interesting article I found was that during the prior summer there where over 500 guests in attendance at the local ball in June of 1941. Presiding over the evening was none other than the Mancini family from Boston and Carmine. The evening guests included the Ambassador of

Japan, Mr. Yuki Matsomora and several other dignitaries from Hirohito's staff. Included with the article was a picture of Mancini, Matsomora, Carmine, Chloe and in uniform, Peter D'Angelo.

"Voile", I thought. I've got you now. Sailor boy works for the Mancini family. Now a huge piece of the puzzle fits into place. Interesting enough there in the photograph was a sixth person, a female, but she had her back to the camera when it was taken and I couldn't make out what she looked like. But listed in the names was, Francesco Ialucci! Could she be Carmine's wife, sister or mother? Who was this female and where is she now? Was she another player in this chess game?

It was closing time at the library and the clerk told me that she was sorry, but that I would have to leave.

I told her "Thank you, it was a most informative day."

She smiled at me as I went through the two wooden doors into the warm Palm Springs air. It was nearly dusk. So, I looked at my watch; it was 5:45 PM. I thought I would go by my office to see if there were any messages and then go home, because tomorrow would be an extremely long day, going to LA and all.

Entering my office, I found two notes, one from Carmine inviting me to dinner and curiously one from Elizabeth. Both messages came in about 4 o'clock. I decided not to answer Carmine's call, but to concentrate on LT Yardley instead. Unfortunately, when I returned her call, she had already left for the day. Therefor I decided to call it a day and picked up my handbag and keys and walked out the door, locking it behind me.

Stepping out of the double doors of the lobby, I saw Nicky the Leg standing by my car. Deciding to be extra careful, I reached into my handbag and felt the coolness of the revolver as I slowly walked up to him. I wanted to make sure I was ready in case he was going to try something.

I said, "Hi Nicky, what can I do for you this fine evening?"

He smiled and said, "My Boss Carmine would like to have dinner with you!"

I replied, "Yes. I received his note. And thank you but you should tell Carmine that I do appreciate the offer very much, but that I must request a rain check for tonight, as I must go to the city in the AM very early as I might have a lead on Chloe. He will understand I am sure. So, I am going home to hit the sack early."

Nicky looked a little shocked that I had declined and said, "Ok, I hope Carmine isn't too mad that you can't have dinner with him."

I told Nicky "Not too worry, it would be OK". I also told Nicky to tell Carmine that I would call him if my connection to Chloe proved to be positive, otherwise, I would call him about what I did find out when I returned to the desert.

Nicky said he would and walked off in the direction of his car.

Driving home I decided that I would be extra careful to see if I was being followed. It was too creepy with Nicky showing up and all. I couldn't take this occupation anymore as a fancy free, $200.00 a week missing purse or missing dog job. This was serious and I wanted to be around to see what unraveled. So, I drove the back roads and side streets just to make sure that I didn't have a tail before I climbed the hill to my house. I even stopped before I got to the corner of Palm Canyon Rd and Sunrise, just to make sure there wasn't anybody behind me. After about fifteen minutes, I drove to the house and was in bed by 10 PM sharp. As I laid my head down, I succumbed to the feather pillows and silky sheets. I knew that I needed to get my beauty rest and be prepared for whatever tomorrow would bring.

CHAPTER 4

Saturday morning at 7 AM, I was walking out of the house
in my dark green herringbone suit, with green pumps and a
black see through blouse. I was ready for the day in L.A.
and the entire hustle bustle that it would deliver. So, I
grabbed the newspaper that was neatly placed on my front
porch by Kenny, the local schoolboy who worked hard
making sure his paper route was neat and tidy, and walked
out to my car. As I turned the key, Big Red began purring
like a kitten and soon I found myself driving about 65 miles
an hour through the roads and highways of the farmlands
and desert properties that stretched through the Riverside,
San Bernardino and L.A. counties. The convertible top was
down and my hair was being tossed around. I could smell
the countryside filling up my nostrils with the sweet and
rancid odors of farming and I thought, "This is great!"
Horses, goats and cattle, as well as fields covered in
tomatoes and corn were everywhere. Farm houses were
scattered throughout the maze of roads and the two-lane
blacktop highway that pieced itself together to get to L.A.

Traffic was light and I was feeling quite pleasant, when I
happened to look back and noticed a black Lincoln Zephyr.
I surmised that it was following me after I kept my eye on
it for two or three miles. I thought I saw that 4-door sedan
before when I stopped for gas in Pasadena. Now I was sure
that it was either Nicky or someone attached to Carmine or
both tailing me. Who else knew where I was headed?
Since there were so few cars on the road I let several go in
front of me and noticed that the Lincoln stayed right behind
me all the way. It was almost 10 am and I was nearly in
Chinatown to meet up with Brad. Rather than going
directly there, I decided to head downtown to lose the tail.
As I pulled unto sixth and Broadway, I hesitated in my turn
so that the rather large limo sedan would drive up right

behind me. Just by chance I thought I might get a glimpse of who the driver was. And as planned, the Zephyr pulled around the corner and for a moment, I saw panic in Nicky's face. He saw that I had stopped my car on Broadway. Just as he was about to run into my car, I popped the clutch and squealed the tires for some twenty-five yards. As I looked back into my mirror, I saw the Zephyr drive to the right as a police car with lights on and sirens blazing came from out of nowhere to signal Nicky to pull over. I thought to myself, "Good timing". This will help me in my own get away without speeding down any of these streets. "Safety first..." as my dear Uncle always says!

When I finally pulled up across the street of The Mandarin, Brad was waiting for me, just outside of Jimmy Woo's Market. I got out of my car and walked up to him, handed him my newspaper and said, "I'll take Sleepy Girl in the sixth."

He turned and looked at me and said, "You know that's exactly what I was thinking. Jack, how did you know that Sleepy Girl was running at Hollywood?"

I replied, "Women can read too!"

He smiled and said that Chloe was still in her room, last, he checked, which was about 9:30.

I told him to stay put and watch for anything "moving or stopping" as I related my story about Nicky following me. Brad replied, "No problem, I don't have anything else to do, it's Saturday!"

As I entered the hotel, the aroma of incense of jasmine and ginger floated through the air. The hotel was mostly in gold trim, red wall paper and rosewood furniture, all curved elegantly in dragons, flowers and Chinese bric-a-brac, as if a king lived there.

I walked up the stairs to the second floor and found her room number and knocked firmly.

A minute later, the door opened and there stood Chloe, dressed in a simple teal green kimono, with black peasant slippers. Her hair was black, straight and cut short, almost boyish. It was not parted, so it lent itself to no style at all, with bangs straight across her eyebrows. Her face was not as round as most Chinese pure-bred women. Her French heritage shone prominently in the narrow face, small pointed nose and not quite "round" eyes.

She smiled and said, "Yes, may I help you?"

I replied, "Why yes you can" and proceeded to tell her who I was and why I had been looking for her.

Politely she invited me into her room which was beautifully adorned in the same type of furniture that was downstairs. The only difference was that the room was ivory white with gold trim. After offering me some tea, we sat in the alcove overlooking the atrium of the hotel. She looked at the tropical plants for what seemed like several minutes and then turned to me and began to speak. "Jacqueline, I can never again go back to Carmine. My life with him and the Family and what they are involved with is not who or what I am. I have committed myself to my new life here."

I replied, "Of course you mean your life with the Tong and possibly being one of their girls doing favors?"

Chloe replied, "No it's not like that, it's just, well I don't want to be involved with who wins this war."

Puzzled by her comment, I looked at Chloe and thought to myself, here is this beautiful girl. How could she be mixed up in something larger than life? What is she afraid of? Is she that scared to talk about it, let alone return to the man who took care of her for years?

Chloe looked up at me knowing that I was pondering her comments. "I knew that Carmine might hire someone to look for me. No matter what the reason he told you, I am also sure that he is looking for me himself. It's important that he control my life so that I do not tell anyone what I know."

Again, I nodded and told her that I realized that Carmine didn't trust anyone, since he had me tailed from the desert to LA, without a reason to do so, or at least I thought.

Chloe said, "Carmine trusts no one!"

I then asked Chloe if Carmine wanted to find her because of what she knew and what she may have already told someone.

She answered me, but almost with a whispered "Yes".

I looked at Chloe, my thoughts were everywhere at the same time. It must be huge. Carmine scared of what Chloe would say and Chloe afraid to tell anyone for fear of what? Was it big enough to deport Carmine or his associates? Or maybe be sent to prison? Whatever it was I needed to know.

I asked Chloe about the Tong and their security to keep her here, protected from Carmine.

Chloe told me that the Tong would not let anyone take her from them, as they were as powerful as the "Mancini family" and just as resourceful.

I said to her, "It doesn't mean that Carmine won't try."

She placed her head in her hands and began to sob.

I asked her again, "What is it that you know about Carmine, his business, the war or whatever else?"

Chloe asked me not to get involved, in which I replied, "Oh no my dear, I am already involved and I've been involved for three days and I've just gotten to first base, as to what all this means. Some way and somehow, you're all involved with it too. The war, the Navy, Carmine and perhaps even Peter D'Angelo. You might even know Elizabeth Yardley and be involved with information coming out of the Navy's Task Force Office in San Diego. So, I need some answers, otherwise, I'll tell Carmine where you are!"

Chloe pleaded with me and asked to keep her hiding place a secret.

I said I would, but only after convincing her to let me know what the hell was going on.

With that Chloe began her story.

CHAPTER 5

Chloe reiterated the story of how Carmine and she met and about her parents etc. At one point I thought I would stop her from telling me the same story that Carmine had already given me, but I had a feeling that it would lead to the information that I really needed, and what "rope & yarn" Carmine was up to, so I let her continue.

Chloe told me that she didn't know Elizabeth, but that Peter D'Angelo had worked for the Mancini family for years, even before he went into the Navy. Peter apparently was a runner for the family, usually carrying money and information back and forth between clients and such.

Chloe went on that she was introduced to Peter about a year ago, when the "family" had an outing in Palm Springs and Peter had come up from San Diego in his uniform. She remembered that he was treated as kind of a big shot or hero for the day. Not like Carmine, but almost as if he was a long-forgotten son, back from his travels abroad. Around the dining table sat more than forty people mostly men, with Peter and Carmine sitting directly across from each other at the far end of the room, between the Don, Tio Mancini and one of the other bosses.

Carmine's sister, Francesca, sat across from Chloe, but said very little to her during the meal or later that evening.

Francesca was kind of strange Chloe said, almost like she held onto power and respect like Carmine, but very secretive. Anyway, during the entire meal, Peter, Carmine and the Don kept up a continuous conversation which no one seemed to pay much attention to except for Francesca and myself.

Chloe said that she had been seated about eleventh from Carmine and from time to time, he would look at her directly and then say something to the Don or Peter. The others on the right side of the table seemed to know what the conversation was all about and in between eating the soup, the salad and then the main course, they would at times laugh and smile, but she figured that it was serious as they were all so intense about what the conversation entailed. The dinner seemed to fly by as if they were trying to finish the conversation and meal at the same time.

Later that evening Chloe was introduced to Peter. Carmine informed Chloe that she would be working with him soon regarding a "project." Chloe didn't think too much about it then, and only bent her head forward and smiled at him.

Chloe then said to me, "You know it's kind of funny now that I am thinking about it, but though I never did see a photographer or any follow up photographs, sometime during that evening, pictures were taken of all of us. I remember posing with The Don, Carmine and his sister, Francesca, and Peter."

Chloe took a break to sip her tea, so I decided to do the same. She then resumed her story and said that in the late summer of '41, Peter had contacted Chloe at her apartment in Santa Monica. He had told her to expect him around mid-day, as he was driving up from San Diego and that he had something for her to get to Carmine. Everything seemed normal, as normal can be around those guys, and so after Peter left, Chloe preceded to make arrangements to meet Carmine in New York. She was to take the package to Carmine and meet him at his office the next day, shortly after noon as they were to have dinner that evening and she was going to stay a few extra days with him to go shopping.

The flight to New York was uneventful, and Chloe checked into the Fairmount after her arrival and waited until 11 o'clock in the morning before heading across town to Carmine's office.

Sitting in the lobby across from his secretary, Mabel, Chloe picked up a magazine to read from the glass and chrome table. About 12:30 Carmine arrived and immediately asked Chloe for the packaged as he dashed into his office. Chloe followed Carmine and stood there. He then tore it opened and she could see that it was some sort of book or binder that said, "NAVY CRYPTOLOGY TOP SECRET".

Chloe noticed that Carmine extracted other papers and folders from inside the envelope with various a red stamp engraved on most of them. For some time, Carmine just continued to stand there and read through all of them, without looking at her.

As in a trance, Carmine never looked at Chloe as he glanced over each piece of paper. So, Chloe went to the bar and poured herself a bourbon & water. She asked Carmine if he wanted one, and he said, "Later my China doll."

Chloe thought it was odd of Carmine to say that since he never called her that before and she almost choked on her drink as she heard the words roll out of his mouth through her ears and to her brain. She thought, what is that all about? But he was so distracted with the papers that she dared not probe about either what the papers were or why he had called her by that name. So, she just sat down and picked up another magazine that was on one of the three coffee tables in his office and paged through it.

When Carmine had completed his reading of all the documents he smiled like she had never seen him smile before. It was kind of like a Cheshire cat, who had just eating a bird. He looked over to Chloe, stretched out his legs and arms and said to her, "Chloe, this was the best news of my life. We have everyone where we want them. And the Family and of course myself are very grateful for both Peter and yourself for delivering these very important papers to us. We now will be able to assist our brothers in both the Far East and Italy in this war."

He stood up went to the safe in the wall, which was behind a painting of IL Duce', standing in a white uniform covered in medals and ribbons, with one hand on his hip and the other hand straight out in front of him. To Chloe it was a weird image, not being Italian, but she never did ask why Carmine had this painting. After he put the papers in the safe, he said, "Well we shall go to dinner in a little while, but I need to make some calls. You can either stay here or go back to your hotel, where I can pick you up for dinner?"

Chloe opted to go back to the hotel, as she was bored and had had enough of his non-attentive actions for the moment. So, she went down to the street and hopped into a cap for the hotel.

Chloe said that whatever the contents in the package were, she never did find out from Carmine, but the activity between Peter and herself became rather busy immediately, almost every two or three days over the next month.

When Peter and she would meet, either she would drive to San Diego or he would meet her in Santa Monica. It was a different location every time and never again at her apartment. Peter always asked her if she had been followed, and he was always nervous and quick to dispatch the package to her and leave. But each time she met with Peter, she would call Carmine and fly the next day to New York.

She had become nothing more than a courier. Sometimes she arrived at the airport and handed it off to one of Carmine's lieutenant's and would then get back on the next flight to L.A. On occasions, Carmine would give her a package to give to Peter. Sometimes it was paper documents, but there were also times that it contained money, she was sure of it, because it felt different and the sound of the package didn't crinkle as much.

At least twice in his office when Chloe stayed overnight and she was brought there to drop off a package, Carmine and several family members would be looking at a map that took up the entire office conference table. There was what looked like islands and ships figurines all painted with red arrow marks drawn on the map. Once she remembered seeing a map that looked like Italy, with the mountains raised and the seas surrounding the country. Along with the toy ships, were tanks and little soldiers in clusters placed on top of the map. Then realizing that she was in the room, she would be immediately ushered out of the office after handing over the package and driven back to either the hotel or airport to await the next flight back to L.A.

Just last week, two days before Peter was arrested, she had gone to San Diego to meet with him. He had told her to come to this bar that was on 1st street, near Broadway. When she got there, she had to wait about fifteen minutes for him to arrive. This was unusual she thought, as Peter was generally on time and was usually waiting for her.

However, on this occasion, Peter was more nervous than she had ever seen him, so she said to him, "Peter what the hell's the matter? Are you in trouble, being followed or what?"

He said, "Never you mind" and shoved her the package as if it were a hot potato or something like that.

Whatever was in there she said to herself, must have been worth a lot, because no one would behave like the way Peter was acting. If it had been routine like the past deliveries, he would have been himself and in control. But that wasn't the case on that day.

Peter then told Chloe, "You need to leave as quickly as possible. Tell Carmine that this could be my last communication for a while, but I will know for sure by next week."

Chloe looked at Peter and said, "OK" and stood up to leave.

Without saying goodbye or anything, Peter turned quickly, looked around the room and ran out the door to the back alley of the bar.

No sooner than he had left, two shore patrol sailors and a civilian burst into the bar and asked, "Anyone see a sailor run in here?"

One guy pointed out the back door! Another pointed at me and said, "The girl!"

Chloe said she could fell her face go flush but didn't want to raise any suspicion and tried to act nonchalant. When the civilian approached her, and flip out his badge, he questioned her. But her response was that the "sailor" was looking for a good time and that she had never seen him before.

With that, the civilian agent dashed out the back, following in the footsteps of the shore patrol.

Shaking, Chloe stood up and walked out of the bar, got into her car and started driving north to L.A. She had never been more scared than that moment.

She was trying to figure out what was going on and thought if she should open the package and see what was in there. She realized that everyone else got excited when she brought it to them, so why shouldn't she know what she was delivering.

Mulling this over in her head, she pulled alongside the road around Oceanside where the Marines have a base. She stopped the engine and reached over to retrieve the package.

Chloe then carefully opened it as to not arouse too much suspicion. In this way she could say that Peter gave her the package and it was open. Inside there were maps, calculations, pictures of ships and numbers written throughout the papers. Peter's handwriting was everywhere with notes of time tables, dates and other Navy information. Once again, it contained several envelopes that read "NAVY DEPARTMENT TOP SECRET".

Chloe closed the package after she read everything once and thought, "I'd better get out of here, go home as quickly as I can and decide what I should do next."

When Chloe got to her apartment, she again opened the package and read all the information several times. It finally hit her that the information contained in this package was secrets of where the Navy was going to be and what the military was going to do over the next several months. She just sat there dumb founded. Why was Peter giving all this stuff to Carmine and what was he doing with it? She felt perplexed and betrayed at the same time and then began to feel queasy. Running to the bathroom, she threw up. After several minutes she was able to compose herself and she walked back into the living room and sat down and grabbed a pillow to hold across her chest.

Chloe thought, "This information was going to be used against the United States." That information frightened her immensely. She knew that she needed to do something. Somehow, she had to get this information into the hands of the government, without getting herself involved. This was too deep for a girl who had in a way been raised by a Mafia family. She couldn't be naive and not care anymore about who Carmine was or the Family or who won the War.

That night, Chloe called Carmine and told him that she was still in San Diego even though she had driven back and was now in her apartment. She said to him, "I had a flat tire and the service station could not fix it until the morning, so I will not be able to fly to New York until tomorrow night." She never mentioned to him what had transpired at the bar with Peter. She just acted as if everything else was normal.

He said, "OK, but you better be here as soon as possible and that he would have one of his men at the airport to pick up the package from her." He also told her to make the ticket a roundtrip on the next plane back to L.A. because he expected another quick package from Peter but would no doubt see her as well, because he would be flying back to

L.A. in a few days. He said he wanted to pick up the next package from Peter directly because of the importance in the operation that the Family was now involved in.

After Carmine and Chloe spoke she decided that she had better get help, hide and get rid of the package she was carrying before the government started looking for her.

Chloe decided to call a friend by the name of May Ling who was part of the Chinatown Tong. Chloe told her that she needed to see someone for possible protection and could she help? Chloe then told May that she knew something about the War and that it was more than she needed to know and that the information needed to be given to the authorities.

May told Chloe to look outside in about an hour and that she would see a car that would take her to safety. May said, "Pack light, just a few things, as you probably would not be going back to your apartment."

Chloe did as May suggested and after about an hour or so later, Chloe noticed a slow moving black Cadillac limousine drive up the street and then down the other side and then return to the curb outside of her apartment building.

Chloe quickly grabbed her things and went downstairs. When Chloe got outside the doors she peeked in both directions of the street and hurriedly walked to the car where the door was now wide open for her to enter.

As soon as she was seated, she went to close the door but the door somehow shut behind her and she was alone in the car with one Chinese man, dressed in an all-black suit, tie and shirt.

She looked at him thinking that he resembled a bull sitting there in a suit that looked too small for him.

Chloe said "Good-evening Sir", but he never responded, he just turned and looked straight through her as if she wasn't even there.

Silent the Chinese driver turned back around and engaged the clutch and drove away from the curb very slowly. After making several left and right turns down some dark and deserted streets forty-five minutes later the car came to a stop somewhere in the middle of Chinatown. Then the black suited Chinese man opened the door from a lever in the front seat, turned to Chloe and nodded at her and then looked at the door.

Chloe looked in the direction of where he nodded and saw that a door was open. She stepped out of the car, looked both right and left for some bearings as to where she might be and then walked straight into the doorway of the building that was open.

Dim lights lit by white candles flickered throughout the hallway. It appeared as a maze. In fact, she thought she was walking around in a circle when another door opened. As she walked through it into another dimly lit room, she looked around. There she noticed seven Chinese men all sitting on pillows, crossed legged, against the furthest wall with black robes on, except one. His robe was white. They all seemed to be sitting in space, but after her eyes adjusted to the light, she could make out all the shapes of the room and reasoned that it was a counter or ledge that they were sitting on.

At times the robes of the monks seemed to sparkle as the light from the candles bounced off the cloth. It was eerie.

A single chair was directly in front of her as she approached them.

The Chinese man in the white robe spoke to her very gently and said, "Chloe, please sit."

Chloe did as she was told and then waited. As the monks stared at her and it felt like forever, however it was probably no longer than a minute or so before the man in the white robe spoke again.

He said, "Do you know who we are and what we represent?"

Chloe told him she wasn't sure.

He continued, "My name is Lien Chung and we are the Tong and have been informed that you are involved in possible high stakes of the world powers, in which you no longer wish to be a part of."

Chloe nodded and thought, "How did he know all of this?"

He continued, "We also know that you currently are the concubine of Mr. Ialucci, who is very much involved with our enemy neighbors in the Pacific. Perhaps you are not aware of the fact that the Japanese have been in our country since 1931, when they seized Manchuria. They also attacked Shanghai in 1932, bombing the city and killing thousands of civilians, including many of our brothers. Even while America was dealing with their own Depression during those years, Mr. Ialucci and his adopted family were aiding to the rising powers of Italy and Japan. It was only fitting that these two countries become a partner with Germany. So you see Chloe, Carmine is a very bad person. He hasn't any loyalty to his own family, who still live in Italy, and who also hate the Dictator, Mussolini. He prefers the side of the Mancini family and their aid to these most un-noble empires."

Chloe felt like a little school girl, sitting in front of the school superintendent, being scolded for stealing some candy, but she realized that the Tong was only giving her an education of what was happening in the real world.

Listening to Mr. Chung, she realized that the Tong was probably her best choice to bring the papers to, as well as for asking them for protection. "Besides", she thought, "Where else could I go and Who would believe me?"

Chloe was a mixed-race woman and she knew that no policeman or government agent would really listen to her story without first locking her up.

Lien Chung then got up from his pillow and walked towards Chloe. As he was nearing her chair, she swore that he was walking on air for his robe was flowing as if there was a breeze, blowing softly throughout the room. It appeared as though he was gliding over to her. He stopped about a foot from where she was sitting and said, "Chloe, please stand up."

As she did, two monks from out of nowhere appeared on either side of her. They stood there as Lien reached out for her package, which she had completely forgotten about. She seemed to be in a trance. Without much thought she raised her hands and gave him the package with both hands and as he turned, he gracefully returned to his pillow, as if he had never left it at all.

Mr. Chung looked at Chloe and said, "Chloe, thank you for this information. Please go with our brother monks who will take you to a room that has been provided. You will not be harmed in any way. You will rest and I will see you after that."

The two monks standing beside Chloe, touched her arms very gently and walked her outside the room through an almost blackened hallway, lit only by candles that hung about every ten feet from the ceiling. They continued down the hallway until they entered another waiting room. This room was also lit by candles, but there were windows everywhere, reflecting the candle lights. In fact, both the black starlit sky and the reflection graced the room in an iridescent glow. After entering with Chloe, the two monks gently bowed and backed out of the room, closing the door and locking it. Chloe was at first a little frightened, with the click of the lock. But then she was taken in by the Chinese art and furniture that occupied the room. There were the usual reds and blacks on the bamboo and hardwood shoji screens, but there was also a large rosewood desk with a matching chair with a red cushion.

Chloe felt relaxed and waited in the room, not knowing her fate, but she sensed that she would be cared for. She walked about and talking to herself, thinking of the past few hours and days. Then a door opened from the side of the wall where a very large Chinese countryside mural was painted. Out stepped a young Chinese boy with a tray of tea, rice and slices of chicken and vegetables. He smiled at Chloe as he placed the tray on the ledge by the twin windows that looked out onto the heart of Chinatown. As quietly and quickly as he came in, he left in the same way, smiling but without uttering a word.

Realizing that she had been up for hours and hadn't eaten anything, she immediately sat down and ate the meal and drank the tea.

Chloe was not sure if it was the tea or just that she was tired, but when she awoke the next morning around nine, she was in a bedroom that was full of nature light, filtered through the windows. Colors of green and white were everywhere. There were also hints of yellow that tied together the curtains, comforter and wall paper. She couldn't remember if she had passed out. She felt like she had been in a dream, but she did remember walking alongside the monks to her bedroom. As she sat up in the bed she realized that she felt incredibly refreshed. Her silk nightgown was white and red tiny dragons. Had she only imagined the dream? No, she knew that she was carried to her bed, because how else could she have gotten into the bed and had her clothes changed.

Chloe looked around the room for her own clothes. Not seeing anything laying around, she hopped out of the bed and went to the closet, where she found not only her clothes, but an entire wardrobe. Trying to figure out what to do next, she decided that she had better dress and find out what was happening. She used the sink to wash up and then she got back into her own clothes, just in case there was some sort of mistake.

When she touched the door knob, the door opened. It was unlocked. She found a hallway, only this time it was lit by the sun coming through the windows high above. On the floor was a white rug with small red dragons in the center, just like her nightgown that were spaced every five feet or so. Every room that she went into smelled like jasmine. The hallway took her to a set of stairs that led her down past two other floors. When she reached the bottom of the stairs a Chinese woman who was sweeping the floor smiled at her and extended her arm and hand out in a gesture pointing to the main dining room.

As Chloe entered the room, she was again gestured to sit down by another Chinese woman smiling at her. Chloe picked a chair where she could clearly see most of the room. The dining table probably sat about thirty or so people. However, this morning she was the only other person in the room, except for the tunic clad Chinese woman, serving her tea, breads and pastries.

The room, like the room last night, had Chinese art and furniture throughout. The table was shaped like a U, and had the Chinese dragon design in the very center of it. And all the backs of the chairs had the very same design curved into them.

After breakfast Chloe walked around the big house and grounds. She felt like she was almost in a fairyland, but she hadn't spoken to anyone. And everyone that she encountered only smiled and extended their hand to her as if to say, go ahead you first.

Chloe was feeling a little alone when around four PM, while she was in the library room of the house, the head priest Lien, whom she had turned over the papers to approached her and spoke.

"Chloe, good afternoon. I take it that you are finding the house soothing and less traumatic than dealing with the powers of the world?"

Chloe answered, "Well, yes, but what about the information I supplied, where am I and what am I supposed to do and?"

Lien smiled and held up his hand to quiet Chloe.

"We have reviewed the papers that you had brought us. I must tell you, that you may have helped America more than you will ever know!"

Chloe was startled by this statement and began to speak, but Lien stopped her again.

"We have sent these documents to our agents in China, other Italian families on the East Coast, as well as to the U.S. Government. Everyone is quite pleased and thankful for this information. The U.S. has agreed to help us in our own endeavor to protect and save as many of our brethren as possible in our own fallen country. Now we must protect you, as we have found out that Mr. Ialucci has hired a private investigator and seems very determined to find you at any cost."

When Lien said this, it woke Chloe up to the stark reality that Carmine would not stop looking for her, now that he knew that she had betrayed him and cheated him out of his information and that both his cover and the Mancini family would surely be in big trouble with the government. He would also know that several agencies would be looking for him along with the rest of the Mancini family.

Then Lien said to Chloe, "Over the next couple of days, you will remain in the Red Dragon House and then you will be moved every week or so for the next several months, until there is no longer a trace."

Lien went on, "Furthermore, I will do anything in my power to protect you, even if it means changing your name or losing my life!"

Chloe sat down in a chair facing Lien, trying to understand what he just said. Her heart began to pound and she could feel that she was about to cry, when Lien sat down and spoke to her.

"Chloe, do not worry about what I have just said, you will be taken care of more than you know. It is my honor to have you here in my home, and you should know that if you need anything, I would try my best to assist you with that request. Please feel at ease here. You will no longer be in any harm whilst you are in my house."

Then Lien stood up and said, "Good-bye Chloe, I shall return shortly after I have taken care of some business. Again, feel free to roam the house and grounds. I shall see you soon. Thank you again."

After Lien left, Chloe thought, "Changing my name! Why? What good would that do? And what did he mean by losing his life?"

That evening while eating her dinner, she looked out into Chinatown. It was raining. This was a tropical storm that had come up from Mexico, so the air was warm and humid. It felt like she should be somewhere else in the world, not L.A. She realized that she was in a way a captive of her own feelings and fears. Two days prior, she had no idea what was really going on in life, except that there was a war in other parts of the world. Today, she knew that everywhere she looked and everyone that she knew was involved someway with the war. She also knew that if Carmine ever tracked her down, he would probably kill her!

CHAPTER 6

I had sat there listening to Chloe's story. It now seemed to piece together most parts of this giant puzzle.

I looked down at my watch and noticed that it was 12:45. I was about to speak, when Chloe got up from the chair she was sitting in and went to the window and looked out. She then turned to me and said, "Jack, how did you find me and what becomes of me now?"

I sat my tea cup down on the saucer at the end of the table and said, "Chloe, how I found you is of really of no importance. But if you must know it was through a friend of mine, who knows one of the local grocers here, Jimmy Woo. You see, Jimmy was a young Navy Chinese Lieutenant based on the Yangtze River in '37. There he had befriended my father during the investigation of the Panay incident. That's when the Japs sank an American gunboat. My dad had gone to several of the villages there to gather up data and the remains of the sailors to bring back to the U.S. There the two officers became great friends and working associates. So, knowing this, I had asked Brad, an associate to chat with Jimmy. In 1939, Jimmy had moved to Chinatown with the help of my dad and though Jimmy joined the Tong as a member, he was still highly regarded by the Navy as a friend and ally. As far as what becomes of you Chloe, I think that it is up to the Tong and maybe even the Navy to keep you safe from Carmine and his friends. For now, I think that I should be included in knowing your whereabouts, just so that there is one person outside of the us keeping an eye on you. I will communicate to Lien through Jimmy, so that he knows what my intentions are and why I should continue to know where you are."

Chloe said, "I am glad that you understand and see why I can never go back to Carmine."

I nodded and got up to leave, but told her to not be afraid and to stay where she was and do as the Tong told her and that I would contact her shortly.

When I left the apartment it was 1:30. I was starved, so I went across the street to see if Brad was still at the restaurant and still "on the job", or had he left?

When I got to where he was at the restaurant, he said, "Well, I'm glad I don't have to wait for you when you go shopping!"

I smiled and replied, "Honey, we were just shopping, that is for information!"

Not only was my associate still on the job, but he had ordered me a Chinese noodle salad, which I was enormously grateful for.

Brad kind of smiled and said, "Jack, did you read your paper this morning?"

I replied rudely, "Sure, in between the cow pastures and the corn fields. No, how could I! I barely had enough time to wake up, shower and put on my pumps to get here on time. Not to mention my ever-present tail gate buddy, Nicky the Leg. Why?"

Brad began to fill me in over lunch on the latest news from the war front. It seemed that our military had lost the battle at Bataan in the Philippines.

As Brad told me this I reached out and clasped his left hand and gave him kind of a school girl's squeeze and smiled. I looked past Brad out through the window up the street and thought, "another loss for us, hopefully we will prevail soon and turn the tide around."

Brad noticing that I had drifted way past him, rattled a phrase at me, "Time and distance Jack are to be reckoned with when at war."

Surprised at this observation, I replied, "In time Brad, America will kick anyone's butt, no matter how far they have to go!"

With that, Brad started to update me on other important stories. "The Japanese Espionage Investigations had continued for almost eighteen months with allegations pointed to some traitorous Mafia family members. It seems that the De Young Committee had printed a report that concluded that the Japanese, along with the help of those turncoat Mafia families had planned to attack the United States and its territories for some time. They had found that the Japanese had gathered information on transportation, refineries and maps of the U.S. military. However, the Naval Intelligence seized a book, from an unidentified sailor at a Japanese restaurant and brothel in Los Angeles recently. This book gave great details on the plan of attack and sabotage of the Pacific coast. Republican Thomas De Young, chairman of the House committee on Un-American Activities was working with the Navy and other agencies in gathering up information pertaining to the Japanese Investigations. His staff had concluded that during a formal dinner last summer in Palm Springs, California, a high ranking Japanese Naval Officer had posed as part of the Japanese Embassy, out of Washington D.C. There he was given several documents containing delicate matters of State. This information was then transported back to Japan via Hawaii, through a spy network established there and then to Admiral Yamamoto, the Commander in Chief of Japan's Combined Fleet. At this dinner were Mafia members from the Mancini family, Carmine Ialucci, his girlfriend, several unidentified U.S. sailors and the Ambassador from Japan. Two nights later there was a going away party for this officer in Little Tokyo, Los Angeles. The Naval Intelligence found out where this party was being held and busted it and carried off the Japanese officer for interrogation. Though the NIS couldn't get much out of him due to diplomatic immunity from the Japanese Embassy, they deported him the next day."

Between bites, I exchanged looks with Brad looking at me, as he half smiled and continued reading me various articles that seemed to tie my puzzle more together. It was amazing how they were all connected.

During the breaks from his reading, we'd look at each other intently. I knew that Bard wanted to make sure that I was paying attention to what he was saying since all the information we were gathering seemed to be directly involved with war and the likes of Carmine and the Mancinis.

Brad then looked back down at the newspaper and continued, "The Mafia in New York would not be involved with the Japanese or Germans, but the Mancini family from Boston apparently had a connection with one Eddy Falcon, a cop in the Brooklyn precinct. Eddy apparently swayed his superiors in allowing both the Japanese and German Gestapo agents to tour the New York police headquarters as part of an embassy exchange program. The agents were then able to obtain additional information regarding the protection of the New York harbor and other local points of interest. Eddy, it appeared, was on the take and connected to the Mancini family and was later picked up by the FBI. He was never referred to again so his whereabouts is unknown."

I smiled at Brad and blurted out, "Ah, one for the good guys!"

Brad continued, "After the German Consulates were closed during the early part of 1940, the Japanese consulate offices were often used as a funnel for messaging information both in and out of the U.S. The Japanese men's clubs (brothels) of New York, San Francisco and Los Angeles were the meeting locations of all parties concerned in their own war plotting and the exchange of military matters. The FBI did in fact turn up additional information regarding the storing of ammunition, rockets, flares, rifles, uniforms, cameras, maps and most of all the arrest of some eighteen Japanese police located in Los Angeles and New York, posing as priests of a religious group."

As I finished my lunch Brad said, "There, timing is everything, you're now well versed on what has been happening in the world of espionage."

I just looked at him and snickered. But I also replied with, "If it wasn't for Chloe, I would have continued to search for lost dogs. Thank goodness for taking the bait from Carmine. You know Brad, I may not be wearing a uniform but I certainly have been enlisted into this war."

Brad nodded and said, "That makes two of us!"

That afternoon I outlined my plans with Brad what I wanted done regarding Chloe.

I needed a tail on her whereabouts at all times. Not that I didn't trust her or the Tong, but that I didn't want Carmine to locate her. And if he did, then I wanted to nab him and keep Chloe protected.

After we had finished Brad called another friend to assist in the stakeout. So, I decided to go see my Uncle Mike at the police station in the Fairfax district. It was probably a good time to get him involved as well, or at least fill him in on my doings.

It was late that afternoon, when I went inside the precinct building and the sergeant at the front desk looked up at me.

I could gather that he was apparently new by his stare as I walked up to his desk.

I smiled at him and said, "Good afternoon, may I see Detective O'Keefe?"

Apparently, the sergeant was a little amused as he looked at me, standing there in my three-piece suit, pumps and blouse. He stood up to look over the counter and then plopped back down on his seat.

I guess he wanted to get a long look at me or to see what color my high heels were. Naturally they were green as I hate it when colors are not coordinated, thinking to myself.

Anyway, I guess he was spaced out or something, as I started to repeat myself. However, he regained his composure and said, "Ma'am, I did hear you the first time."

He kind of snickered as he asked the question, "Who may I ask is looking for him?"

I said, "Sergeant, please tell my uncle that his niece, Jack is here."

With that he leaned back in his chair smiled and snickered again. He then said to me, "Your uncle now is it. How come I don't know you Jack, if that is your real name. A woman dressed up in a man's suit with high heels on. Come come now. You don't look like any niece to me."

About the time that I was about to punch this guy square in his fat face, when my uncle's broken English floated through the squad room. "Jack, Jack, my fine lassie, it does me heart grand to see you again."

With that, Uncle Mike walked up to me smiled and put his arms around me and gave me such a bear hug that I thought I would lose my breath.

As he kissed me on my cheek, I looked at the sergeant and then straightened myself up and said, "Uncle Mike, this here sergeant hasn't been very nice to your niece. He has insinuated that there was something wrong with what I was wearing and that I might not be your niece. I also believe that he was thinking that I might be your..."

Startled, Uncle Mike looked at the sergeant and said, "I want to see you in my office right now."

I waited about five minutes in the main squad room until my uncle finished with the sergeant. There was a lot of yelling from Uncle Mike's office. And when the sergeant returned, his face was a little red and all he said was, "Your uncle will see you now Jack."

He then let me through the gated area and I walked to my uncle's office and sat down. Meanwhile Uncle Mike calmed himself down and went to get coffee for the both of us.

When he returned, I began to tell him what had been going on over the last few days. I only told him about Chloe, Carmine and enough to connect everybody without going into details of any of the secret information that I had gotten from Derek.

When I was done, he looked at me with that concerned look of a father, and said, "Well Jack, you apparently have stepped into the 'circle of chance'. To me, you've got yourself involved with the Navy, the war, many of the crime bosses and now the Chinese in less than a week. How did you do all of that Lassie? Every car license number you gave me checked out to some big-time crook from L.A. or Palm Springs. You really are in the bosom of the snake and I don't like it one bit."

I said to him, "Well, I can't just step out of this now Uncle Mike. Too much is at stake and there are a whole lot of people who are involved besides us. There are people and countries that need to be salvaged from the crime and espionage goings on of the Mancini family. We've got to fill in the holes that have been created by these guys and either lock them up or deport them, to stop the damage to America and her Allies. And I won't be satisfied until the Navy, you or the Feds get all these bastards behind bars."

My uncle then said, "Jack, that's all well and good, but what about your role. You're right in the middle of this mess. How do we get you out?"

I replied, "You don't. I'm the only one who can piece together all the players and get them to show their hands, in order that one of the agencies is able to arrest them. So,

I've got to stay in this circle and keep it open to all the players and lead them down the path."

My uncle just sat there shaking his head. He smiled that big Irish grin at me and then said, "Well, are you coming for dinner, your Aunt Dorothy would love to see you?"

I just smiled back at him and said, "Yes".

That afternoon I was able to catch up on some of what was piling up on me, even though I wasn't at my own office. My Uncle set aside an office for me to use, so I called Brad to check on Chloe and then called my office and spoke to the part time secretary to see if I had received any calls. Uncle Mike had given me some additional background information on the rogue Mafia members that made what I was doing that much more important to stay in the game. It seemed that months following Pearl Harbor, the Allies lost over 120 ships to German U-boats off our coast. The U.S. Naval Intelligence in New York decided that it needed to collaborate with the Families who controlled the docks to assist in patrolling and keeping them safe. The Navy had termed this "Operation Underworld". It was led by known other than Lucky Luciano. He had been in jail, but somehow through negotiations he was able to be fancy free as long as he assisted in the war effort.

After Uncle Mike had finished his business for the day, I was able to catch him up regarding the other information I had found out. We then walked out of the precinct and got into our cars and headed to his home.

That evening as I sat there at the dinner table with my uncle and aunt and their kids I thought to myself, here I am sitting in this normal household, and tomorrow I'll be back engaged in the war efforts. I looked at little Marie and

Billie and wondered if James and I would have had a good marriage and children and church on Sunday. Sweet moments of time are so precious; you just never know where it leads to or if it ever happens again!

CHAPTER 7

Sunday morning at my Uncle Mike's house was like
stepping back into my own childhood. The difference
between my dad and my uncle and aunt's house was that
my father raised me, as my mom had passed away from a
long illness at the time I was nine. Here in my Uncle's
house the radio was buzzing with the news of the war,
while my Aunt Dorothy was cooking breakfast and Uncle
Mike was out in the driveway washing his car. It seemed
fairly normal for 1942, but it wasn't.

They lived in a new neighborhood that was called North
Hollywood, located in the San Fernando Valley. It was just
over the hill, north of Hollywood. Beyond my uncle's
neighborhood was nothing but farm land with orange
groves, avocado fields, strawberry patches and oak trees
sprinkled throughout the sprawling Valley. It seemed
pleasant enough of an area, no crime to speak of, just a
couple of food markets with paved and dirt roads and
streets where there were wooden sidewalks. And the
people you did see, they would greet you even if they
didn't know you. Most of the homes were on one level.
This new type of floor design had been the rage in
California home construction for several years before the
war had started. Now the housing market like so many
others were on hold, as all supplies and materials were
subject to the war effort.

Like Dorothy in the Wizard of Oz, I felt like I was in a
dream. So after I came back to reality, I got myself ready
for the day. I then meandered into the kitchen and sat
down with my Aunt.

She said, "Jacqueline, I am very worried about what you have gotten yourself into lately. Your Uncle told me last night. I know if James were still alive..."

Just then I looked at her and began to cry.

My Aunt placed her arms around me and said, "I'm so sorry Dear. I didn't mean to hurt you or bring back bad memories. It's just that, well I guess I'm just concerned."

I looked up at her after I had stopped sobbing and said, "That's all right Auntie, it's been hiding inside me for a long time and I really do need to finally let it all come out."

As if it had been planned, Uncle Mike came through the door and the two of us women straightened up and just looked at him. Irish women are, well damn proud. Probably too damn proud for their own good, if you know what I mean. So, I wiped away my tears with a napkin and had a sip of coffee. Uncle Mike knowing that he intruded into our conversation, just said, "Excuse me ladies", as he walked into the living room, knowing to mind his own business.

My Aunt then reached across the table and squeezed my hand. There was nothing else to say, so I smiled at her as we both drank our coffee and continued to chit chat about the neighborhood gossip and the kids.

That afternoon, I called Derek at 2 PM. He promptly answered the phone and said, "Hello".

I told him it was me and he replied. "Jack, I just got done taking a nap, having returned this morning at 7:30AM. I was going to give you a call, to see if you could come down tomorrow?"

I replied, "Derek I'm in LA, at my Uncle's house and I thought that I might come down late this afternoon, if you didn't mind."

Derek replied, "Mind, not at all, in fact I'd love to cook a new dish for you that I picked up in the islands. Yes, come on down, besides we've got a lot of catching up to do."

I told Derek that I would be leaving in about a half an hour and that I should be there no later than 6:30.

He said, "Aloha" and hung up.

Getting ready to leave, I told Uncle Mike that I would be in touch with him as soon as I had a chance to get updated by Derek and after I had updated him with my findings. I told my Uncle that I would have Derek call him to coordinate their efforts to see if they or the police could stop the leak from the Navy or civilian side so that we all could close in on whoever the traitor was.

At 2:35 PM I started to drive back over the hill to Los Angeles so I could get to the Santa Monica Boulevard that connected with the Pacific Coast Highway. PCH as everyone called it, would take me all the way to San Diego and Navy Housing, which was next to the base and the 32nd St gate.

As I was driving past the Los Angeles Airport, I glanced in my rear-view mirror and saw a Zephyr some three car lengths behind me. Initially I didn't think much about it, but as I continued to check its whereabouts I noticed that it didn't move out of position as I drove for the next five or so miles. Then I asked myself, "Could it be another tail? If so who was following me, how did they know where I'd be and why was I being followed?"

74

I decided to try and see who was driving, so I began to slow down to allow the car immediately behind me take the hint and drive around. Now I was down to two cars.

Driving through the towns of Manhattan Beach, Long Beach and Sunset Beach, the unknown car stayed on my tail. I thought about going to the Long Beach Naval Air Station to rid myself of whoever was driving, but decided that if I did this, I really wouldn't discover who might be trying to keep tabs on me.

I thought it's better to let the tail follow me as far as I would allow it before I tried to dodge the car.

Needing to stop for the ladies' room, some petrol and a cup of coffee, I decided to pull off at the next available location. This would also give me a chance to see if the car would drive past or pull off the road so I could see who was driving.

I found a service station close to the Newport Beach area. This town was a small fishing and boating village with cute little curio shops and large red tile with pure white painted houses, spaced out alongside the road.

The service station was on the corner of PCH and Dover Rd. As I was driving up to it, I quickly made a sharp left and pulled into the station.

The Zephyr barreled past the station and I wondered if I had lost it for good or if the driver was smart enough to wait for me down the road.

The guy at the station was looking at me rather strangely as I got out of my car and the dust from the road drifted past me to where he was standing. I guess he had never seen a woman wearing a man's suit, particularly in high heels, so I gathered that he was a little confused about what he saw. Nevertheless, he carried on as if he had known me all his life.

"Ma'am, can I help you today?"

I said, "Yep, fill it up please and can you tell me where I can get a cup of coffee."

The attendant raised his hand to scratch his bald spot on his head then pointed down the road and said, "Well seeing that this here is Sunday and not much of anything is open anyway, I would have to tell you that down the road a piece, about two miles is Katie's Kafe. Probably still open and she cooks darn well too."

I said, "Thank you."

After I did my business at the station, I looked for the Lincoln. It seemed to have disappeared. So, I got back into Big Red and went through the gears making a left to get back onto PCH.

Down the highway, like the attendant said, was Katie's Kafe. I found it on the right side of the road. It looked like a pretty good stop as it was set back from the highway and was about 50 yards from the water's edge with plenty of beach for sunning, off its wooden deck.

However, as I drove into the parking area, I noticed the Lincoln had once again gotten behind me. After I parked Big Red, I opened the door and saw that the Lincoln had pulled to the far end of the parking lot. Deciding that I needed that cup of coffee anyway, I went inside and ordered a cup. I then asked where the ladies room was located and the waitress pointed towards the rear of the restaurant.

Not having to use the rest room, since I had just gone at the service station, it was good excuse to walk back to an area that I could see anyone coming into the café. I noticed the waitress setting the cup of coffee on the counter and right after she did this, the door opened and there stood Nicky, looking throughout the room. I ducked back into the ladies' room with the door just open enough to see what he would do.

Peering out the door I noticed that there was a kitchen door just past the rest rooms, and across from where I was. So, I waited until Nicky sat down at the counter. I heard him ask the waitress if she had seen the young woman who came into the café. She motioned with her arm and hand back towards the rest rooms. He turned around and looked back, but didn't see me so he then turned back facing the waitress and asked for a cup of coffee.

Seeing that I had a chance to hopefully leave Nicky in the dust, I quickly walked into the kitchen, after quietly closing the ladies rest room door.

There I noticed a large coffee urn and cups that sat alongside it. I poured some coffee in one of the take-out cups and placed a lid on it. Then I reached in and took a dollar out of my pocket and laid it on the counter.

I then walked casually out to the back and looked around the corner at the lot. The Lincoln had pulled in and was parked in a way to drive straight out onto the highway. No time to lose I thought, so I briskly walked to my car, jumped in and turned the ignition key. I then slowly backed her out hoping that Nicky wouldn't see me leave, and drove to the edge of the parking lot where I had to wait for a few vehicles to drive past before I could drive out onto the road.

As I looked into the rear-view mirror I saw Nicky running out of the café to his car. Now knowing that Carmine wanted to keep tabs on where I was going and who I was seeing, I didn't think that I was in too much trouble. But I decided to be cautious anyway.

Driving down the road, I looked at my watch. It was now 4:40 PM and dusk would soon be approaching. I thought this isn't going to be much fun trying to figure out in the dark if the Zephyr was following me or not. I couldn't remember how the headlights were formed and what kind of beam reflected from it, so unless the Zephyr had something peculiar about the headlights, it was going to be a very long drive to San Diego.

As I continued to drive into the darkness of the evening I'd notice a vehicle behind me every so often, but there seemed to be no specific vehicle type staying close to me.

However, I continued my vigil anyway until I saw a diner on the road close to the town of Oceanside. I decided that if I didn't get something to eat and drink, I'd be a zombie by the time I got to Derek's.

Even though it was on the left-hand side, I pulled into the diner called Charlie's. There I used the rest room and had two cups of coffee and a freshly made cinnamon roll. I couldn't resist. In my opinion or maybe I was just starved, they were probably the best lightest and tastiest rolls I ever tasted. There were served with powdered sugar and cinnamon that covered the inside and outside. I thought this guy should be making these for all the dinners of

California. He could retire just from selling these damn rolls.

Anyway, I was going to call Derek but knew if I were to say anything, he would have the Navy come looking for me. So, I passed on phoning him. Besides the Lincoln was nowhere to be found or at least I thought?

Looking at the clock on the wall, it was nearly 5:30PM, so I knew that if I got back on the road right now, I could just make it to Derek's on time.

Leaving the dinner, I took in some heavy breaths from the early night air and got back into Big Red to pull out onto PCH and as I looked left to see if the lane was clear, another car was driving on the side of traffic towards me and its lights shined on the Lincoln, which was parked about twenty yards from the diner on the right side of the street in the dark.

Damn I thought. He's still following me. I could see Nicky sitting at the wheel from the passing car's headlights. His eyes seemed to bug out as he saw my car pull out onto PCH. My guess was that Carmine wanted to know where I was going, so I pushed my foot to the floor to get into traffic and see if I could get down the road before the big sedan could follow me.

It seemed that I had gone about thirty miles without seeing Nicky and the Big Sedan, when suddenly, the Zephyr was behind me. And I mean right behind me, as if trying to run me off the road.

A bit nervous from the aggressiveness of the Zephyr, I pressed down on the gas pedal, asking Big Red to put more space between the two cars. But the Lincoln seemed to respond with no hesitation and stayed directly behind me, not giving up one inch. My only hope was that I knew this road probably more than Nicky and that I might shake him down around the Del Mar area, which was ahead of us about twelve miles.

As I was approaching the waterfront town, I remembered that it had a bridge that only one car could pass over it at a time. That was it I thought. Nicky would have to wait at the light while I went through and then by the time he went over it I could be miles away or hiding some place in the shadows down the road.

We both slowed down as we came into town. I was sure that Nicky didn't want to get stopped by the local cops, so he stayed a little further behind me so as not to attract any attention to his driving. This town was known as "ticket town", as the cops were forever stopping cars and issuing tickets. I didn't know if Nicky knew that, but he appeared as though he knew. The cops probably would have thrown him in the clink just for looking like a thug and driving through their town. Del Mar was a horse racing town but also an area where lots of wealthy folk lived. That said, they ran their town like any other Mafia Family would, by controlling the ins and outs of who lived and worked there.

As I approached the bridge there was one car already stopped at the light with the gate down. I slowed to a stop behind it. As we both waited, Nicky gingerly placed the Zephyr about a foot or so from my car as we nudged up to the light.

After the gate swung upwards, the car in front of me drove over the bridge slowly then it was my turn to wait for the light to turn green. When it did, I placed my foot on the gas pedal all the way to the floor as the gate popped up and

Big Red raced across the bridge before Nicky could get through the gate.

I breathed a sigh of relief for the moment, but realized that I had to do something to make sure that Nicky was off my tail, so about four miles from the bridge, I pulled off the road on the left side so I could see when the Zephyr went by.

Just as I thought! Some five minutes later and the roar from the Lincoln screamed around the corner heading south passing the area of weeds and rocks that I had parked Big Red.

It was now my time to play chase, so I gunned the engine of the Buick and peeled out into the highway after Nicky. I knew that after a while, if he hadn't found me then he would either slow down or turn around and head back to the Desert. Hopefully, he would just forget about tailing me altogether and go home.

I kept my distance from him in the dark and allowed several cars from the side streets to enter and get between us. But as I approached La Jolla, where the mountain road juts out over the ocean, I came up on a section of it where a road construction crew was working on the right side of the highway. It was all lit up by lights from the crew. Thinking I was safe, I slowed down and drove up into the lighted area glancing to the right and then to the left. I almost froze as I saw the Zephyr approaching me in the left lane. Shrewd Nicky had apparently figured out that I wasn't in front of him but behind him, so he must have made a u turn to double back. As he slowed down his car almost to a crawl coming towards me he looked like he was about to slam into my car.

Before I could react, and no sooner than I had figured out what his next move might be, the Zephyr lurched forward with full speed. With that I pressed my own gas pedal to the floor and held it there.

But at that very moment I realized that I was going to be hit, the question was, "how bad?" So, I kept my foot anchored to the carpet. I could see Nicky trying to turn his steering wheel more to the left, so in that very moment, I quickly took my foot off the gas and slammed on the brakes, holding the steering in a straight direction, but Big Red began to fish tail to the left as the Lincoln slammed into Big Red.

Both cars were now spinning out of control. Luckily for me, Nicky had spun my car towards the left lane. Even so, some of my life began to roll before my eyes as Big Red slammed into the side of the mountain and came to a complete stop.

The engine was still running but my mind was still spinning. It took me a couple of minutes to get focused on what had happened. The son-of-a-bitch tried to run me off the road and over the side of the cliff. He tried to kill me!

I got out of the Buick a little shaken, but reality came into focus as I realized that I should never drive with high heels on particularly if they have had an accident. Trying to stand up with them on was a mistake, so I stooped down and took them off.

I couldn't feel the pain from the rocks, dirt and pebbles, as I stood there in bare feet looking at the tail end of the Buick. What a mess, I knew that instant that Melvin would be smiling that "I told you so" grin next week when I dropped it off at his place for repairs. Oh well...

After gathering my wits about me I realized that I hadn't heard a crash or explosion, so I looked up and over across the road where the construction crew was standing.

I then walked over to see what had happened to Nicky and boy was I surprised. The Zephyr was tittering on the side of the road where the construction crew had been working. The car was half on the road and half in the air. Nicky was slumped against the steering wheel, and I thought, "It's a good thing that the tail end of the Lincoln had some extra weight, otherwise Nicky would have been part of the rocks below and dead. Not that he didn't deserve it, but then I probably shouldn't think like that!"

The foreman who now saw me walking out of the shadows came running over to me and asked, "Ma'am, are you all right? Do you know why this guy would want to run you off the road? We all saw what happened even in the dark?"

I responded by saying, "You know I've never seen him before, so I don't know what this was all about, and yes I am just fine, thank you."

I suspected that Nicky wasn't dead, just passed out from the excitement and perhaps he had smashed his head into the steering wheel. I couldn't tell.

After we all stood there looking at the Zephyr for a moment, the foreman started yelling at his men to move the crane over to try and hook it to the Lincoln.

Walking with the foreman, I told him that I was leaving and he kind of got a little rattled at me and said, "Don't you want to report this accident to the police or sheriff departments? After all, it looked like this guy wanted to kill you?"

I said to the foreman, "No, I think that the guy driving probably made a mistake about who I was or maybe he was drunk".

I told the foreman I'd be going and he then turned around again and started yelling at his crew about what had to be done to get the Zephyr back on the road. He also told one of his guys to drive to the road house and call it in to the cops.

I in turn just walked back to my own car. The poor Buick was resting in a heap of mountain dirt and brush.

As I got back into Big Bed, I looked at my watch. It now had a crack in the center of the face. The crystal was broken and the time was now a constant 6:45. Well I thought, "I'm never late for dinner, except for tonight. All I want to do is get to Derek's without any more problems."

I kept my fingers crossed with regards to how the Buick was going to respond. I didn't know if the wheels had been bent or if the axles were still in place or if they were cracked. I just didn't know, nor did I give a damn.

I turned the key and started Big Red up. I listened to her purr like it was brand new and didn't hear any knocks or chugs, so I smiled and said to myself, "Thank You for watching out for me, whoever you are."

As I shifted the gear into reverse I did hear something rattle, but figured that it might just be some dirt or rocks hung up in the axles or in the shaft areas. I didn't want any additional mountain dirt on the hood or under it, so I took it real slow as I backed the car up.

After I slowly drove the Buick out into the center of the lane, I stopped and looked towards the construction site. No cars were coming in either direction. I saw the construction crane trying to pick up the Lincoln from the edge of the road. Nicky was wide awake now and screaming at the foreman and crew as the mechanical beast lifted the car up.

I smiled and said to myself, "You got another day to live you bastard." Hopefully the foreman would keep the car up in the air until the police arrived. No doubt they would keep Nicky on "ice" until Carmine or one of the other family members came to rescue him out of jail.

I shoved the gear shift into first and the car lurched forward a bit and as I drove past my latest brush with death I felt really exhausted.

I suppose it all finally hit me that I was tired from driving, being followed, and tired of my poor car getting damaged again. I just needed to get to Derek's.

I finally got to the 32nd St gate at 7:20PM. The guard at the gate popped tall and said, "Good Evening, Mam". He then looked at my DOD ID card and said that Commander Kent had been asking if I had arrived.

I smiled and said, "Thanks" and drove through to Derek's house.

It was on Starboard Ave facing the harbor. The lawn stretched out about 10 yards in front of the house. Knowing Derek, he probably finessed his way of obtaining this house as his residence. As I recalled from my childhood, it really was meant for a Captain or Admiral. It had way too much space for a Commander. But then again Derek was on staff. Rank did have its privileges.

No sooner than I had gotten out of the car door, Derek was standing there as I turned around. He could tell that something was wrong, that something had happened, but he smiled and moved to me as close as he could, placing his arms around me and holding me tight.

We didn't speak for several minutes. He kept lightly kissing my hair. I just melted into the moment. The cool ocean air felt good against my warm cheeks as he continued to smother me with affection.

When we finally broke apart, we just looked at each other. Destiny, Derek's dog, was nuzzling her nose between our bodies, and as I looked down at the lab, I patted her head and she licked my hand, making me feel that much more loved and secure.

Derek reached into the car for my handbag and small suitcase, then moved me from the car as he shut the door. If he did notice the damage he didn't say a word. He and the lab walked me into his house. There was some music playing in the background. I was sure it was Jo Stafford singing, "Come Rain or Shine", but I felt like I was in a trance. Nothing seemed real. Or maybe it was too real. It really didn't matter. For the moment life stood still and I was in my own cocoon.

The fireplace that burned brightly lit up the living room. Through the alcove I saw the dining room lit only by candles.

Derek took my bags and set them down and then took my hand again and led me to the dining room. He placed his hands on a chair and pulled it away from the table. He looked at me and smiled and without speaking I sat down. He then walked to the other side and took the Cabernet and poured it into the two wine glasses that sat in front of each dinner plate.

I took his hand in mine and he reached for his glass and held it up and said, "To you Jack, I'm glad you're here, safe and sound!"

In a way, I felt like a little girl being comforted after waking up from a bad dream.

I looked at Derek and smiled. I knew that I needed to feel like a woman tonight. No bad guys, war or Navy lurking about, just two people. A night that just Derek and I would share that was a need, love or just lust. Whatever it was, I needed that feeling and release.

As we ate dinner, we talked about what we might do together in the morning and throughout the day. We also chatted, like lovers often do, about making plans for another time, another adventure and another place. We knew that we needed to forget about the rest of the world for now and concentrate on each other.

Later that night, Derek and I loved each other as much as any two people 'in love' could have. Yet neither of us wanted to admit it.

I knew that I might be in love with him and Derek with me. But we were both afraid to tell each other how we really felt. Our past and present seemed to bend and bind us but also separate us from each other. James and me. Derek and his duty to the Navy. The loss of his best friend, and the fact that we both were involved in the very essence of World War II. It was a crazy time.

When we finally drifted off to sleep, I thought I would sleep like a baby and I did. I didn't even hear Derek get up in the morning for his usual exercise routine.

While I was still fast asleep, Derek called Elizabeth and told her what his schedule would be for the day in case anything important came up. To Derek, the LT seemed to be normal in her response to him as he hung up without thinking anything about her.

When he finished with his Navy business, he decided to let me sleep some more and went to the kitchen to prepare breakfast for his "houseguest".

Still in "lala land", I was dreaming of Derek making love to me when I was awakened by Destiny licking me on the face. I wrestled with the big dog until we both landed on the floor with a huge thud. Perhaps it was partly from my nakedness landing on the hardwood floor, or just that Destiny weighed 70 pounds. Nevertheless, the Big Dog was still licking my face and I was madly laughing when Derek appeared in the doorway with a biggest grin on his face. He said, "I'm glad that my dog can make you laugh, I might have a chance of courting you then?"

I returned his question and comment with, "Only if you offer a shower to this naked lady!"

I then jumped up, kissed him on the cheek as my breasts brushed up against him walking through the doorway to the bathroom.

He just smiled and shook his head.

Monday morning was full of bright sunny skies and breakfast chatter was still in lovers' tones. I knew that both Derek and I would have to face up to the next challenge of the WAR soon, but for now, we might as well go along and enjoy this sweet moment in time. Soon enough I thought I would be coming out of my love mode, getting ready to do battle with the world again. Sad, I thought, I think I really could love this man. It's a nice feeling that I feel each time I am near him. Why can't it be like this all the time...? Oh yeah, the War!

CHAPTER 8

Following breakfast, Derek surprised me by telling me that we would be going sailing on Derek's twenty-foot sloop, "THE IRISH ISLES". I had been out in it one time before when my Dad was still alive. After we drifted out through the channel, we passed by the Tankers, Cruisers, Freighters, Destroyers and Cargo ships that were making themselves ready for deployment overseas. Sailors and Marines were everywhere on the docks, handling and passing boxes between themselves, in long lines like a conveyor belt. We saw them loading food, ammunition and bombs, yet I tried not to think about the reason for all this. I just wanted to enjoy the day and pretend that life was just wonderful.

Still being a bit naïve, I didn't want this special time to end, yet even as I pretended, I knew that both Derek and I would have to return to the reality of life and the War later that day.

After sailing on a calm and peaceful ocean a bit, we anchored off shore about 200 yards. We swam a bit in the cool Pacific Ocean waters and then had a beautiful picnic lunch. Afterwards we turned the boat around and started slowly heading back to the harbor. Derek and I had put the sloop on auto pilot much of the day and had made the day special that seemed to last longer than usual, making love and speaking to each other in the most intimate way. We were making plans about tomorrow and next week by the time we pulled the boat back up to the slip, where the sloop would wait for her next outing. Derek's admin assistant, Lieutenant Yardley was standing there on the dock waiting. She seemed a bit nervous, fidgeting and had this strange look on her face and barely acknowledged me as I stopped by the cleat on the dock to tie up the boat. I looked at Derek, but didn't think he saw what I saw as he shut down everything on the boat. She yelled to Derek that Captain Stark from NIS was in his office and wanted to speak to him in private and to hurry.

Derek looked at me and was about to say something when I replied with my eyes as if to say, "I understand." So I hopped back onto the boat and we gathered up our things from the cabin below and climbed out of the sloop and started to walk down the dock. As we did, Elizabeth walked immediately up to and past Derek, standing between us and not allowing me to get any closer to him. Finding this strange because I had just gotten off the boat with him, I decided that I would show a little force in this matter and said, "Excuse me Derek, would you mind waiting for me!"

He turned around and saw that he had walked some distance from me and that only Elizabeth was behind him.

He said, "I'm sorry Jack, I must have been preoccupied. "Forgive me?"

Elizabeth retorted with, "Commander, I must insist that we hurry, Captain Stark said it was most urgent!"

Derek turned to her and replied, "Lieutenant, I'll be there as quickly as I can, don't sweat it!"

I could see that Derek was a little upset with Elizabeth, so I walked past her and up to where he was standing and said, "OK my love" loud enough so that she could hear it.

Walking further down the dock, I could see a car parked right outside the gate that allowed you unto the dock. I noticed that the engine was running and that it wasn't a Navy vehicle, because most of cars in the motor pool were

91

Fords. This was a black Chevy, with four doors, that faced each other on the side so that when you opened them both up, it looked large enough to be a limo. I couldn't see who the driver was as I walked down the dock alongside of Derek.

As we were approaching the end of the dock, I accidently dropped one of the towels that I was carrying. I stopped and stooped over to pick it up and wham!

Derek had already reached the gate and as he opened it and heard the scuffle as Elizabeth grabbed me from behind and threw me over the side of the railing into the water.

Derek's face was in horror as he watched me fall over the side and as he began to run down the dock to come to my rescue, two thugs from the car had slammed open the gate and grabbed a hold of Derek from behind. He tried to wrestle from their grasp, but Elizabeth was lending a hand to push all four of them through the gate to the waiting car.

As I plunged into the water, I rolled into a ball as I did not know what I would hit once I landed in the water or if it would be the edge of the rocks. Once I realized that I was in the water, I knew that I had to grapple for my own life. So I kicked and pushed my feet as hard as I could and was able to stop the panic of drowning and leapt back up from the water to the side of sea wall. As I got my footing on the rocks, I tried to crane my neck up to look past the railing to see what was happening with Derek. By this time, I saw that he was being dragged and tugged into the car with Elizabeth helping them all from behind as she closed the front passenger door. Because of the slime from the kelp and sea weed, I had a hell of a time climbing up unto the rocks which would lead me back up to the street.

Continuing my climb, I heard the car squeal from the parking lot unto the street as I finally reached the top to swing my legs over the railing. I didn't realize how banged up I had gotten in those very few short minutes, but as I got up unto the street I took an inventory of myself. I saw that I was bleeding from my left leg and from my left elbow.

My mind now raced on, "Good thing I had been wearing my boat shoes, as I must have the hit bottom or the rocks when that bitch threw me over the side, otherwise I would have probably torn up my feet as well."

My clothes were thrashed. The light blue shorts and wind breaker were cut up, almost shredded from the rocks. Knowing that the boat docks weren't too far from the base dispensary and hospital, I opted to head there first. I could call the base security office to make my report from there. Fortunately for me, I was still a Navy dependent granted to me from my dear departed Dad and his years spent working for Uncle Sam. Being able to use the facilities was now one of the perks I received.

With no one around the docks, I kind of hobbled and walked out of the parking lot and towards the hospital, trying to replay every moment that had just occurred.

In my haze, I heard a car honking its horn at me as I headed to the dispensary. It was across the street going in the opposite direction. I looked up. It was Maggie, my Navy bud. I smiled, "What a life saver" I thought!

She stopped the car, jumped out without closing the door and ran across the street to find out what had happened to me and why I was walking down the street and looking like a drowned rat.

"Jack, Jack, what the hell happened to you" she asked as she reached me and put her hands on both my arms, as if to hold me up.

Though I was about five inches taller than she, I couldn't help feeling like my mother had come to rescue me.

Maggie helped me back across the street and into her car. Then she ran to the driver's side, jumped in and rammed the gear shift into first as she popped the brake and off we went heading to the hospital. Maggie knew that I needed some sort of medical attention fast, so she waited for me to tell her what had happened, so I explained what had just transpired and how Elizabeth and the two thugs kidnapped Derek.

She told me that she had gathered some information for me and that nothing would surprise her at this point regarding the War and who was involved. Knowing that this was a horrendous crime, she stopped by the Shore Patrol's office first so that I could give them a quick verbal account. We told them that I would come back to the office later to fill in the blanks. They notified the gates as we stood there giving them the "nickel" brief. They told the guards to be on the "look out" for the black Chevy, but I already knew that it too late and that it would have already left the base and that LT Yardley was in control of Derek's life for now.

Much of the rest of the afternoon I spent in the hospital getting probed and taped up. Not until they started probing me did I find out that I had also injured a rib, which the doctor told me would take some time to heal properly and that I shouldn't be playing any rough house with any of my friends for a while. I just looked at him and laughed. He gave me some pain pills to help me through the next couple of days or so. He also told me not to drink or drive as the medication might me to feel sleepy and cause some drowsiness.

I said to the doc, "Don't you think that's exactly what I need at this point?"

He looked at me with those puppy dog eyes and just shook his eyes. I guess he didn't think my statement was funny.

When I had finished at the hospital, Maggie drove me back to the Shore Patrol office to fill out the report on what had happened.

Maggie had informed me that there was a Captain Stark with NIS, who was working with Derek on the Peter D'Angelo case.

I told Maggie, "Yardley kept telling Derek that Stark wanted to see him in his office. Even though she was lying, no doubt the Captain will be working on his kidnap and whoever the hell Elizabeth is."

Maggie replied, "Yep, but for the moment, Stark is at Pearl Harbor and wasn't expected back until Tuesday."

I snapped, "That doesn't help us right now."

While still at the Shore Patrol office, the Commanding Officer, Captain Thompson was notified of what had taken place and he immediately came over to get the full report and speak with me. He knew my Dad a long time ago and was very apologetic about my injuries and all. But his main concern was what Derek and I were working on, since someone would kidnap him and try to injure me. So he pressed me with several more questions. In fact, I almost felt like the guilty party.

Still I told him nothing. Not that I didn't trust the Captain. It was just that what Derek and myself were involved in was way over the head of the Captain. War concerns and issues were not really for public scrutiny or for that matter for their information. Playing dumb, I just played along and said that it must have been because of something Derek had been involved in.

The Captain again told me how sorry he was and that they would do everything they could to locate and rescue Derek. The C.O. then called his superior, Rear Admiral Franklin to notify him of the incident. Though the Admiral was not in town, his staff said they would get this news to him as quickly as possible. The C.O. then asked me if I could stick around a day or two. I told him I could because I wanted to know as much as what they would allow me to know, in order that I might aid them in their search for Derek.

I told the C.O. that I would stay overnight at Derek's house. He said fine, but that he would have the shore patrol police the area on a regular basis for the rest of the day and night.

A little past five PM Maggie drove me back to Derek's house. Fortunately for me, Derek had only recently given me a key. But as we drove up to the driveway I noticed that the screen door to the house was wide open. Not knowing what was going on, or if someone was in the house, both Maggie and I crept up to the door and placed our heads up against each side of the screen.

Maggie had a revolver in her car and ran back to get it in case we needed a little fire power. When she returned, we again leaned against the screen. After an additional five minutes of not hearing anything, we decided that it was safe to go inside. Though Maggie was ready to fire the pistol at almost anyone, or anything, we moved slowly as we entered the house. I then flipped on the outside light and the living room light at the same time to get a better look inside the house.

It seemed that Derek had had a visitor or two. As we moved through each room, we declared the house was in complete shambles. Every book had been torn from the bookshelves. Every drawer had been pulled out and dumped on the floor. And as we moved from room to room, we noticed that every cushion had been pulled from the chairs and sofa. Upstairs, the same held true. Every room, including the bathroom had been turned upside down.

Toothbrushes, along with a razor, shaving lotion as well as the soap dish were either on the floor or lying just outside the doorway to the bathroom. His bedroom was the hardest hit, with the pillows and mattresses sliced and the insides spewed all over the floor. Even the kitchen was not saved from this raping. Everything that had been in the refrigerator was now on the floor, along with every pot, pan and dish, not to mention every piece of silverware. The house looked like a bomb had gone off inside.

Maggie finally found the phone and looked at me and said, "Girlfriend, you're really in the thick of it this time. I've got to call this in!"

Noticing something strange, I yelled out loud, "Destiny, where is Destiny?"

Maggie still on the phone said, "Who, Destiny?"

I yelled back, "Destiny, the dog", as I began looking around again and opening closet doors. Upstairs and downstairs I went looking for her, calling her name. I couldn't believe that she wasn't responding to my voice! Where was she?

Through the screened door, leading to the back yard, I looked out and saw something in the middle of the yard. I burst outside and ran across the lawn and came to a complete stop, where Destiny was laying.

Without panicking too much I got down on the grass and placed my head to her stomach. She was still breathing.

By this time Maggie had followed me out to the back of the house. She told me to step aside and that she would look at the dog. She said that she was the volunteer at the pet clinic on base and that she could at least tell how much damage there was. She opened the dog's eyes and mouth and listened and smelled her breathe. Maggie told me to go in and call the clinic because we had to take Destiny there right now!

I did as I was told and in the meantime that short Lieutenant had picked up that 65-pound dog and was racing through the house as I hung up the phone, and followed her to the car.

After putting Destiny in the back seat with me holding her firm, Maggie sped to the clinic running a couple of traffic signs.

Upon arriving at the emergency entrance, Maggie again picked up the dog and raced inside yelling at the veterinarians and volunteers to clear a room and bed.

The vet on duty was Commander Farina. He calmly listened to Maggie as she was spouting out all this jargon, as I stood there panicked. The doctor then turned to me and said, "Please wait out in the lobby."

I was about to respond, but Maggie smiled and said, "Go ahead, I'll be out in a couple of minutes or so."

I turned and walked back outside into the waiting area. I couldn't believe that those bastards would also hurt a dog. "You've got to be inhumane", I said to myself.

About fifteen minutes or so, after sitting and then pacing around the clinic, Maggie came out of the room where she had taken Destiny. Maggie smiled and said, "Jack, we were just in time. I didn't want to tell you but whoever tore up Derek's place had poisoned Destiny. She was almost in a coma from the shock to her system, but Farina pulled out his magic wand and she will be fine after a few days of rest and treatments. They will keep her here until she has fully recovered."

It finally hit me, as I broke down and began sobbing. I kept on saying, "That bastard Carmine, he is going to pay for this…"

By the time Maggie had gotten me calmed down and back to Derek's house, I found a pillow in the living room that hadn't been torn to shreds and sat down on it and looked around. What on God's green earth could these maniacs been looking for. Maybe by now, my own house had been turned upside down as well. Was Carmine and the Mancini family looking for something that either Derek or I had? Maybe they thought that I would give it to them if they kidnapped Derek? Was Derek's capture because of the information that only he had? Or was it what the Navy had? We had stirred the pot up so much that they resorted to additional criminal acts to protect themselves. I was sure of it. And all I could keep saying to myself was, "Those bastards will pay for this!"

CHAPTER 9

After Maggie made the second call out to the Navy
departments in the local area, she relayed that shock waves
hit all the different agencies and commands with regards to
Derek's kidnapping. All the way up the Chain of
Command in the Navy there would be a lot of finger
pointing and blame. She went on to say that there would be
a lot more protection and secrecy put into place at NIS and
the Commanding Officers.

It wasn't until about 9:15PM that the shore patrol, CO of
the Base and city police had left Derek's house. Once
again, we answered tons of questions, some of them were
the same as before, along with what we thought might have
happened here at Derek's house. It looked like the police
took fingerprints of almost every square inch of the house.
There was plenty of dusting powder all over the place now.
And as we began to clean up the house both Maggie and I
started sneezing so much that we started laughing. It was a
funny moment in a not so funny situation.

As we tried to place everything back into some kind of
order, we found a sealed bottle of Bombay Gin and decided
since we had had a bad day that we deserved to have a
drink. We then searched the pantry for a bottle of olives.
Happily, we found it, unopened and untouched. Then we
dumped half of the olives into each one of our water
glasses, added some ice and filled the glass up to the top
with the gin.

Discussing what we should do next, we agreed to walk over
to the sea wall that stretched down the street, across from
the house. There was a pretty good view of the city to the
right and Coronado straight ahead of us.

We sat there, a little bit melancholy in the black of the night, looking at the city lights and played back to each other what had taken place earlier in the day.

By the time we had finished our recollection, our glasses were empty and we knew that the best thing for us to do was to go straight to bed. We then staggered back across the street to Derek's house and went to sleep in the living room, where we had made up two sleeping areas on the floor with pillows and blankets.

Though I slept all night it was a restless sleep, as my mind kept on seeing Derek's face and poor Destiny laying there in the yard, almost dead. Mixed feelings crossed my mind. One minute I felt happy and I could see myself grinning at Destiny that she was alright. Then the next moment I also felt great pain knowing that Derek was being held captive. No matter what I thought even in my state of dreamland, I knew that I had to find him and find him fast!

When I awoke Tuesday morning I felt that all too familiar fog and chill in the air. Apparently, Maggie had been up for an hour or so, as there was the smell of fresh coffee and she was already dressed in her uniform as I saw her hurry by me to go to the bathroom.

I stretched on the floor, between the sheets and the comforter. I felt like a wild cat waiting to spring into action.

It was now my turn to prepare myself for the day. My thoughts homed in on my efforts to get Derek back safe and sound. Maggie and I again discussed everything of the previous day just to make sure that we hadn't left anything out. We wanted to make sure that we hadn't forgotten a single thing or a single lead that would find Derek. Then

Maggie pulled out of her briefcase two folders. She said, "I almost forgot!" One of them was marked in bold letters "TOP SECRET/CONFIDENTIAL".

Maggie handed it to me and I ripped opened the folder to look through the documents. They all pertained to the Mafia bosses, the Navy and the connection on how they were all a part of the war effort, both home and abroad. There were many photos of several meetings between all parties concerned and in one of the photos stood Peter D'Angelo in uniform next to a few of the Dons and Rear Admiral Franklin, the CINCPAC Fleet. Peter showed up every time you turned a page.

"Who could have missed these connections", I wondered? Peter seemed to be one of the main characters throughout the pictures. Was he playing both sides against the middle? What was his connection with the families? No wonder he had an ear on everything that was being planned by the Navy. Every page I turned there was a picture of Peter's mug being photographed.

The next folder Maggie gave me was labeled, "LT Elizabeth Yardley". As I opened it up Maggie also handed me photos. She too was in several photos pictured with Peter, the Mob bosses and Rear Admiral Franklin. There was one at the formal dedication of the destroyer, "USS Steadfast". Then there was a photo that tied it all together for me. It was a picture that I had seen before at the library in Palm Springs. Only I didn't know who the woman was then as her face was hidden. But on this cool San Diego morning reading this TOP SECRET information, it all came together. The face in the photo was Lieutenant Elizabeth Yardley. Carmine Iialucci's sister!

I placed the folder down, looked at Maggie and said, "Did you know that Elizabeth was actually Francesca?"

Maggie said, "No, not until you asked me to run the file on her, and then all this stuff came pouring out. We're not sure how she slipped past all the scrutiny that we all were placed under. Even her file is clean. There is nothing that shows of her heritage line to Italy or the company she was keeping. She went to Vassar. Her family as noted in her personnel records was third generation English. However, after this stuff was put on my desk, I had both NIS and the OSS run a check on her and now somebody will have a red face and probably an early retirement from this little mishap."

Two incidents, very critical to the war were overlooked. The Japs bombing Pearl Harbor and now the Ialucci family knee deep in the Navy's business and as War manipulators.

"How could this happen no longer mattered" I told Maggie. It was now time to stop the Mancini family and get these traitors out of the country or better yet, in prison, where they belong, before anything else turns up on the wrong side.

Maggie then gave me some more troubling news with regards to how convoluted everything was. She said, "A British source has stated to our intelligence that during 1941-1942 there were several members from the German Army that looked to assassinate Hitler." She went on to say, "Somehow this was tied back to or through Pope Pius XII, who apparently was a negotiator and playing on both sides of the War. He had befriended Mussolini, who had killed Italians and Jews. But he was looking to eliminate the Mafia from Sicily and he approved of Adolph Hitler, even though there was strong evidence regarding the deaths of thousands of Jews. Even after the Polish Ambassador pleaded his case to the Pope confirming the concentration camps, Pius never accepted the deaths of so many people. The Vatican's Christmas broadcast in 1941 drove home a speech requesting that a new world order led by Christians, come about. Pius was promoting Fascism throughout Europe. He even looked the other way when Franco committed murder of hundreds or even thousands in Spain as well. Somehow he was able to justify all this by stating that he was against communism."

Maggie then confirmed one of my darkest fears. Because of Mussolini chasing the Mafia out of Italy, the Navy had stepped in to ask their help. She said she could verify that Meyer Lansky had breakfast with Lucky Luciano's lawyer, Moses Polakoff, the District Attorney Gurfein, and the Office of Naval Intelligence (ONI). Apparently, their discussion was about the German U-Boats who had sunk 71 merchant ships off the east coast. Luciano was able to set up the meeting, even though he was in jail. It was through his network that the Navy used the Sicilian Mafia to control the waterfront to keep out the German spies.

Flabbergasted, I just looked at Maggie.

She shrugged her shoulders and said, "Jacqueline, it's hard to know who to trust. Everyone seems to be out for themselves. Because of this there are so many double and triple agents. Apparently, the War makes someone a hero one moment and then the next time, he's a terrorist. No one is perfect and hardly anyone can be truthful. I suppose they all use the same people whenever they can."

After a numbing conversation with Maggie, I just sat there for a while as my brain tried to place all this new data into the corners of my mind. Some things I understood, while other events just tore me up.

I still needed to find Derek, so I decided to get back to the task at hand. I couldn't change the players or politics of the War. So I called Brad and told him some of what had happened. I instructed him to be very cognizant of Chloe and to call the Tong to ask for a meeting. I figured that we had to turn up the pressure to see what Carmine and or the Family might do next. I also knew that this was definitely real and that everyone involved was susceptible to being harmed by this circle of characters. I let Brad know that I would be up to LA as soon as I had gotten done with the Navy and that I would call him as soon as I got there.

Next, I called Uncle Mike and filled him in as well. He was worried as hell about me, so I kept telling him, "That I was all right and not to fret."

He couldn't understand how this had happened, particularly on Navy property. I told him that it wouldn't have happened unless there was stupidity amongst the Navy higher ups. That said, he calmed down and said he would help me in any way that he could and to call him when I got back to the city.

As I was speaking to Uncle Mike, I could hear him yell to his sergeant to put out an APB pronto on the Mancini family for kidnapping and possible conspirator charges. He told me that he would be able to hold them for a long time on these charges, as we were at War and no attorney would be able to get a client released until a formal court date was set. And based on the War effort, it might not be until long after the War.

106

Uncle Mike also said that he would contact the Sheriff offices in the other nearby counties and have any other Mob associate that was in the Riverside or Palm Springs area picked up for "questioning". He informed me that he would also send out an arrest bulletin to other cities, particularly on the East Coast and up the California Coast.

Maggie left around 8:30 to go back to her office to try and dig up any additional information that she may have missed, though I couldn't imagine what, after everything she had already told me.

I let her know that I would head back to LA shortly, as I thought that this is where they would have taken Derek and that I needed to meet with the Tong family. But before Maggie left she told me that she would call my Uncle's precinct office as soon as possible if she found out anything more.

I then rang up Captain Stark's office to see if he had returned from Pearl. His secretary told me he had, but was in conference. So I said to her, "Excuse me Miss, would you kindly tell him that it's Jack Riley. He will come to the phone and speak with me."

She kind of snickered, but did as I requested and in a few minutes, Captain Stark was saying. "Yes Jack, can I get together with you this afternoon, at my office?"

I said yes, but it would have to be early as I was going to LA.

He said, "Let's meet around 12:45." I told him "can do" and hung up.

I made some more calls, one to Melvin to give him the lowdown on my poor car, Big Red. He just laughed and said, "I told you so". He told me that he would send someone over in the morning to pick up the car and bring it back to the Springs for repair. He asked me to make sure that his guys could get on base.

I chuckled and told him, "Do not send any Italian looking guys as it would be hard at this point to get them through the gates. Otherwise, I will set it up with security."

I could hear Melvin reply. "Aye Aye Captain", as he hung up.

I then called the clinic to ask about Destiny. The nurses said she was doing just fine and that she was out for a walk in the kennel area already this morning. However, the nurse also said that they would keep her there for a few extra days just to make sure she was OK. Smiling to myself, I could see her happy face and then thought of Derek. "Damn those Dagos!" was all I could think of.

Wanting to put additional heat on the Mancini's, I decided to call Carmine's office. It was time to really crank it up on this "meatball". His secretary, Ida, told me that he was not in, as he had a meeting in the morning and was not expected to be in until after lunch. I said, "Fine, kindly leave him a message that I called and that I'm coming to get him, whether he's in New York or California!"

The secretary answered with, "What did you say?"

I told her "Just tell him exactly how I told you."

"Yes Ma'am" she said and hung up.

At 12:35 I was walking up the steps to the Naval Intelligence Service building. Maggie had set it up for me to borrow an unmarked Navy car from the transportation pool. As I walked through the main door, I noticed two Marines standing behind a counter that looked like a barricade. They were armed to the hilt with a rifle strapped across their bodies and a handgun hanging from a ready holster. Being dressed in my favorite navy-blue pin striped pleated skirt, with a cream color silk blouse, no collar, navy high heels, no stockings and a navy blue double-breasted jacket I felt I was dressed appropriately for the day.

The Marine Sergeant though looking at his paperwork on the counter, politely said, "Good Morning Mam, may I help you?"

With that I looked at this all too familiar 6 foot 6-inch-tall "Jarhead" and said in a kind of southern accent, "Why yes you may!"

The Gunny shifted his face up from the paperwork and smiled and then yelled my name back at me in that Georgia accent of his. "Jack. How the hell are you?"

I replied in my southern belle accent again, "Well, just fine, you hunk of a man!"

We both laughed, as the young corporal standing next to the Gunny, twitched and looked at both of us with a strange face, as if to say, who the hell is this woman?

Gary Jackson then came around the counter and gave me the biggest bear hug I think known to man or for that matter known to any woman. He let go and continued to look at me and say "Jack, Jack, I can't believe it's you, how the hell are you and what are you doing here?"

As it turned out, Gary and I had known each other for almost fifteen years. Gary had become my father's orderly, when my Dad was promoted to Commander, way back when. He traveled all over the world with my Dad and kept him safe from any harm that would have befallen him. He remained with my Dad until my Dad retired. Gary was, as my father told me many times, "more like a son". When I was a teenager, I had a crush on Gary, but never pursued it because I knew that it was not appropriate to try and get between my Dad and Gary. If there was substance on male bonding, this was it in the most extraordinary way. I knew that my Dad had to occasionally defend his relationship with Gary, regarding some Admirals, Captains and even with my late fiancé, James. But by my Dad's insistence, Gary always attended every function that my Dad was present at. Gary was not only a bodyguard, but also my Dad's confidant.

I told Gary that I was here to see Captain Stark. He said, that he had heard about the kidnapping, but didn't know who was involved with the incident or who the Captain had assigned to the case. I told Gary that I would ask that he be assigned and only him. I didn't know who else I could trust from the staff.

Gary told the corporal to notify Stark's office that I had arrived.

Laughing it up a bit with Gary relaxed me. It felt good to be around a man that I could trust with my life. After a few minutes, the Captain's administrative assistant, Mrs. Agnes Bellflower appeared in the lobby. She introduced herself, standing behind the barricade and asked me to come on in.

I told Gary that I would see him before I left the building and proceeded through the gate at the counter and followed Agnes to the Captain's office.

As I walked through the doors to a conference office, I found eleven people sitting around a large table. Eight men and Maggie stood to introduce themselves, while the two civilian women sat in the chairs looking at me. They seemed like other admin type assistants to me, but I didn't know for sure.

The first person I met was Captain Stark, who was a shorter man, about 5'6 or 5'7. He was bald and a little on the pudgy side and looked a little mischievous. But I gathered that he knew what he was doing. After all, he couldn't have become a Captain unless he knew something or someone. There were three Commanders. The first one introduced to me was Commander Martin from the staff of Admiral Franklin. The other two Commanders, Jones and Bain were from the Navy Department in Washington D.C. The two Lieutenant's Burnett and Chase were from NIS. There was a Detective Smiley from the San Diego Police Department and Lieutenant Colonel Murphy from the Marines Security Force. Standing was Maggie who just nodded at me.

After the introduction, we all sat down. The table was filled with charts and files strewn all over it. In front of me were the same items that I had seen that morning from Maggie. I figured that they had her pull all the files on anyone or everyone involved that they could think of.

At that very moment and three hours north in LA, Derek was being beating as he sat in a chair in a warehouse. One of Carmine's men had tied him up. Every time they asked him a question and he didn't answer that punched him in the face, or kicked him in his legs. After a while he passed out from the amount of punishment and pain he was enduring. But the men brought in their "doctor" who verified that he was still alive, and gave him smelling salt to help wake him up. This continued until Carmine got to the warehouse.

Upon arriving, Carmine told his guys to stop and then said to the doctor, "Keep him alive. He is no good to me dead, at least not yet!"

The doctor patched Derek up as best as he could, but his left eye had taken quite the beating and was so swollen it was closed, so he could only see somewhat good out of his right, where it had not been the main target in the pounding of his face.

Derek was having a hard time and could barely keep awake. He was numb with pain throughout his body. He hoped that someone would find him, as he didn't know how much more he could take before his body would shut down.

Carmine sensing Derek's demise, told his men to back off for now and to just make sure that he didn't escape. There would be time enough later if he needed some more prodding. His main concern at that very moment was Chloe and the Tong. He would deal with the Commander later in case he needed him as part of an escape plan to leave the country.

CHAPTER 10

Back at the long table meeting, Captain Stark started the conversation by telling me that "everyone at this table is sorry about this incident in regards with Commander Kent, and that they all would do whatever they could to find him and bring severe penalties to his kidnapers."

After some additional small talk about Derek, Commander Martin asked me a few questions. "Ms. Riley, can you please tell us any additional details regarding why you believe that Petty Officer Peter D'Angelo is connected to the Mafia and why you think that he is probably involved with this kidnapping as well?"

Before I could answer, he asked me another question. "Also Ms. Riley, would you also please tell us your findings on LT. Yardley, Commander Kent's assistant and her connection to Peter D'Angelo?"

As Commander Martin started to speak again, I cut him off. I thought I had better lay it on the line all that I knew, in hopes that the Navy would fill in some of the blank areas that I was missing.

So, I began. "Commander, the recent findings of the true identity of LT Yardley as Francesco Ialucci, the sister of the Mafia crime boss Carmine Ialucci, not only connects Peter to them but also connects them directly to Admiral Franklin and his own knowledge of the Mafia and their association with the Navy. The direct links of all these parties involved, the correspondence, the photographs taken at more than twenty events have now connected them to Navy ships, personnel and in most cases, movements around the world. All of this information whether willingly given to each party or not, has been going up and down this

"Jacob's ladder" like running water for some time. And Commander Martin, I am quite surprised that you have no or very little knowledge of this at all?"

Commander Martin, fidgeting in his chair, said, "Ms. Riley, I am merely the Admirals Staff Officer, what he does in his time off and who he rubs elbows with is his matter, not mine!"

"But", I said to the Commander, "You are his right-hand man, who plans and makes sure that he is supposed to be where he is at almost every moment of his day. Why then did you not know these people yourself?"

Apparently, I hit a nerve because the Commander shifted in his chair and started to refute my concerns, when Captain Stark jumped in.

"Ms. Riley, let's try and stay on the course to find Derek and get his release. Regarding Commander Martin, the Navy will investigate his side of the story."

I responded with "Ok, but not one of you in this room or in Washington D.C. wants to admit it that you just screwed up in allowing both LT Yardley and Peter D'Angelo into the Navy. Even if you knew and were using this pipeline to give out wrong information, it's killing our sailors and marines in faraway places."

Passionately I continued on. "The Navy Department knew about LT Yardley and her association to the Mafia. However, you neglected to inform the man that she was working for. And now, he's in captivity by her and her brother, who has sent me on some wild goose chase to find a woman that knows that she can spill the beans about the Mafia's involvement with the Japanese and the Navy. I wouldn't be surprised either if the Mafia were not involved with the Germans as well, as their only loyalty is to themselves, not to any one country."

Just then Detective Smiley said, "Jack, you don't mind if I call you that, right?"

I looked across the table at him and just nodded. He went on. "Jack, do you have any idea where they might have taken Commander Kent?"

I replied with "No!"

He then asked, "Is it true that you know where Carmine's girlfriend is? Chloe, right?"

I said "Yes."

"Well" he said, "I think that they still need her to put their own puzzle together on how much Commander Kent knows and who he told, and whether Chloe can help or not. And I am sure that they probably want you as well to find out how much you know and to secure themselves. As they probably don't know how much you have already uncovered and who you have told, I am sure they don't want to take any more chances than they have to!"

Commander Bain, of the Navy Department chimed in, "What is it that we can assist you with, Ms. Riley?" We can't go back or even make any excuses, for what the Navy did or didn't do, we can only go forward. And if we want to get Derek back alive and out of this jam at the same time, we need to offer you our complete cooperation. This will at least keep the American public unaware of who these intertwining personalities are and what businesses they are involved in, so that we can better serve our country, without mucking it up any more. We are not pleased at all about our involvement with all these Mafia figures. However, we needed their help in controlling ship building, piers, harbors and other hardened areas that the government does not need to be involved with, nor has the personnel and or the means, but we had no other alternative to excel our own war efforts."

Captain Stark then said, "Commander Bain, I think that the Navy Department should give Ms. Riley any and all information regarding offices, warehouse locations and or meeting places that you all and the Ialucci's have met at, or that you were aware of. I will inform Rear Admiral McCoy, my boss, all that I know and all that I will know by tomorrow. No doubt, he will speak with your boss and others on "the Hill", including the CNO and Admiral King, about this collusion."

Captain Stark continued, "Commander Martin, you must find Rear Admiral Franklin and recount this story verbatim. You must then tell your Rear Admiral to hand over to me immediately, all correspondence that has occurred between himself and any Mafia or associate affiliated with the Mafia. I am also instructing you to inform him that I will be asking for his resignation and retirement through my chain of command by tomorrow, based on just what I have in my possession. There appears to me to be enough information to justify my stance and to request that he be arrested for his actions. I am not saying that the Admiral is a traitor, I will let the attorneys figure that out."

Commander Martin said he would try and contact the Admiral, who was currently on leave. Martin said that there was no answer at his office or home and that he'd have to drive up to Malibu to see if he could locate him.

I looked at Commander Martin and knew that he was lying about his involvement. He was the main person to manage the Admiral and his day to day routine and appointments, even if he were on leave, yet here he was in this room lying to us all.

Captain Stark then said, "LT Burnett, I want you to be the liaison officer between detective Smiley and this office. LT Chase, I want you to be the liaison officer between this office and Ms. Riley. Jack, you can call me direct anytime, if you feel you need to. LT Colonel Murphy, I want a full-blown investigation of what happened on base and give it me by tomorrow 0700. I also want you to work closely with Detective Smiley in trying to connect any links between LT Yardley, Petty Officer Peter D'Angelo and this base."

Again, Stark asked me, "Jack, I know you have your own reasons to get to the bottom of this whole mess, but I would appreciate it very much, if you would keep me posted with any new information that you obtain, so that we can all help each other in apprehending these criminals. Any thoughts on where you will start first?"

I looked at Commander Martin and then said to Captain Stark, "Probably with Rear Admiral Franklin! He has got to know something about where Derek might be kept and what information has been given to Carmine and the rest of the Mancini family."

The Captain then said to me, "Jack, please go easy on him for now, we will be investigating the Admiral, his entire staff and everyone else close or involved with him. This may have been the leak for everything the Navy has been involved with during these past several years, but we won't know till we hear his side of the story."

117

I told Captain Stark I would, but I also kept my fingers crossed.

Standing up, Commander Martin excused himself so that he could try and contact Admiral Franklin. With that I inquired, "Commander, would you mind if I went to see the Admiral?"

Commander Martin replied, "Not at all. In fact, it might be good if he heard these questions from a civilian, before the military started making inquiries of his meetings."

I said, "Thanks." However, my thoughts were rolling in my head that started with my Dad and what he would have said and done, because if this Admiral was the traitor, he needed to be taken out the back door and shot in the head. I could hear him saying, "You can't be acting as the good guy and reaping benefits from the bad guys. That dog don't hunt in my book!"

Captain Stark ended the meeting and I excused myself to all, so that I could make some calls and begin my trek up the coast to see this Rear Admiral Franklin.

Agnes was able to direct me to an office to use to make my calls. Once again, I called Brad. This time I asked him if he had put together the meeting with the Tong. He said he had. It would be at 7 or 8 PM on Wednesday night. I told him that that was perfect. I then asked him about Chloe. He told me know that everything was quiet and that neither Carmine nor his associates were seen around looking for her. With that, I told Brad that I would be in LA tomorrow and would call him when I got settled.

As I got into my car to leave, there was a knock on my window. It was Lieutenant Colonel Murphy.

I rolled down the window and the Colonel said, "Ms. Riley, I knew your father. He and I served together many times. I would appreciate it if you would patronize me, by allowing the United States Marines to shadow your movements. I would very much like for Gunny Jackson to become that bodyguard who also once upon a time protected your Dad."

I answered with a giant smile, "Yes thanks, but only if the Gunny is dressed in civilian clothes, I don't want it to be too obvious."

The Colonel grinned and sort of chuckled and then said, "Very well, Mam."

As I began to drive out the driveway, I saw Gunny opening the door to a black unmarked 2 door Ford. He had already changed into "civvies". Clever man, I thought of the Colonel!

I smiled to myself, knowing that I had a Good Samaritan within my beck and call. As I drove up the Pacific Coast Highway every so often around a bend, I would see that black Ford, blending in with traffic, never too close, yet never too far away either. I thought my Dad was pretty damn lucky to have the Gunny for his confidant. Now it's time for me.

I looked at my watch. It was 2:30 PM. I knew that we wouldn't get up to Malibu until nightfall as it was about a four to five hours drive. So, I decided to push on as far as I could and spend the night at one of the hotels along the sand.

Driving along the highway I thought part of the puzzle had to be the bombing at Pearl Harbor. Rear Admiral Franklin was there when it happened. He was the assistant

CINCPAC. And even though he will undoubtedly be forced to retire, he had to have been involved even then. Too many connections between him and the Mafia not to have been part of the overall story.

It dawned on me that the clock was ticking on Derek's life, not to mention other Allied military personnel, across the world. This was just like what Derek had told me regarding all the hush hush chatter about Roosevelt. Apparently, the President knew that the Japanese were going to attack Pearl, but not when. In knowing this, it would allow the United States to enter the War alongside the British as promised to Churchill. It seemed like there was a lot of politicians, not to mention, criminals, regular civilians and military involved in either trying to cover up or keep the war going for their own rewards. In my opinion, it didn't matter now, we needed to take down both Germany and Japan and that's all there was to it!

As I continued my drive I noticed the heavy fog that was sitting off the coast, waiting to roll over the highway. I knew it would not be long, until sunset and the dampness would set in on this California highway. The sun was peaking over the fog into the water giving it an eerie glow. The mountainside was aflame in orange and would be pitch black shortly. Very weird, so I turned on the radio, and the Glenn Miller orchestra was playing "American Patrol". I thought, isn't that just what we are doing!

Driving the Navy Ford was not like driving Big Red. It would under steer at almost every corner or bend, so I had to compensate for it by tapping the brake and the gas pedal at the same time as I went around each curve.

Just as I passed the northern San Diego produce fields, I noticed a strange looking car behind me. It was some sort of foreign made, maybe Italian or German. It only had the driver, no passengers. I kept looking at it because there are not many of these types of cars here in America and because it was staying about 25 to 50 yards behind me. I thought I remembered seeing this car parked the night at Pasquale's, when all the Mafia members where having dinner with Carmine. Though I couldn't see the driver, the hairs on the back of my neck stood up. I just had a funny hunch that it was Nicky or even Carmine himself behind the wheel.

As I continued up the highway, I had hoped that Gary had taken notice of this car too, as Gary was another twenty or so yards behind the foreign vehicle.

Rolling along in the Ford, I continued to drive up the coast, not thinking too much of my "tail". I figured that whoever it was they were just following me to find out where I was headed, not to try and harm me. However, I paused, "How did they know where I would be in the first place?" "Who was the leak from the meeting this afternoon that told them where I was going?"

I pondered this for some time and kept coming back to Commander Martin. It was just too obvious not to be him. He was assigned to the Admiral and was always with him no matter what or where. It would have been impossible for him not to be involved, like he mentioned and lied about in the meeting.

North of San Diego was dotted with fields of lettuce, green peppers, onions and tomatoes for miles on end. The area was a farmer's dream, where one could raise almost anything all year long. Further north, I drove through the orange trees of Orange County. They were so thick that they hid the mountains and at times the ocean from view.

Every area and town that I went by had its own distinctive smell. The coastal air was incredible.

After we had driving another hour or so, I decided that I needed to stop for coffee and some bathroom relief. The Texaco service station that I frequented was up the road and not too far from where I was, so I decided to make the "pit stop". I remembered that there was a small dinner next to it, where I could grab coffee to go. When I arrived, the attendant came out and I told him, "Fill it up please, I'll be in the coffee shop".

Walking in I turned to look over my shoulder. The Italian car had stopped about five feet from the driveway entrance of the service station. It was sleek and red. I still couldn't make out who was in the car. I figured it was safe for now, particularly since I knew that Gary was somewhere around and not too far behind me.

I visited the women's restroom and then sat up at the counter to have my coffee. I could see Gary drove in and pull his Ford on the other side of where my car had just gotten gas. He apparently asked the attendant to fill up his vehicle and then walked towards the diner nonchalantly and through the door and looked at me for just an instant before heading for the men's room.

Based on that slight meeting of our minds, my assumption was that he knew that the foreign car was outside waiting for me to get back on the road.

After Gary came back out, he asked the waitress for a coffee to go. As Irma looked at Gary with a big smile and said, "That'll be twenty-five cents handsome", Gary reached into his pocket and placed fifty cents down on the counter and was about to walk away, when I walked up behind him to pay for mine. Irma just looked at me and said, "That'll be the same for you Miss!"

As I was reaching into my purse for the change, I felt the air from the opening of the diner's door brush the skin of my legs. I felt all those hairs of mine stand up on my neck and I knew whoever was following me was standing close by.

Gary had grabbed the door from the intruder and walked outside looking back at me. I had turned slightly and heard a voice, "Well if it isn't Sam the P.I. Nice to see you again, Jack!" It was Nicky staring at me with that missing tooth grin.

I looked at Nicky and asked him, "What brings you to this side of the mountain? The last time I saw you, you were hanging from a crane. I guess you were able to get loose?"

Nicky said "Through no help from you Jack! Carmine's a little peeved with you. He wanted me to locate you and keep an eye on what you have uncovered on Chloe. He was wondering why it was taking you so long?"

I said to Nicky, "Tell Carmine that the P.I. is working on it and when I have something to report, I'll contact him."

Nicky said "Fine, I'll pass that on." Then he sat down on the stool closet to the door and asked the waitress for a coffee. Irma didn't say a word but proceeded to pour a cup and bring it to Nicky.

I turned back to Nicky as I began heading out the door. Nicky, placing his cup back down on the saucer, said, "See you 'round beautiful!". I just squinted my eyes and said, "Yeah", as I walked out the door.

Gary was standing by his car chatting with the station operator when I stepped back into my car.

I looked at Gary and then through the window of the diner to see if I could see Nicky. He was still sitting at the counter, but he was watching my every move.

I turned back around, turned the key and the Ford's engine came alive. Shifting into gear I thought to myself, I know now that Carmine and probably the Mancinis assumed that I had contacted the authorities with information that could tie them all together. This would cause the Mob great trouble if they didn't get rid of me. I felt it from that look in Nicky's eyes. I knew that I needed to be extra careful even if Gary was around. The Mob wanted to know where I was and what I was doing so they could quietly remove their number one problem – me.

As I pulled my car out of the driveway onto the highway, I looked at my rear-view mirror and could see Nicky getting back into his car. I pushed the gas pedal all the way to the floor. The Ford heaved forward a bit as I popped the clutch. Down the highway, I was way ahead of Nicky and couldn't see his car. Fortunately for me, Gary had gotten right behind me, so I at least I had some protection, now that I knew who was following me.

Even though I couldn't see Nicky, I had a feeling that he was still following us and that all three of us now traveled in unison along PCH. After another hour had passed we drove into the town of Seal Beach. We were just coming up on the Long Beach Naval Shipyard and I considered going in there to shake off Nicky, but I thought it would be too obvious, so I continued on.

Close to Santa Monica now, not much had happened. We were still all in tow, rolling up PCH in the dark. At times I could see the foreign car far behind me from the street lamps.

By the time that we were close to Malibu and Zuma Beach, it was around 7 o'clock. This is where the Rear Admiral lived.

I remembered that a little motel was on the left-hand side of the highway. I knew that I needed to keep Gary close by and yet lose Nicky. We were all traveling at the same speed, when I decided to shut off all my lights, in order to make a left-hand turn into the street where The Sandcastle restaurant was. This was a way to let Gary know what I was up to. Then as we were rounding the bend and approaching the intersection, I slowed down which made everyone do the same and then I gunned the engine.

This alerted Gary to pay attention to what I was doing. Gary kept his car back, which forced Nicky to stay behind him. Then Gary moved a bit towards the center lane of the highway to block any view of my actions that Nicky might have.

Completing the bend in the road, I made a left-hand turn.

Gary then stepped on the gas which left Nicky behind unaware of what had just happened.

Nicky couldn't see where I had turned as Gary's vehicle rolled left, right and then again left of the center line. Gary once again pressed the gas pedal all the way to the floor, driving past the road that led to the restaurant, with Nicky right behind him.

It was about 20 minutes later that Gary came back to the restaurant without Nicky following him. My guess was since it was so dark out on the highway, Nicky didn't know that I had turned off and just kept driving after Gary made a turn into a house driveway. No doubt Nicky suspected that I had just driven fast to get away from him.

The plan worked. Now Gary and I could relax without our tail.

Gary had pulled up behind me in the parking lot of The Sandcastle. It was busy for a Wednesday night. He got out of the car and came up to where I was waiting.

"Jack, I was kind of aware of what was happening but I didn't quite know what you had up your sleeve."

I told Gary, that the goon driving the car worked for the Mafia kingpin Carmine who was up to his "knickers" in the disappearance of Derek and the undermining of our national security. I suggested that we eat and then drive up to the motel, which was a short distance away. I recommended that we leave one car at the restaurant and come back in the morning for it, just in case Nicky had doubled back and was still looking for us. I didn't think that Nicky was smart enough to know that Gary was my bodyguard, but I didn't want to take any chances.

Unbeknownst to Gary or myself, Nicky was following me but for different reasons. After the Navy meeting took place, Commander Martin had called Carmine, to inform him that I was in route to see Admiral Franklin. Carmine told the CDR that he would send someone to the Admiral's house to make sure that there was no conversation. The CDR understood what Carmine was saying and sent Nicky.

Nicky was smarter than I gave him credit for. He called CDR Martin and asked him what I was driving and from where. He then drove out and placed himself at a position along the highway and just waited for me to pass him. This way he just followed me and then proceeded along to Admiral Franklin's house after I had given him the slip.

Nicky woke the Admiral around 1 AM claiming that he needed to talk to him. After petting the dog, he gave the dog a treat that was laced with poison and he then killed the Admiral and threw him in the pool to make a statement. Nicky was as ruthless as any Mob member could be. He was sometimes called by his nickname, A.C., as in Al Capone. He had no feelings for murder. He just did it.

CHAPTER 11

After having a pretty decent meal of salad, swordfish and mashed potatoes, I asked the owner if I could leave my car overnight and he said, "Sure." With that we jumped into Gary's vehicle and drove out of the parking lot, making a left onto PCH and headed north for a few miles where the motel was. We checked in and asked for two rooms. The clerk looked at us funny, but never did ask us why? However, we paid him in cash in advance with a tip to wake us in the morning with coffee, so a smile spread across his face and he went about his own business.

We never did see Nicky again that night, so I figured that we were in good shape. Besides, in my opinion, he was never that smart. Little did I know what Nicky was really up too and that I had miscalculated him!

After I took a shower, I washed my underwear and hung them close to the fireplace, so they would be dry in the morning. I did however, ask the clerk for an iron, so I could press off my outfit. I wanted to be quite presentable to the Admiral on Thursday.

"There's nothing like living out of a purse", I thought to myself. Fortunately, both Gary and I were able to obtain some small samples of shampoo and a travel tooth brush with toothpaste from the night clerk.

I laid down on the bed in just the towels wrapped around me. They were a little rough, yet they kind of aroused my breasts as I stretched for the phone to make a few calls. "I think I am in need of Derek", I confessed to myself. Then I shook my head and said, "Back to the real world, Jack", so I called Uncle Mike to find out if he had come up with anything? I also filled him in on what was happening out here on PCH. He told me that he would send out a couple of cars to locate Nicky and his Italian automobile and put him on ice for a day or two.

As usual he told me that he was worried as hell about me, even though Gary was shadowing her. So, I told him "not too worry about it."

My Uncle was able to get his hands on some of the members of the Mancini family. But they weren't the principal ones that we needed to have locked up, but he was keeping them behind bars for the moment.

He told me to check back in the morning for an update, as he was also able to pick up a few more family members in Riverside and Palm Springs for "questioning". He informed me that his counterparts in New York and Boston had confirmed that they had arrested eight of the top figures so far and that there were more to come.

It was about ten o'clock when I called Melvin. He lived above the garage, so he always answered the phone after hours. He sounded tired, but joked with me anyway about Big Red. He told me that it was all ready for me when I got back and not to worry about it.

I rolled over to the side of the bed and hung up the phone. I was felling exhausted and immediately fell asleep after laying my head on the pillows. All I could think about was Derek, Destiny and me out on his boat. It made for a pleasant and soothing dream.

In the morning, Gary was promptly knocking on my door at 7am. "Jack, hope you don't mind me waking you, he said?" However, when I opened the door, I was already dressed and ready to go.

We decided not to risk getting a "cup of joe" after all, from the desk clerk, so we drove back to pick up my car and then we both drove up to a diner that was along the way to the Admirals house. We talked about Derek, my Dad, and the war. We found that we were kind of catching up on old times.

Then Gary asked me to tell him as much as I could and the details of Chloe, Carmine and whatever else I thought. Knowing Gary, I knew that he wanted to get a mental picture in his mind to assist me in any way he could to free Derek and deport Carmine.

I asked Gary about Commander Martin. Did he know anything about him and his background? He told me no.

I then said, "We need to get going to visit with our Admiral Franklin. I want him to tell me the truth of his involvement before the Commander gets here. We also need to get the Admiral to hand over to us anything that connects him to the Mafia or associate affiliated with the Mob. I should tell him that Martin will be asking for his resignation and retirement today but I think I'll let the Commander be the bearer of bad news."

I didn't think that Gary was surprised. In fact, he agreed. Being in the military, there was always someone out of character that was discharged or even sent to prison. Though bordering on treason was something else.

I commented that the Admiral probably knew where Derek might be kept and if so he may have been in contact with Carmine or the Mancini family already.

I pondered the question, "Was the Admiral linked to President Roosevelt in the theory that we all knew we were going to war, as Derek had mentioned to me before?"

Before I could answer myself, Gary said, "Don't you think we need to go?"

"Yes", I said to Gary, "Time's a wasting. Let's go see the old Admiral and put this piece of the puzzle together."

Gary and I then jumped into our cars and headed out into PCH and drove towards the Admirals estate.

As we rounded the curve to Broadbeach where we could see the Admirals house overlooking the coast, we turned right and drove up the long road.

When we pulled up to the circular driveway, we stopped the cars and Gary and I got out and walked up to the Admirals house. It was just shortly before 8AM.

It was a little eerie as the sun was just coming over the hill behind the Admirals house, throwing its light on the huge anchor centered in the circular driveway. The only sounds you heard were the ocean in the distance and the faint cry of a seagull.

We knocked on the door. There was no sound. We then rang the doorbell, which sounded like a Navy bell ringing. Still no sound or answer at the door.

Gary said to me, "Jack you stay here and wait for the Admiral, and I'll go around the back to see if I can find a way in."

I said, "O.K., but I am not going to wait too long."

Gary just snickered. "You haven't changed a bit Jack. You were impatient when you were a young girl and a teenager!"

Gary then disappeared to the back of the house.

Looking at my watch I noticed that some five minutes had passed before the door opened. It was Gary looking at me with a grim face.

As I pushed past Gary, I heard him say, "Jack, the Admirals dead! It looks like he drowned in his pool. No wonder Commander Martin couldn't get a hold of him. When I jumped over the fence I went straight into the house to look for him. When I didn't find him inside, I looked out the back and towards the pool and saw something in the pool. Not a pretty sight!"

Almost running to the pool, it hit me what Gary was saying. The old Admiral was lying face down, naked with his uniform of blue and gold floating to one side of the pool.

I told Gary, "Don't touch anything".
We just stood there, dumbfounded looking at the dead Admiral.

I then said, "I'll call both my Uncle Mike and Captain Stark. They will want to know immediately. More than likely they both will want to send their own detectives and all to the house to look for clues. This is almost getting to be routine with me, people missing and dead bodies wherever I go."

I told Gary, "Before I call, let's look for documents, any documents that might help us. I'm not sure what they are or where they might be, so we need to tread lightly throughout the house, without leaving any fingerprints."

Gary looked at me and said, "Right, lead on Jack!"

We spent what seemed to be minutes, but it was an hour and a half, scouring the house for anything that looked like it would help.

We used towels to open the doors to closets, carefully not disturbing any evidence all the while going through uniforms, pockets and even the insides of shoes, neatly placing everything back into its original location.

We stood on chairs to rummage through the boxes of storage items, finding an occasional picture and letter that we just throw in an old empty "seabag", so that we could look at the items later.

"We will have to go through everything when we get to Chinatown or at the precinct", I told Gary.

By the time we had gone through all of the Admirals personal belongings, including his room that was set off the side as his office, we had a full seabag filled with stuff. Who knew what we would find in there, but it was a start!

We checked behind photos and paintings on the walls. We even looked under the naval paraphernalia.

When we were done I had Gary throw the seabag in my car and then I called Uncle Mike and Captain Stark, to inform them of the Admiral's demise. While Uncle Mike listened to my story, he told his sergeant to firm up that his precinct would send over two squad cars. When I was done with Stark's office, as he wasn't in just yet, the Lieutenant told me that she would have the Navy's NIS office send up several officers, including staff to see what had happened. In the meantime, Gary kept looking in more places, just in case we missed something.

After we had completed our search, we went into the living room and sat down on a couple of ottomans.

We discussed the fact that the house hadn't been messed up and that all the doors seemed to have been locked. Gary told me that he had to enter the house through the dog door in the kitchen to get in. Good thing the Admiral had a St Bernard otherwise Gary would have had to break down the sliding glass door on the porch.

Unfortunately, the poor dog was dead also, lying on the floor of the porch, but there was no blood, so it appeared that he was poisoned, so that he wouldn't bark. Whoever did the job was pro, we both agreed.

"Could it have been Nicky?" I asked Gary.

Gary said, "Yep it was probably him, because it was just too convenient for Nicky to have been on the road only to tail us. Certainly, there had to be a leak from the office meeting."

As I was about to tell Gary who I thought it was, the door opened which surprised both Gary and myself and we both jumped up into a stance to protect ourselves. But standing there with a set of keys in his hand was Commander Martin.

When he saw us, he looked rather surprised. "Ms. Riley and Gunny Jackson", he said.

I responded with, "Good Morning Commander. I didn't expect you to be here so soon?"

The Commander replied, "Didn't you remember that I was to come up and get the Admiral ready for his investigation?"

I said, "Oh yeah, but didn't realize it would be this early! However, I need to tell you something." And then explained what we had found.

I was looking at Commander Martin and he seemed to be non-responsive to what I was saying.

Then he finally said, "Well Miss Riley, have you found anything or touched anything? I suppose I should let Captain Stark know."

I looked at Gary and then back at the Commander. He was way too nonchalant almost non-emotional about the Admiral's death. I found him to be peculiar with his attitude. I was sure that he knew something or was up to something. Yes, it dawned on me, I don't like this guy! This officer was on the Admiral's staff. Maybe it wasn't the Admiral after all that knew everything. Maybe it was the Commander instead? Why did he have a set of keys to this house and why was nothing in this house tossed about and why was there no struggle? In other words, what the hell happened here? The Admiral must have known the person inside the house with him. The Admiral had to have let in whoever killed him. No doubt about it!

Seeing the scowl on my face, as I took a long look at Martin, Gary chirped in and said, "Commander, let's go back to the pool area so I can show you where the Admiral's body is."

Thirty minutes later two squad cars arrived, along with my Uncle Mike.

He said to me in his broken Irish English, "Another fine mess little girl. That circle of yours keeps getting bigger" I responded with, "Trouble just keeps following me along on this one Uncle."

The police began their process of looking for clues, fingerprinting as much of the house as possible.

The Commander, Gary and myself drifted off to one side to let the police do their jobs. That afternoon, Captain Stark and his staff arrived. All of us huddled around the dining room table to discuss motives and anything else that might shed some light on this bizarre situation.

My uncle didn't think that it was suicide, but wouldn't really know till an autopsy was performed. On the other hand, Commander Martin thought that it was suicide, because he said the Admiral had been acting strange lately.

I stared back at Martin and said, "No I don't think so!"

Captain Stark on the other hand, couldn't bring himself to agree with the Commander, as he said he had known the Admiral for years and just couldn't believe that this is the way he would want to die, even if he was in the middle of something that was destructive against his own country.

I myself believed that he was murdered, but didn't state my feelings to the group. I felt it was too timely with Martin at the meeting yesterday and then showing up first thing this morning and acting a little too strange for me to believe anything differently. Besides, if Martin got here by nine, what time did he leave San Diego? He would have had to driven up last night sometime?

It was nearly five thirty in the afternoon when we all left the Admiral's house. Dusk was settling in. Gary continued to be my shadow and I was thankful that he was.

Nicky had long disappeared and Martin had appeared.

"Who did the Admiral let in", I asked myself. One of them for sure. It was way too obvious to me, though no one else could see it. The whole thing had gotten way out of hand. In the meantime, we were still left back at square one trying to find Derek.

I realized that it was time to call on the Tong to help me in this search. Besides, I knew that they had a score to settle with the Mancini's and Carmine for involving Chloe. I decided that when we got to Chinatown, I would call Maggie to dig up the info on who Commander Martin was.

We drove to the part of Main Street where it runs from the Latin neighborhood to the Chinese section. It was now around 7:15PM and the streets were still busy with shoppers and merchants going in and out of the many stores that sold food and veggie items. It was a busy little place with stalls in front of every store.

I drove to the Mandarin to hook up with Brad and Chloe. Gary was right behind me as we drove through the alleys and back streets to the hotel. I didn't want any more surprises, even if I was on the Chinese turf.

We pulled up behind the hotel, which faces due east on 1st St. The Chinese have a thing about design and order in their world. There we found an alley that was a dead end, where we parked the cars, after first backing in. This way we could easily drive out if we had to in a hurry. Gary and I then went through the back entrance of the hotel and up the red and golden stairs to the third floor where Brad was supposed to be.

It was now 7:50 pm as I knocked on his door. Gary and I didn't hear anything, so we knocked again. Still no answer. It was locked.

Gary asked if he should break it down. I told him "no" and then took out a couple of bobby pins and worked the lock to let us in.

Brad wasn't in the room, but his room was in total shambles. My first thought was, "damn", as I sprang out of the door, with Gary following me in my tracks on our way to the fifth floor where Chloe's room was.

As we reached the floor, Jimmy Woo was coming out of Chloe's door. He looked at me and said, "She's gone." I said, "How, what happened! I thought she was safe in your own backyard"?

Jimmy responded, "We were all getting ready for the meeting that was to be held at 8 across the street at the Dragon House Restaurant. Brad and Chloe were going to meet with me at 7:30 and then wait for you in the lobby. When they didn't come down, I went to find out what had happened, as the Madame couldn't reach either of them by phone. As I have now found out, the Tong had pulled off their guards for about a half hour during the afternoon. No one would have thought that the Mob would find not only find her, but also that this would be the exact time when we would be the most vulnerable and no one to protect her. I suppose we are all at fault in this fiasco."

CHAPTER 12

I looked at Jimmy, shaking my head. This whole damn day seemed to go straight to hell with one disaster after another.

Gary started to question Jimmy on anything that he might know about why the Tong had pulled off the guard.

Jimmy just kept saying, "I do not know except that it was all our fault."

I sat down on the chair where I had sat the last time I was with Chloe. Nothing in the room seemed to be touched. I was sure that they had both been drugged, but by whom. How did they get in? It had to be one of the Chinese Tong member's trying to make a name for himself or to get even for something.

Gary continued to snoop around the room and Jimmy kept on apologizing, when I finally said to him, "Shut up"!

I then told Jimmy to go across the street and tell the Tong what had happened and that I will come and see them now and ask for their help.

Jimmy said, "Jack, are you sure you know what you are doing. Your father had asked for help before. They are like the Italian Mafia, in that when they do a favor for you, you will have to do a favor for them."

I looked deep into his eyes and said, "We are both doing each other favors at the same time, so I don't believe that I will be left holding to any pay back. We are both in need of each other regarding Chloe and Brad, so I fear nothing about it. You could say it's an eye for an eye!"

Jimmy got up and said, "OK, Jack, you're the boss, but I also want to help."

I almost jumped down his throat showing my emotions of losing Brad and Chloe but held back and said, "Jimmy, you already have done your share. Thanks."

He turned and walked down the stairs.

I looked at Gary and said, "Would you be so kind to see if there are any aspirins in this apartment? I have a dreadful headache and I need to gather my thoughts and put together a plan when I meet the Tong. Besides, I need to call Maggie and find out about our Commander Martin."

Gary answered me as he went into the kitchen, "Yes Ma'am, I am sure happy that I've tagged along to fetch you some pills. It's a big job, that's why this Marine is doing it!"

I laughed and told him to go to hell, jokingly of course.

The apartment reminded me of a Basil Rathbone and Sherlock Holmes movie. Two bedrooms, one bathroom, a sitting room and a kitchen. Not much in the way of a struggle happened here. Very interesting I thought. Why not, did Chloe know her intruder?

I reached for the phone after finding my handkerchief just in case the police needed to dust for fingerprints, provided the Tong would allow them to even do this. I phoned Maggie and got down to business. She informed me that the Commander was in fact in Pearl Harbor when the Admiral was there and that his records were a little shaky. They couldn't quite connect all the periods in his life, yet there he was standing tall in the U.S. Navy.

140

I half-jokingly said to Maggie, "Damn the war starts up and then suddenly the Navy Department has all kinds of security holes. What are they doing not checking on the validity of their personnel?"

Maggie replied, "Don't know, but after the First World War, the Navy Department had terminated about 100 temporary civilian personnel, who oversaw processing security and background checks, who used to validate school records, previous jobs and references, etc."

I was astounded by what she told me, so I had to ask the million-dollar question, "So who was responsible for closing that Department down and why wasn't it manned by Navy personnel?"

Maggie snickered and told me, "Admiral Franklin. He recommended that it be closed down, because there was no need for such a Department."

Gary had come into the room and set my aspirins and a glass of water down next to me. I gulped those aspirins down as Maggie went on with some additional facts on the Commander.

Then I said, "Maggie was Commander Martin with him at that time?"

She said yes, that he was with him for some twelve years. He initially was selected for this staff position back in 1930. And that's when they closed down the processing site. Martin was an Ensign at that time.

I gave unusual comment "Christ" over the phone.

Maggie then gave me the biggest bomb, "Jack, I hate to be the one to tell you this, but Peter D'Angelo escaped from the shore patrol! After interrogating him, they decided to take him to the brig at Coronado. On the way, another car ran the shore patrol vehicle off the road into the sand. They then forced the shore patrol sailors at gun point for the release of Peter. They had taken the car keys from the shore patrol and busted up their radio, so it was hours before it was called in. The shore patrol was able to give a description of the two people who held them at gun point, one was a woman who I believe was Elizabeth Yardley and the other was Commander Martin, though both of them were in civilian clothes."

"What the hell", I said, followed by "Jesus Christ".

"Maggie", I asked, "Who else knew that this would be much larger than anyone ever could imagine? You need to call Captain Stark and fill him in. I wouldn't be surprised if Martin was from the old country too and was able to get anything and everything from the Admiral without the Admiral knowing what he was doing. I feel bad for the old Admiral; he didn't deserve to die like that, unless he was in it as well. I guess they decided that he was no longer useful or that he could spell the beans on all the players."

I asked Maggie to keep me posted; that I would probably be at my Uncle Mike's house but if not, he would know where to get hold of me.

After hanging up I said to Gary, "There's got to be some clue in this apartment that will give us some inkling where the hostages have been taken. How about you search through the other bedroom and this sitting room for anything and I'll search through Chloe's personal stuff!"

142

Gary said, "A-OK boss", as he walked into the other bedroom.

I heard him say, "I don't have a clue what I am looking for, so I'll wing it!"

I chuckled and said out loud, "Neither do I but when I find it, I'll let you know."

Rummaging through her dresser drawers, I found nothing except fine lingerie, all made in France.

I checked the night table, and found that all her jewelry was still there, or at least that is what it looked like to me. Nothing seemed to have been moved or out of place.

When I had finished, I went into her closet. I looked in her hatboxes, only to find matching hats for the shoes that were in the shoe rack, up off the floor. She definitely knew style. All the dresses hung on neat wooden hangers and looked untouched. However, there were more kimonos then dresses or skirts. I wondered why. Yes, she was Chinese, but she didn't live here in her community until just recently. It had to be the Tong who supplied these to her. I wondered if Carmine liked his girlfriend in kimonos or dresses? Did he even recognize that she was Oriental? A little question that might be important or maybe not!

Ironically, almost all the labels on the dresses were stamped the same, "Manufactured by the Unions of America, Los Angeles". And all of the ones I looked at also said, "Material imported from Italy and China". An interesting marriage I thought.

Looking in the handbags, I noticed that most of them matched the shoes and hats, but there were two that were just leather, one brown and one black. I looked inside the Black one and it said, "Made in Italy". But in the Brown one had a claim stub from the Hotel Fonterra in Bel Air. I had heard of it but didn't know anything about the place. Perhaps it would be something for me to follow up on later.

Meanwhile in the sitting room, Gary had located some loose photos stuck in between some pages throughout the books on the shelf. He said out loud, "You'd get a kick out of these, Jack."

I said, "Ok I'll be right out."

As I came out of the bedroom, Gary handed me the photos and to my surprise, there in front of the La Fonterra Restaurant marquee, stood Admiral Franklin, Commander Martin, Carmine, Chloe and the noted Tong High Priest, Mr. Chung. Geez I thought, very interesting, all of them seemed a bit too chummy for my taste.

I said to Gary, "We've got to go over and see what Mr. Chung knows. If he is on the level and wants Chloe back, then he'll play ball. We'll see."

I knew too well not to call the police for their help, but I did leave a message for both Uncle Mike and Captain Stark, what I was up to and that I would contact them later.

Gary told me that based on what Jimmy had said that it had to be an inside job because of the shift change at the prescribed time, it probably allowed an opportunity to kidnap Chloe and Brad. He also agreed with me on the meeting with Mr. Chung. He stated that we would more than likely need the Tong's help if we wanted to rescue Chloe and Brad.

I told him that he was right, so we quickly went downstairs and across the street to the restaurant where Mr. Chung was waiting for us.

I was hoping that Jimmy had been able to run interference prior to our entrance and that the Tong would not act too unkindly to me or Gary.

Depressed by the fact that everything I was involved with seemed to be going nowhere fast and that I felt like I had an albatross on my back, I was anxious to get on with our meeting.

Kind of half smiling at me as we crossed the street, Gary was up for anything. I could feel his "ready to spring into action" persona. He reached for me and gently pushed me forward but held onto my collar, as if to say he was right with me in regards to the task ahead.

Walking up to the restaurant door, it swung out towards us. There was a huge Chinese fellow that held the door. He was at least six feet five inches and about 300 or so pounds. Though Gary was an inch taller, he looked like a stick next to him. He just nodded his head to go forward through the door to the left.

Through this door we found ourselves immediately in a square chamber with one red light bulb directed in the center of the ceiling. The cloth walls looked like they were dark red, but we couldn't tell in this light. It was about five by five, and I was thinking to myself, good thing I am not claustrophobic. I would have met my match.

Gary and I backed up to each other and kept our eyes open for anything that might come at us. About two minutes passed before another door opened up in front of us. We couldn't tell if they were scanning us with some sort of device or what was going on, but those two minutes seem to be an eternity in the red light.

With no one to greet us we stepped out into a large hallway. Though I never heard a sound, I then realized that we had been in some sort of an elevator that moved so slowly that we never felt it shake.

I figured that we were now deep inside the Tong sanctuary. I noticed that the double door in front of us had a huge hand carved red dragon on it as we entered this part of restaurant building. There was a massive fish pond with a bridge over the entryway to the dining room. Walking into the main room, it was enormous, with hand carved chairs and tables everywhere.

In the very back of the room was a table where Mr. Lien Chung sat. He had two other associates sitting on either side on him and was being attended by three Chinese waiters; two women and one man. He saw us enter and motioned for us to join him. With that, we proceeded quickly to the table.

As we walked towards it our eyes were becoming accustomed to the light. I noticed that only candles lit up the room. They were attached to the sides of the walls about six feet up from the floor and about three feet apart.

There were also candles on the floor that were encased in some sort of metal and glass at the top, which stood straight up about four feet. They acted as a path to the table centered in the back of the room. The reflection of the candles only increased my own anticipation of our meeting. It may have been one of the few times that I can remember really being nervous. The palms of my hands were moist

146

and I could feel my underarms sweat, along with beads of perspiration on my forehead.

Monks stood between the candles on the walls. Each one was in a different color kimono. It looked a rainbow around the walls. The colors were bouncing off these holy men making the ceiling look like stars in multi colors. It was eerie, sort of sacred looking, yet the room oozed power and intensity.

Lien did not stand as we approached, but smiled, nodded and then with palms up he turned them downward and slowly lowered them as if to say sit down please.

Jimmy appeared out of nowhere and stood next to us.

The three of us then sat down directly across the table from Lien and his associates. I still felt nervous, particularly because this was my first meeting with them and that my back was to the front door. I didn't like this at all. Unknown territory and underground somewhere to boot. I was definitely out of my element.

Lien spoke first, "The 'Brothers of Oil', are not as trust worthy as your government had thought, yet they still use them which has now come back to haunt them. I think that at this point we must take it upon ourselves to deal with our Italian friends, before anything else happens that would hinder our own existence in America."

I started to respond when he had stopped talking for that brief moment, but then he clapped his hands once.

Somewhere out of the dark behind us three monks approached the table. The monks sat down a golden dragon design tray of tea and almond cookies.

Knowing that I should wait to speak I just sat there. Then Mr. Chung continued. "Jimmy has requested that I help you and though I originally disagreed with him, I thought about the fact how General Chennault and his Tigers were at this very moment assisting me and my countrymen, trying to rid the Japanese from the hills and towns of my homeland. So, I must in return try and help you rid these Italians who I believe have overstepped their territory and could cause additional harm to me, Chinatown and my people who I care the most for!"

Again, as I was about to speak, Lien cleared his throat and motioned to the waiters to pour us our tea.

Lien then reached towards his own cup and smiling said, "Please, take some tea. I know of your day, so all you need to do is relax so that we may proceed in discussing these tragedies and the ways to correct them."

Politely, I reached for my ceramic cup that contained an etched gold and red dragon flowing around it. I looked at Lien. He sat there where the lights and shadows created a glow that surrounded him. He was almost like a heavenly being, dressed in a Chinese tunic of white with the gold dragon embossed over his heart. The dragon was spitting out red fire. It had to be a positive sign, though the dragon looked menacing.

Both Jimmy and Gary were looking at me as if to say, go ahead begin the conversation. However, I knew it would be impolite until Lien spoke some more and only then would he ask me to state my questions to open up the conversation.

Lien, sensing that we had relaxed yet knowing that we wanted to discuss the situation began. "Ms. Riley, I must first tell you that I am most sorry for the travesty that has occurred today. Through my humble sources, I have been told that you are a good person and that you have only gotten involved in this nasty business of family and war because of your own association with Commander Kent. Initially I had been told that you were employed by Carmine Ialucci. That said, had you been, we would have never had this meeting. Nevertheless, you are involved today because of the bridges that have connected the land and the sea. What I mean by that is that the families of the East and the West, who are all embroiled in their own wars of their brethren, have linked us all together. And as you know, we are all looking for the best results in this world war."

He reached down to raise his cup to his mouth. We all followed suit, so as not to distract him or to insult him.

Lien continued, "My people on the mainland are being slaughtered by the thousands from the Japanese. America definitely suffered an almost crushing blow at Pearl Harbor. And the Italian families are employed by the Navy to help them control the harbors. Yet it is the same families that have for their own purpose and purse strings, tried to work on both sides of this war. This is not without calamity. America and American pilots have now tried to rescue the Chinese people from their own defeat. Because of this double dipping from a certain Italian family, I will now help you and will turn the Red Dragon loose on the families that are traitors to my American home."

"Ms. Riley, while I have trusted almost no one since I first landed on these shores many years ago, I have also trusted very few round eyes. Not one of them that I have trusted has ever turned against me, yet I am cautious of all motives of the "European heritage". I and the rest of the Tong are

149

not like my Mafia associates. Once I am honored by you, I shall honor you forever. With that said, I am most willing to trust you, for who you are and for what I see in your eyes. We will resolve these unfortunate circumstances for both of us and shall again dine here in my restaurant in the future during a happier time."

Lien then held up some documents that were in front of him. "Now we must exchange all information to determine how to resolve our puzzle."

I placed my cup down and looked at Lien. Knowing that I shouldn't try and fool this man, I told him almost everything, at least everything that was not secret or classified. Even Gary looked at me several times, as if to say, "You got to be kidding".

But I had some questions of my own and decided to quiz the High Priest. I asked Lien why they had left Chloe alone, when they knew what kind of danger she was in.

Lien responded. "Ms. Riley, unfortunately we had made a critical mistake by using some new staff members, not yet mature enough to relieve each other in a staggered fashion. This is something that will never ever happen again, I can assure you."

I then said, "Lien, no sense in beating a dead horse. I'm glad that you have already taken measures to correct your security problem, however how did Carmine know when to abduct Chloe, even if there was a leak on the Navy's side, who or what was the leak inside your own organization?"

Lien looked down at the table and then looked at me and said, "I humbly regret this misfortune and ask you to forgive me, for we have already located the source of our troubles. It was one of our own who had full knowledge of where Chloe was. This person also knew everything regarding our own operations and betrayed us and now that person has been eliminated."

"You see", Lien continued, "At one time, Chloe introduced us to Carmine and his associates. She thought she was doing the right thing. It was a business proposition that did not fair too well, drugs, money laundering and prostitution. When it was over, neither Carmine nor I, would be friends any longer. The families took positions against each other."

I said to Lien, "May I know who it was?"

Lien said, "I'd rather not say, but if you really must know, it was my youngest son! I am sure that during those meetings and subsequently thereafter, Chan, my youngest got involved without fully understanding his own actions or consequences. He was smitten with some of the worldly riches offered by the Mancinis. And he was most impatient with life and what one needs to do to learn about it."

Stunned for a moment, but trying to be indifferent, I looked at Jimmy and Gary. I knew what Lien had meant. In my own little brain, I wondered, "How do you kill your own son?" But decided not to even ask that question.

After about an hour, Mr. Chung said to me, "I will gather my services and people together and we will locate Carmine today."

I responded quickly, "No, please wait for a few days while I gather up some more information from my uncle and of course from the Navy Department. I do have a few leads, like the Hotel La Fonterra."

Mr. Chung spoke up, "Hotel La Fonterra, it is at that very restaurant that all the Italian families get together and discuss business. It is also a neutral area, where no guns are allowed. It is I believe, owned by Herb Stein."

I responded with, "I believe that you are right, but I also found a claim check in Chloe's purse, so I know that she had been there before."

"Yes, I know", Lien said. "Unfortunately, my daughter sometimes accompanied Carmine there!"

A shudder ran through me. My mind was yelling at me. I then looked at Gary and Jimmy again. Gary looked surprised, but Jimmy showed no emotion.

"Holy crap", my mind shouted, "First a son, now a daughter! I see where all the connections are located in this disaster. I couldn't believe what he had just told us, so I continued on."

"I also found an address for what looks like a warehouse, though I am not sure where it is", I said to him.

Mr. Chung nodded at one of the monks, who quickly and quietly approached me to retrieve the address. I stood up and gave it to him, but remained standing.

The young monk gracefully took it to the high priest and only after a moment of reading it, he handed it back to the monk who then returned the note back to me.

Mr. Chung said, "I know where this is. It's almost downtown on Wilshire at 7th. It is an easy drive from Bel Air where the restaurant is. Do we want to go there first or to the restaurant?"

I said, "Neither for the moment. I need to know what you know about the Italians."

Mr. Chung, smiled and said, "I have from time to time been engaged with them purely for a business transaction. In fact, it was olive oil that I was buying and they in turn wanted raw silk products for making clothes, but I never would put it past them that it was used for something else, like bomb making. I have been to both of the locations that you have noted, so at least I am familiar enough with their layout."

I jumped in and asked, "What do you know about "Unions of America"?

Mr. Chung said to me, "Ah yes. That is controlled by the Mancini's and where they manufacture and distribute their goods from. It is at the same warehouse where we discussed our mutual business together. Why?"

"Well, Mr. Chung", I said, "It is also on almost every label of Chloe's clothes."

Lien looked surprised at me and then said, "Yes this is one of my dealings with Carmine, but nothing more!"

Still standing, I said to him, "Mr. Chung, your business is your business, but for the sake of this country, now is the time to put both of our resources together and get those people who we love the most back into our lives. I will contact you like I said in a couple of days, but I want some additional information cleared up before we go down there, guns a blazing. Is that agreeable with you?"

Mr. Chung smiled and said, "Jimmy has told me a lot about he and your father and that you are a strong woman. I like that. I wish my Chloe was the same, but I'm afraid that good fortune is not part of her chakra. I will however, wait for your call. But if it is longer than two days, then you must know that I will have to act without you. You see I know that the Mancinis are getting things ready to leave the country, though I am not sure where they are going with the war of the worlds taking place. Perhaps back to Sicily. But I do want to get my daughter back before they go, even if I must negotiate for her. So, for now, it will be up to you and your resources to find her first. You know I can't bargain for your other two friends, you do understand that. It would be unethical."

I said, "Yes, I do understand, but I will get back to you before you have to go at it alone."

I looked at Gary as to say it's time to get up and then turned to Mr. Chung and said, "I will call Jimmy when we should meet again. Thank you for your time and attention to these troubling matters."

I bowed and out of the corner of my eye I saw Jimmy and Gary stand up and bow as well.

I hadn't seen him get up, but Mr. Chung bent over at his waist from where he was sitting. He said something in Chinese to Jimmy that I couldn't understand as we began our walk back out through the maze of candles.

CHAPTER 13

Once outside, the air rushed into my lungs refilling the
space that had been breathing incense and candle smoke.
Suddenly, I felt very alive. My muscles began to relax and
the sweat against my skin chilled as the cool air began to
dry the moisture.

I turned to Jimmy and said, "What did Lien say to you?
What is this thing about his daughter? Whose daughter? Is
Chloe his concubine?"

Jimmy laughed and smiled that wide grin, showing all his
teeth. "No, no. Chloe is really Mr. Chung's daughter. But
she doesn't know it. In fact, neither does Carmine. You
see, her adopted parents were related to Mr. Chung. He
and the stepfather were brothers. His brother could not
have children, so when Mr. Chung had a child with the
local Hong Kong city police chief's daughter, it turned out
to be a very embarrassing time for all. You see, when Mr.
Chung was young, he oversaw one of the local gangs and
was running guns and gambling. He knew that he would
lose the child because of his operations and the legal mess
anyway, so he took his Chloe and had her adopted by his
brother, so that she could be raised properly. However,
after the death of Mr. Chung's brother, he investigated
what had happened to her and where she was. He found
her in the arms of Carmine. Even when Chloe was sent by
Carmine to Chinatown back before the war had started to
hook up the Family with Mr. Chung, he knew but didn't
want to say anything to her at that point. So, he decided to
wait till the time was right to get her back in his life and tell
her the whole story. Well that time has never come. Even
when she appeared in front of him to discuss what was
going on and why she fled from Carmine, Mr. Chung
couldn't bring himself to confess and tell her the truth. In

fact, he was going to send some of his monks to find Carmine and kill him. And then this happened."

"Wow, this is like a World Series game, way too many curve balls", I said.

Gary laughed and Jimmy smiled and then said, "I think that Mr. Chung was going to tell her today in front of you. That's why everything was to be perfect!"

"Yea" I said, "Perfect like a circle, but now that this one is broken that we have to fix."

"Jimmy", I continued, "You need to talk to everybody and anybody on this street. Find out anything if you can, then call me at my…

"Uncle Mike's?" he said. "Yes yes, I know the routine. Your dad did the same thing. I'll call you later tonight."

I then turned to Gary, "You need to start earning your keep. I want you to go to the two locations that we have uncovered and snoop around. No one yet knows who you are, unless Commander Martin shows up. In which case, I would just shoot him."

Gary looked at me wrinkling his forehead. "Really he says?"

I said, "I know. I shouldn't have said that, but he's been lying to me ever since I met him. So as far as I am concerned, take his butt down!"

I gave Gary my Uncle's phone numbers to his office and to the house. I also told him that if Martin is 'hanging around' with the Mancini's that he should call Captain

Stark and have the shore patrol pick him up for questioning.

Gary shook his head, 'I'll call you later if I find anything or not. I'll probably stay in Long Beach at the Naval Station tonight and then catch back up with you in the AM."

I said, "Roger that!" And then we all left.

As I got back into my car, I had a funny feeling that I was being watched, so I took some extra precaution leaving the area and kept an eye peeled for any tag-a-longs.

Monitoring the rear-view mirror there appeared to be a Chrysler that was keeping as close to me as possible as I drove down several streets before turning unto Highland to get to my uncle's house. It stayed on my tail the entire time. I never saw a face, so I couldn't tell if it was The Tong or if it was Nicky, but somehow I felt safer driving through Hollywood.

When I arrived, it was well past midnight, so I just tiptoed in and went to bed. I looked out the window and saw that the Chrysler had parked across the street. I figured that I was well protected being at my Uncle's and all, so I decided that I would deal with it in the morning.

I found a note from my Uncle who left it on my bed, detailing some more information from Jimmy. Though it was not enough to keep me awake, it just added more to the already bulging case against the Mancini's and Carmine.

There was also a glass of water on the nightstand and a sleeping tablet from Aunt Dorothy. She must have known that I had been having a hard time sleeping lately. I passed on the idea hoping that being this tired would allow me the sleep I needed. So I climbed under the covers and thought, "Tomorrow was going to be crazy, I was sure of it, so I had better rest up!"

CHAPTER 14

When I awoke in the morning, I realized that I had slept all night without the help of the sleeping pill. After taking a shower and finding some fresh clothes in my room that I usually leave at the house, I got dressed and went into the kitchen.

Both my Uncle and Aunt were having coffee when I walked in. I told my Uncle about the car that had tailed me and that it had parked itself outside of the house. With that he immediately went and looked out the living room window and found that there was no vehicle across the street. He became very concerned and told me that he didn't ask one of his detectives to follow me, but that he would have a car follow me now, since Gary was off doing something else and he was a bit troubled that whoever it was would be brazen enough to come to his neighborhood house.

As usual, he gave me the speech about being worried for my safety and I of course tried to appease him with, "Gary's got my back and all." But I don't think he believed me. There the conversation ended as Aunt Dorothy hugged me and said, "Be careful Jacqueline."

With that we both left around 7:30 to drive to the precinct. Looking back several times in my rear-view mirror, I noticed that no one was tailing me except for the Police Ford that was about a block behind me, per my Uncle's insistence. I tried to figure it out and it dawned on me that perhaps it was the Tong or someone from the Mancini side of the fence, so I would keep it in the back of my mind for now and ask Mr. Chung later.

When I had gotten to the precinct with my Uncle, the sergeant that had been on duty the last time I visited was once again on duty. This time however, I was clad in a dress of spring colors and he was more polite and just escorted me into my uncle's office, as my Uncle went to find out if there was anything pending.

The sergeant trying to make up for the previous embarrassment asked me if I wanted some coffee to drink. I smiled and said in a southern voice, "Why thank you sir, but I must decline. This late in the morning, it gives me gas." I then busted out laughing and the entire place looked up at me and then at the Sergeant and started laughing as well. Not sure if everyone heard what I had said, but they were laughing at him anyway.

My Uncle, who was in another office came out of it and just looked at me and shook his head and said, "Jacqueline are you being nice to the Sergeant Hill?"

I just looked at both of them and started laughing again. It took me a few minutes to finally calm down. It must have been from my frustration and fear that I reacted that way. Probably better than crying I thought.

Finally, Sergeant Hill started laughing as well, so it proved to help break the ice and tension of the moment.

My uncle and I finally got down to business at hand and started putting together a plan. One was to flush out the Mancinis, and one was to find Derek, Chloe and Brad. Poor Brad I thought, I always get him into something.

"Depending on what Gary finds", I said to my Uncle, "In two days we should storm the restaurant and the warehouse. So, you need to get those court orders ready so we don't have any hiccups."

Uncle Mike said, "No problem, Judge O'Shaugnessy is on duty today and he'll do it just because."

I told my Uncle, "I want to use the Tong to get into the warehouse, no sense in losing any of our men in case there is a shoot-out."

"Fine", my uncle said, "But I have to send some of my officers there as well."

I said "Ok, but make sure they are Asian, so they blend in. I'll also send Gary with them to keep us posted."

I then got up to leave and my Uncle Mike asked, "Where are you going now, to the Mandarin?"

"Yes", I said, "I want to look around again. I am sure that I can find a clue or two that didn't catch my eye the first time there."

My uncle said, "I'm sure you will, you're like a bird dog, looking for your kill!"

In the meantime, Gary, who spent the night at Long Beach had gotten into his car and drove up highway route 1 to Los Angeles. It was a dark and gloomy day, with clouds and heavy fog pelting the City of Angels. In the fine mist, he pulled unto Alameda St. and headed for the warehouse. But first he noticed that a Chevrolet was behind him. He didn't give it too much thought, except that as he turned the corner and made his way to Wilshire, the car seemed to stay right behind him.

Gary decided that it was time to get a real good look at who was driving, so he slowed down and waited for the next light to turn yellow and stopped sharp slamming his brakes on. The Chevy also slammed on its brakes. Now as Gary waited for the light to turn green, he was able to get a good look at the two gentlemen in the front seat. One was Nicky but the other one he wasn't sure of. Maybe he had seen him before though he couldn't remember where or when.

Just as the light turned green, Gary popped the clutch and squealed the tires as he tore to the next corner at 1st Street, about 25 yards down the street. There he floored the gas pedal and turned left into an alley. The Ford squealed again and before Gary knew it he came to North Main. He turned right and then at the next cross street, he turned right again, back onto Alameda. When he came back up to the alley, he stopped. He saw the Chevy slowly driving down the alley, so Gary backed up and then turned right into the alley to follow the Chevy. As the car got to the street, Nicky apparently looked in the rear-view mirror and saw the Ford behind him. This caused Nicky to make a quick right. Gary pressed the pedals again to the floor to get to the street. By that time, he had a good view and saw the Chevy making another right. He paused for a moment to try and second-guess what Nicky would do. Nicky who wasn't the brightest person Gary ever knew, since Jack and Gary had lost him once before up in Malibu, thought that he would play the odds and pull over on the right in front of some other car to park and wait to see if Nicky came back around to look for the Ford. Five minutes passed and then Gary saw the Chevy through his rear-view mirror make the turn from the alley. Gary slumped down in order not to be spotted and watched the Chevy drive by slowly.

"It worked" Gary snickered, as he raised his head to watch the Chevy drive past. After a few minutes of verifying that

Nicky hadn't seen him, Gary started the engine and drove to the corner and turned left to head towards the warehouse, which appeared to be the same direction that Nicky was going. Pulling into the traffic to follow him, Gary kept at least three cars behind Nicky. Like a parade, Gary followed him to 6th and Wilshire.

Nicky apparently was so busy berating the person in the other seat, waving his hands and turning and yelling at the other guy that he didn't see Gary following Nicky, as he drove slowly onto Jameson Street to drive up the ramp into the warehouse. Gary looking from the corner of 6th could see the Chevy disappear into the warehouse.

Then Gary figured out how close he could park without being noticed, so he made a right turn and parked the car up the street about 15 yards from the ramp to the warehouse. This way he was out of view, yet across the street from the entrance.

Gary got out of the car and stood there for a few minutes. He watched as several lights were turned on in the building, particularly on the second floor. It was now almost 9 in the morning, as he casually walked to the corner. However, it looked like eight thirty at night with the morning fog hanging itself over Los Angeles like a blanket of death. Everything was basically dead silent as Gary looked at the building again and noticed the sign "UNIONS OF AMERICA". Gary was convinced that it was either a front or a sweatshop.

Waiting for a few more minutes to see if anything else would happen, a Zephyr came down from the ramp area. Placing his one leg up on a water hydrant to tie his shoe, he noticed that there was only the driver in the car as it turned right, heading for Hollywood. The driver was the same guy that was riding shotgun with Nicky. Fortunately, he never saw Gary driving so even when he looked directly at Gary, he didn't recognize him. However, as the lights from the intersection illuminated the inside of the Zephyr, Gary caught a glimpse of Carmine sitting there alone in the back seat. Torn between wanting to follow him or find out what was in the warehouse, he opted to stay on his original course.

So where was Nicky, Gary thought. For a minute, Gary contemplated finding a phone and calling Jack, but unlike all his training and skills taught him, he then decided to go into the building alone, with no backup and find out what was in there first.

Gary decided to walk on the other side of the street from the warehouse to get a better look into the ramp area. He noted that there were a few huge houses across from the warehouse, where trees lined the curbside. He could see that there was a light at the top of the ramp, but nothing more. Walking further up the street along the houses, Gary tried not to be noticed and crossed over to begin his way back to the ramp. He felt like he was in Paris with his old unit, when they crept up to the monastery and captured the German scientist, Von Gilbert, only this time it was just him. He had no back up!

Stopping within ten feet of the ramp, he then ran and jumped to the wall of the ramp in almost one step. He listened. The only thing that he could hear was his heart. He then inched his way to the opening of the ramp and peered into and up the ramp. No sign of anyone, so he stepped around and clung to the wall leading up the ramp. He knew that he had to run up as fast as he could, because of the light. He also knew that he had to break the bulb, so that anyone on the street or inside the warehouse would not be able to see him once he got inside. His training taught him to find a pebble or stone and heave it as he sprinted for the top.

He looked on the ground and besides his right foot was a small piece of building material stone from the wall. He reached over and quickly picked it up in one movement. He then looked at the light. It had an opening between two strips of steel casing that wrapped around from side to side. He would have to be accurate in his throw otherwise he would just hit the steel and not the bulb.

As he stepped backwards a little from the wall, he heard a car turning the corner. He didn't know if it was going to turn into the ramp driveway or not, so there was no time now to do anything else except to throw the stone and make a run for it.

In a split second he heaved the stone and by the time the shattered pieces of glass had fallen to the ground, Gary had hurled himself into the garage at the top of the ramp, clinging against the wall in the dark.

The car that spooked Gary, never came up the ramp, but the breaking of the glass had brought a guard out the office mid-way down the garage, so Gary hid behind a couple of barrels that were in the corner.

The guard looking towards the ramp to see what the noise was about started rambling on in Italian to another guard in the office. Gary looked on as the guard outside threw up his hands and then went back inside the small office.

There were some cars and trucks parked on both sides of the warehouse. But it was still very sparse and so getting to the stairs would require some luck.

Gary crept along the wall trying to keep his shadow to a minimum. When he got to about twenty feet from the stairs, he squatted behind the Chevy that had been chasing him. Standing up behind the huge car, he looked inside. It was empty. Not much he could do here, but he decided to let out the air on the left tire, so he uncapped the stem from the tire and slowly let the tire go flat. It took longer than expected and a couple of times, he thought that he let out too much too quickly, because the sound from the escaping air seemed to make an incredible hissing sound, but fortunately the Guards where making so much noise themselves in their card game that they didn't notice anything.

When he got done, he looked at his watch. It was nearly 10 AM. He thought Jack is probably pacing at her Uncle's wondering what was going on.

Just then the phone rang in the office and the same guard who had come out of the office before, picked it up and rattled off something, then turned to his partner and said something again. He then raised his arms in the air and then started towards the stairways. As the guard began to walk up the stairs, Gary heard the door open from the shack.

The other guard came out but started walking in the other direction, as the big Italian headed towards where Gary was hiding. He stopped for a moment to light a cigarette then looked at the Chevy. He cocked his head sideways, and then muttered something and took another drag from his cigarette and continued towards the stairs. Starting to walk up the darken stairwell, Gary quickly crept up behind him and just as he sensed that Gary was there, Gary's arm and hand were coming down in a chopping motion over the bridge of his nose.

166

As Gary hit him, he moaned and dropped to the floor. It was an awkward punch, but somehow it worked.

Gary decided to drag him upstairs in case the other guard came looking for him. He had a hard time with the Italian, but finally came to the last step. Gary set him down with his head flung forward towards his lap. He was still breathing, barely. Gary then took the Italian's belt and tied his hands behind him and took out his handkerchief and placed it in his mouth, in case he woke up. He then placed him against the corner of the landing and looked through the right door glass window leading inside. Gary listened for sounds. There were none.

Gary then looked down the left hall through the glass of the swinging doors. There were several doors along the hallway. Not a good protection scenario he thought. He slowly opened the right door and tied this against the railing with a shoe lace from the Italian who now slept behind the open door.

As he entered Gary could hear something but it was from several yards down the hall. Creeping towards the sounds, it was weird as he walked along the left side of the hallway. There was just the hall and doors about every twenty yards or so, with nothing in the hallway and no other adjoining hallways. The first door Gary came to was locked, so he continued on his search. The next one he came to was open. Gary cracked it just a bit to see what was inside. There he saw tables on the right-hand side, piled high with what looked like dresses. Interesting enough, but on the left-hand side these tables were filled with ammunition belts and guns and holsters. Noticeably, there were some tables that had some sort of explosive or part of an explosive next to pieces of clothing.

Unions of America Gary thought, it was a union of the bad guys supplying each other. Carmine and the Mancini family were probably labeling this stuff as clothing merchandise for the families at home. The problem with it was that it never got to the people, only to the "families". It was more than likely sold off to help pay for whatever the Mancini's were getting in return. Gary knew that Jack would be quite surprised at this little operation.

Then Gary heard someone speaking coming out of a half open door, so he ducked inside out of sight into the room across from where the door had swung wide open. His eyesight adjusted and there in the room he saw Nicky. He was sweating a bit and breathing hard and looking a little pale. Gary thought, they must have found the guard he had tied up.

Gary looked back into the hallway. The other guard from the shack was standing there and said something to Nicky as he shook his head and then turned around and went to the next door down the hallway.

Gary stood still waiting for someone to come in. But no one did, so he crept over to peer out the windows. It was looking straight out on 6th Street, so he wouldn't be able to use this as an escape route, unless he wanted to jump out and break his neck.

Gary then walked back to the door. He cautiously stood there for a moment. He didn't hear anything else so he slowly opened the swinging door and then walked alongside the wall towards the end of the hall looking and listening. The next door handle he touched was locked. Even though his instincts told him to break in, he figured it might have caused too much noise, so he opted to wait for his return trip, before venturing inside.

Quietly continuing he found the next door open. As he stepped inside, he looked from side to side and heard something. Then he saw someone. It was Brad, or at least from what Jack had told him about Brad. He was tied up in a chair in a corner of the room by the windows. He looked semi-unconscious and quite bloody. As Gary walked over to him, Brad slowly raised his head and said, "No more, please" and his head bobbed back down.

Gary felt sorry for the guy. Gary said aloud, forgetting where he was, "The bastards gave you a pretty good lacing which was probably not your favorite part of helping Jack!"

Brad just muttered something, as Gary began to untie him. But just then the door opened. Gary knew he'd have to fight whoever came in the room, and he was ready. As he stood up and turned around, he saw Nicky.

With a smile on Nicky's face, he said, "You are right, we did give him a pretty good time, don't you think? And you, I don't think I've had the pleasure of really meeting you, Mr.?"

"Jackson", Gary responded. "And if you don't mind, I am taking my friend here with me. Any objections?"

"No, I don't have any", said Nicky. "But my boss, well, he'd be a little you know, upset with me, if you know what I mean."

"Well", Gary said, "You will just have to tell him to look me up, if he has a problem! I am in the phone book."

Nicky laughed. He said, "Well Mr. Jackson, I'm sorry but I can't let you or your friend leave the premises, so if you don't mind", as he pulled out a revolver and aimed it straight at Gary.

For a minute Gary thought, maybe I can bait this goon instead. So, Gary said, "Nicky, how about we do it the man to man way. Put your gun down and we'll fight like men and if I lose well too bad, but if I win, I get to take ol' Brad with me and we leave peacefully."

Nicky laughed and then smiled again and said, "Sounds like a very gentleman thing to do. If I win though I get to kill you both like I killed that old Admiral. Fair enough?"

"So it was you then", Gary asked. "Fair enough."

Nicky answered, "Yes, that old guy thought I came to give him money, but you know he never saw it coming when I slammed him in the head. Then I had to appease that damn dog. He was huge even for me. So, I gave him a little extra taste that took him down quite rapidly."

Gary sneered and retorted, "Nicky, I am no dog or old man so prepare to meet your maker!"
They both cleared the floor of the tables and chairs to the sides of the room, as they kept their eyes on each other. This was going to be a death match. One that Gary hoped he was up to.

Nicky laid the gun down on a table by the door, as Gary took off his jacket and walked to the center of the room. It reminded him of a gymnasium. It felt that big.

Then Nicky walked directly in front of Gary. Now the room felt smaller. Being six-six, Gary thought he was big. However, Nicky was six five, and carried a lot more weight on him than Gary. This would be a fight of warriors. Gary would have to use his brain on this goon, no other way out of it.

As soon as Nicky got to the center of the room, he leapt straight at Gary, causing Gary to fall backwards on to the floor, with Nicky slamming him to the ground.

Rather than punching Gary, Nicky more or less wrestled with him, as to taunt or play with Gary. However, Gary was able to slide onto one side of Nicky and unlatched himself from his grasp then jumped straight up.
Gary felt the pain in his chest where Nicky had crushed his ribs a bit jumping on him, but Gary had no time to nurture this as Nicky himself was light of foot and quickly rolled over and jumped back up as well.

Deciding to rush Nicky with a karate kick, Gary jumped at Nicky with both feet and landed a direct hit on his chest before he could grab Gary's legs. Gary felled to the floor but managed to role himself left and jumped back up as Nicky hit the floor, cursing him.

Again, Nicky stood up, a little slower and now a little more than pissed off. This time Nicky came at Gary straight away and when he did, Gary was able to sidestep him and quickly threw a chop at his neck that doubled Nicky to his knees.

Over in the corner Brad came awake, yelling at Gary to kick "Nicky's ass"!

Nicky was shaken. But standing back up, he charged right after Gary with all the pain that he was feeling and all the anger that was in his heart.

Gary was close to Brad by the windows as Nicky raced towards him, arms flailing and roaring like a lion. Gary squatted down as Nicky got to within two feet and then Gary grabbed Nicky's left leg with his right hand and the center of his shirt with his left hand and tried to pick Nicky up and throw him against the wall. Sensing that it would be a mistake to try and lift Nicky, Gary just shoved him hard, using Nicky's motion to jettison him.

Unfortunately for Nicky, the window sill was low and the speed that Nicky was traveling at and Gary's movement was just enough to push poor Nicky threw the window, left of where Brad was sitting, wide eyed and gawking at the action.

The window shattered as Nicky went through it and then it was over.

Gary looked down on the street. No one was there. Nor were there any cars cruising down the street. The corner light was blinking off and on and the haze was giving light to a Los Angeles orange sky morning. Gary thought that he was lucky at least for the moment. He was sure that Nicky was died. A pool of blood ran from the side of his head onto the pavement that Gary could now see. Even though it was only from the second story, between Nicky's weight and the toss through the glass windows, he surely perished in the fall.

Brad was half laughing from the side of his mouth. He kept saying to Gary, "I don't know who you are, but that'll teach 'em to mess around with Jack!"

Gary finished untying Brad, as he was rattling on. Finally, Gary said, "Shut up! We need to get out of here."

They walked over to the door. Gary looked down at the table and took Nicky's gun. It was an Italian Beretta, which didn't surprise him at all. Gary peered out the doorway and then told Brad to follow him closely because he was sure that the other guard would be running upstairs any minute.

No sooner than Gary had uttered those words to Brad, the door opened wide from the stairs and there were the two guards with guns drawn. Gary had thought the other guard was out of action, but apparently, he made a mistake. All Gary knew was that they needed to get out of this place alive. One guard shot off a couple of rounds. Gary returned fire, hitting him in the chest. He collapsed. The other guard backed into the stairway, the door closing behind him. Gary said, "Crap how do we get out of here now?"

Brad was tugging on his arm.

Gary said "What?"

Brad pointed and said, "We go through that right door there and the stairwell goes outside through a private door."

Gary nodded for him to lead the way.

They both ran across the hallway as the other guard saw them and started shooting. Gary shot back, not knowing whether or not he had hit him, though the sounds ricocheting around him told him otherwise. The guard was still alive or functioning, so they needed to run like crazy to get out of the warehouse.

By the time Gary and Brad had crossed the street and gotten inside the car two people were standing over Nicky looking at him. However, Gary didn't see the guard come down the ramp after them, so he assumed that either he had taken a hit or he was on the phone calling for back up.

Peeling out of the parking space, Gary put the pedal to the floor to get away from the warehouse. The car tires squealed for about twenty yards, and it wasn't until they had driven about four blocks going towards the Fairfax precinct that Brad started to talk. Since his jaw was in bad shape, Gary told him to stop talking, because there would be time enough for that later, as he kind of figured how much pain Brad was probably feeling. So, Brad just sat there and smiled a crooked grin.

Gary informed Brad who he was. Poor Brad tried to laugh but only could mumble, "I knew you were connected to Jack. She is quite the gal, you know."

Gary said, "I do" and then told him that they would go the precinct where her Uncle Mike was and to just sit back and relax.

By the time they had gotten to Fairfax, it was almost 12:30 PM. The L.A. sun was blazing through the haze.

Helping poor Brad stagger into the precinct Gary took hold of him as they went through the doors. Brad looked ragged and battered himself as they walked up to the counter. The sergeant on duty buzzed the station and several other cops ran from the back and downstairs to surround them.

Gary asked if it was OK to reach in his pocket to retrieve his wallet for his ID and laid it in front of the sergeant and asked him to call Detective Mike O'Keefe to get the lowdown on who they both were.

The sergeant punched the buzzard for the Detective and waved the other police officers away. When he got off the phone, he told Gary and Brad to take a seat and that he would be out in a minute. The sergeant then offered them some coffee. Both Brad and Gary just waved off the offer and went to sit down when Jacqueline and Mike ran out to greet them.

Jack's face had a look of relief and motherly concern. "Holy crap", came out of Jack's mouth!

CHAPTER 15

It wasn't until 5:30 that we all left the precinct. Uncle Mike had had a team of doctors and nurses filtering in and out of the station looking after Brad and Gary. Lots of ice packs and some stitching took place on Brad and he could only mumble out of the one side of his mouth, since the other side needed some mending. Then Uncle Mike insisted that we all go back to his house and spend the night. So, he called Dorothy on the phone and told her, "Dotty me lass, arriving with some guests. Be there in a half an hour from now. Make up the spare rooms, we will have company tonight."

In the meantime, Uncle Mike had sent a few squad cars over to the warehouse. He instructed them not to pick up anyone, but to get their names and addresses, so that they could follow up on the story they were telling. When the cars got there, the street was filled with many of the surrounding neighbors along with Carmine and several other persons of indistinguishable persona. Carmine trying to sound like the victim, told the officers that he had been robbed and that the thieves had killed two of his employees. The lead patrolman called the precinct to leave the info for Uncle Mike. He said that Carmine wanted to file a complaint and might know who did this.

In the meantime, Dottie was trying to be a Mom to us all with drinks, dinner, dessert and helping us clean up. She felt bad for Brad, who was trying not to laugh too much and only could speak out of one side of his mouth. Brad did say to me in that mumbled voice, that I now owed him big time! I told him, "Yeah, I'll take care of you, after your better!"

Later that evening we all went to our sleeping areas assigned by my dear Aunt. It was the end of another day of pain with just a few more answers.

In the morning as tired as I was I got up as my Uncle started banging around in the kitchen. I had slept on the couch, having given up my room to both Brad and Gary. I wanted to get cracking on this case, with Nicky out of the way. I now felt that Carmine would be making other plans to leave the country, as he probably felt vulnerable now and that he surmised that we knew what he was up to and that we would be hunting him down.

After everyone was up, showered and eaten, we all made calls and then headed to Fairfax with Uncle Mike. We agreed to set up the command center there, since this case was both military and civilian related and we both could reach someone 24/7. We knew that Carmine would not come to the station to file the complaint as he stated to the patrolman. It was more of a bluff on his part. However, more than likely he would be packing up and moving out as fast as he could.

Calling Maggie in San Diego from the precinct I asked her if she could find out any additional information that she could give us so we might locate our remaining hostages. She told me that Captain Stark was trying to obtain some additional data from the Naval Department regarding Carmine and the Mancini family, but it was information that the Navy apparently didn't want to give out, even stating to the Captain that it was "above his rank" for such intelligence.

With this non-compliance by the Navy, Uncle Mike and I concluded that either someone was way in too deep or that the Navy was still using the Mafia and was protecting their investment in any anyway they could. We were sure that they didn't want this going public. There was already too much speculation about the entanglement of both "institutions" for the war relief effort and Congress was already trying to find out the inside story.

I figured that after the war there would be a committee formed to investigate the Navy's doings and no doubt there would be a price to pay by some high-ranking Navy Department personnel based on what was uncovered. But for now, it was "full speed ahead and damn the torpedoes."

Brad, bless his heart, was back on the phone, mumbling to his editor and telling him a pretty good story of what had happened. Both my Uncle and I decided that we should let Brad recount the whole story to start heads rolling and for some hard ducking amongst our Navy brethren and Mafia families. His editor told him that his column would run in the late afternoon edition and then recap it in the morning again.

Brad had given us some hope because Gary found him alive and was able to recount to us some pretty good information. Of course, with Gary finding the additional ammo and guns as well, this of course sealed the deal. And that info was then given to the Feds as well as to the Navy for their own digestion of the situation.

Brad told us he believed that Chloe and Derek were alive, because after they had been abducted from the apartment, they were all tied up together for a day at the warehouse. Then Chloe and Derek were taken away to another location, but Brad didn't know where it was, except that he thought that he overheard Carmine talking to Nicky about Sardinia.

Not amused or even frightened by the thought that they were trying to take him to Italy, I calmly asked Brad, "How did Derek look?"

Brad said, "Fine, except that he was pretty messed up. It looked like they had worked him over good." Brad then told us that Chloe on the other hand was being very verbal, so they stuck a handkerchief in her mouth to keep her quiet.

From Bard's information I followed up with another conversation with Maggie. I asked her to check on ships departing for Italy, whether by the Navy or commercial. I needed to know what their schedules were, to and from. No doubt we were sending over tons of supplies, especially since they were sending over General Dwight D. Eisenhower to London or North Africa, according to the rumors. Yes, there was concern that one of those ships may have been owned or operated by the Mancini family and that's where they would hide Derek and Chloe.

Maggie told me, "I've heard from the brass channels that it was up to 'Ike' to close down this war in Europe. I pity the guy. The Nazi's were pretty well entrenched in Europe now. He would have to send over probably a million soldiers to undo the noose around the old world's continent."

After we chatted some more I told Maggie, to stay in touch and to let the precinct know of any new information.

As I hung up the phone I overheard my Uncle telling the sergeant to send over to the warehouse additional crime and finger print inspectors. He said, "It would be hard for Carmine or anyone else to take anything from there now, since it was considered a crime scene and under city police surveillance."

179

The day zipped by as we planned and scheduled our meeting with the Tong and the tracking of the Families. I had gotten pretty determined to get through this case with a victorious ending and to have Derek back in my life, or as much as the Navy would allow it. So for now, I needed to push forward with every bit of information and knowledge that I could find, steal and use.

After the sergeant called in from the warehouse, we all thought that it would be a good idea if we all went out there and scouted around the building ourselves. Then about 2:45 we headed out.

Arriving in broad daylight, the place looked like any other warehouse on the block. I guess that was the idea, so no authorities would come knocking and snooping. It was a pretty good ploy till now.

The policemen had broken all the locks from the doors, so that we could get a good look inside the rooms. One room with an elevator had barrels, filled with garments on the top and bottom and guns and rifle ammunition in the middle. Another room had crates, filled with rifles on the bottom, covered by a fake bottom with hats on top.

Every single room had been used for assembling and packaging for shipping. However, there was one room that looked like the central point that was used to process all the shipments. It contained boxes of invoices and shipping documents. Looking at these containers and such we agreed to sift through the mounds of paper that was on the desk and tables in front of us in case there were any additional leads. As we discovered, there were shipping documents for almost every major port in the world.

Trying to second guess Carmine, I told everyone to look for a ship specifically bound for Italy and to let me know if they found any.

After about 45 minutes, Uncle Mike was the lucky winner. He said to me, "Jacqueline, it looks like that they are heading back to Italy. There are several manifests here showing both supplies and people being shipped out on various vessels.

I got up from the chair I was sitting on and went over to where he was. There he showed me the documents that indicated the number of people going on the different ships to Sardinia. Interesting enough, these were only the carbon copies. The originals had to be at some other place.

We started digging around on more desks and then we found them. Every single name from Derek and Chloe to the Mancini's were on a manifest. They were schedule to leave out of Boston on the...

Crap I thought, the date was never put in. Then I said out loud "BOSTON? "We've got to find them now before they ever get a chance to leave the state. It will be havoc if they all get back together with the Mancini's in Boston."

My Uncle said, "I'm on it. I'm going back to the precinct to call Boston. We'll get back in touch later. You have a car right Jacqueline?"

I nodded and said, "See you later Uncle."

Gary and Brad came over to where I was seated. Gary asked, "What's our plan now?"

I said, "I don't rightly know, but we need to find out any information that would lead us to Derek and Chloe."

Gary asked, "What about the restaurant? Shouldn't we go there tonight and try to squeeze someone for some more info?"

I said, "You are probably right. It's almost 5 now. Why don't we all meet there at 7:30? I've got some other snooping to do. Brad you go with Gary. You guys check out where the Mancini's are in Boston and as much info that you can gather up in a couple of hours."

And with that I headed to downtown center city, as the boys went to the L.A. Times office to try and dig up anything else.

When I got downtown, the guard at city hall was ready to tell me that I couldn't come in as it was after hours, then he looked up and saw a familiar face.

He said, "I know you but I can't remember from where."

I said, "It was at my Dad's funeral, Captain Riley, I am his daughter."

The guard responded, "Oh Yes, I remember now. The skipper and I were long time associates back in the grand old days. He and I and a guy by the name of Jimmy Woo used to get into some trouble. Course that was then and now I'm an old guy. Nevertheless girl, what did you say your name was?

"Jacqueline", I responded.

"Yes well, what is it that I can do for you?"

I smiled back at the guard. He was probably about 60, but looked about 80. I said to him, "I was wondering if I could look at some of your city records on building drawings? I am working on a case with the Navy's Investigative Service and need to find out about buildings that are now under investigation."

The old guard said "Sure, they are upstairs on the second floor in the first office on the right."

I thanked the guard and then proceeded to run up the steps to the office. I had an idea of what I was looking for, but I needed the names and addresses from the plans of the buildings.

I started with Carmine and found that the warehouse plans had listed the Bel Air Hotel as his home and office. Then I started to look under Mancini. There I found several more buildings and addresses, with their addresses listed as the Bel Air Hotel as well. But there was one building down at Terminal Island at the wharf that had an address located in Boston. "You bastard", I thought. I'm on your tail now.

Now armed with information on the buildings located here and the Mancini address in 'Beantown', I ran back downstairs to say goodnight to the old guard. I then hopped in my car and went to the Precinct to see if my Uncle was still there. Fortunately, he was.

I gave him the addresses, but told him not to do anything just yet, that Gary and I were going tonight to La Fonterra and that would meet back here tomorrow to discuss our next plan of action.

Meanwhile about ten minutes from the Fairfax Precinct, in an old movie studio storage building that was used for copied movie reels, sat Derek and Chloe tied together with bandanas tied around their mouths. The building was located at 616 Formosa, near the Formosa Restaurant, an old Hollywood hangout where anybody who was anybody could be seen, all day long. It was a Chinese style restaurant that catered to the studio moguls and their stars and some infamous characters as well. Outside the walls were painted a pink color. Once you walked through the double doors that looked like Chinese art, the inside was aglow in a pink rose color. It was like being on a movie set looking very mysterious and unnerving. Everything had a shadow around it from the lighting. Not sure if it was meant to make everyone look better or worse, but then it was Hollywood...

Anyway, in the dim light of the restaurant Carmine was talking to Peter D'Angelo about what they would do with Derek. Peter argued that he should just shoot him while Carmine stated that he would need him as a hostage and a pawn if they got into a tight spot. When the conversation ended Carmine had won out, so that was that.

Derek, drained from the beatings he had taken, tried to surmise his position. He knew that if he was going to make a break, it had better be soon. But taking Chloe with him now became the issue. He motioned to Chloe jerking on his arms and trying to wake her up. She'd been sleeping for a while, but Derek figured that it was no time like the present to get free.

Chloe was bothered by Derek's moving around behind her and said between through the cloth in mouth, "What the hell are you doing?"

Derek likewise speaking through a bandana said, "I'm trying to get us free. Can you reach into my back-right pocket? There's a small pen knife there and you need to get it out."

"OK", Chloe said trying to reach around with their hands tied together. She was digging into Derek's pocket, when the doors opened and Peter came in.

"Ah, there are the two love birds", he said laughing. "Guess what, I have good news for you. Both of you will live for another day. Carmine has spared your life Commander, though heaven only knows why. One of your buddies aced Nicky and he's pretty upset, but I guess he figures that he can use you somewhere down the road, dead or alive. Me, I would have killed you on the spot and left the damn broad tied to you, just to make sure that she knew what would happen to her if she tried anything."

Derek felt Chloe go stiff from Peter's conversation. She was now very frightened for her life knowing how Peter felt.

Peter then went to the desk in the corner and was digging around when Carmine came in and said, "I see all is right with the world in here. That's good."

"Chloe", Carmine continued, "I guess by now your Dad, the Great High Priest of the Tong will be looking for you? But don't worry I'll work it out with him to keep you with me, one way or the other. I like the way you look and also the way you know make love!"

Chloe eyes swelled up with tears. She despised him. She was disgusted by everything that existed around him. But she was also happy that she finally knew the truth about who her father was. She prayed that he would rescue her from this maniac and kill him for all the terrible things that he had done. She loathed him.

Carmine chuckling a bit turned to Peter. "I am going to the club. I ordered up some food so make sure that our guests get to eat and when you are done here, close up and meet me there."

Peter nodded and Carmine left. Peter continued to sit at the desk and rifle through papers, while Derek and Chloe just sat there bidding time. About a half an hour later, there was a knock at the door. Peter went to the door and said "Thanks, I appreciate it". He then closed the door and walked back to us holding two bowls of rice. "You better get used to it, you'll only be getting a few items to eat, this being one of them."

Peter then unhooked Derek and Chloe carefully from behind and tied their hands together facing each other. He then told them to stand up and then kneel down. Almost falling over, Derek and Chloe were able to get into position. Peter then took the bandanas off and said, "No screaming or I'll put the mouth pieces back on, and you won't get anything to eat, understand?" He then put the two bowls between them and said, "Pleasant night. You will need to eat and rest. We have a very long journey tomorrow."

He then shut off all the lights except one lamp that was on the desk. In the dim afterglow, Derek and Chloe had to wait until their eyes got acclimated to see where the floor and bowls of rice were.

Kneeling there in the darkness Derek told Chloe "Let's eat first, and then I'll be able to think more clearly."

They managed to hold one bowl at a time to feed each other with the spoons that they were kindly provided even though their hands were still tied. When they were nearly done the door opened again, this time it was the goon who had held Derek while Peter beat the hell out of him.

The goon just looked at them eating and then turned around and closed the door without saying a word.

Derek said to Chloe, "We need to whisper since we have a chaperone."

She nodded her head as they continued to finish their meal.

Derek quietly told Chloe that they needed a new plan since the pocket knife was now out of reach of both them.

Starved, it took them only a few minutes to finish the rice.

Derek examined the room. He looked closely at the table where Peter had been working. He motioned to Chloe for the two of them to stand up very quietly. After standing up they almost fell over again from kneeling and sitting too long. Their legs ached. Groaning, they took very short steps to the table where Derek had seen the letter opener. They both had to lean over the table to extract it. Then they made their way back to where they originally were sitting. As they were trying to sit back down, the door opened again and the goon looked surprised by the fact that they were standing.

Derek sensing the goon's surprise said to him, "We were stretching after the meal, after having sat so long!"

The goon said something incomprehensible and came over and grabbed the rice bowls from them and grunted "Sit down!"

Derek hiding the letter opener up his sleeve, motioned to Chloe and they both sat down together.

Then the goon retied them but forgot to tie the bandanas across their mouths as he left.

Derek was then able to maneuver his arm to get the opener back out. He held it so that he could saw the rope between their wrists. Derek had to take a break every so often because with their hands tied together he had to raise his over Chloe's which put an additional strain on his wrist as he pushed the opener back and forth. It took about twenty minutes to finally free themselves.

At last the rope fell from their hands. They both looked at the door, thinking that the goon had known what had happened. But the door didn't open.

Derek then untied their feet, telling Chloe to keep quiet by using a hand signal. Standing up, he stretched and squatted to get his blood flowing again and his body relaxed. Chloe kept looking at him and mimicking Derek. Then he took her hand and he led her next to the door. Both of them pressed their ears against the wall to see if they could hear anything. It was almost dead quite.

Derek looked around the room. He had the opener in his pocket and his pen knife, but now looked for something to either pry the door open or to hit the goon with it as he came through the door.

In the corner of the room was a mop and large industrial bucket. Derek quietly walked over and picked these up. He figured if one didn't do it, the other one would.

He then whispered into Chloe's ear his plan. She was to sit back down and scream and as the goon came through the door, he would see that only she was sitting there and would be looking for me, ready to shoot or hit him. He wouldn't have notice that Derek would have tripped him by then with the mop and smacked him with the bucket to cancel his dancing ticket for the evening.

All went well with the plan, as the goon saw stars as Derek punched his lights out.
With that done, Derek stooped down and took whatever he thought was useful and necessary from the goon, money, wallet and gun.

He then took Chloe by the hand as they crept out of the building like cats walking alongside the wall and out into the Hollywood night.

Chloe told Derek that if she could get to a phone, she could call the Tong and they would send a car for them. Derek was not too sure about it, but agreed to on one condition, that he could call the cops.

She said fine.

They went looking for a phone and found one at the corner of Fountain and Sierra. There was a little Jewish neighborhood market with a phone inside.

Both calls took about 5 minutes. And within ten minutes after they made their calls, a dark emerald green Chrysler limo drove up in front of the store waiting to pick them both up.

The Hollywood police hadn't known about Derek or Chloe abduction, or at least the sergeant of the watch couldn't recall this being on the APB. However, he said he would look into it and contact the other local divisions throughout the city.

Derek told the sergeant to call Mike O'Keefe at the Fairfax precinct just as the car pulled up in front on the store.

Chloe said, "Come on, the car's here." Derek let go of the phone and ran outside behind Chloe.

Wang Chu, the first lieutenant for Mr. Chung was opening the door and greeting the rumpled couple as they entered the car. The big sedan disappeared like a dream from the corner, as if it never was there. Fifteen minutes later they were in Chinatown pulling in front of the Metropolis Club. This was an all Chinese Revue club. [4]

The couple got out of the car. By now it was raining hard. They both went into the Club and down the corridor by the hat check room into an office that was at the end of the hallway.

Mr. Chung was there with a big grin on his face and his arms stretched out towards Chloe. She ran to him crying and they both hugged and kissed each other.

---

[4] The Metropolis Club was patterned after the Robert Low club in San Francisco. In fact, they shared dancers and singers, and it was part of the tour to play at both clubs.

Derek standing there felt a little out of place but then Wang Chu who followed them into the Club gave Derek the sign to sit down.

Derek was not sure what would happen next, but decided to trust his instincts and relaxed.

When Chung and Chloe finally got through their moment of happiness and renewal, Mr. Chung looked at Derek and then said something to Chu, who left the room through a deep red velvet door on the right.

Then Mr. Chung walked over to Derek and sat down in the chair across from him. He said, "Commander Kent, I am in your debt for saving my daughter's life. You are a brave soldier to have escaped from the Mancini family. Your friend, Jack Riley will be quite impressed with your escape, as much as my daughter and I am!"

Derek responded by saying, "Sailor, you mean sailor!"

Mr. Chung bowed his head and said, "Oh yes, pardon me for my incorrect comment. But first you must rest and have some tea, or would you rather have something stronger?"

Derek said, "Both actually. If I could have a glass of bourbon over ice and some tea that would suite me just fine! I would also like to get a hold of Jack, if you know where she might be?"

Mr. Chung said, "Yes I believe I do, but we may not be able to contact her this evening as I believe that she is out looking for you, but I will call my contacts to notify them that you are safe and here with me."

Derek said, "I need to know what has happened since my capture and who and why these mugs are involved."

Mr. Chung said, "In due time Commander, in due time. First you relax, drink and have some food that I can offer you. Wang Chu will be back with towels and fresh clothing for both of you. You may use the facilities here and then stay here till your comrades have been contacted. I wouldn't want you to be recaptured tonight under my own roof."

Derek said "What, what do you mean?"

Mr. Chung said, "Well, it's like this. In business we have strange partners and this evening the Mancini family is scheduled to come to the club for dining and entertainment and to settle up for some of our dealings. I don't want them to know that I already hold the high card, the Ace of Spades. As your Jack Riley and I had put together this little plan that she would raid their club looking for both of you, while they were here tonight. So, I don't think that we want to do anything different, else it would raise suspicion. They are even going to raid their warehouses and shipping docks to look for you. That said, I want to see how this plays out between all parties before and if I tell the Mancini's that I have you and Chloe. Our dealings are sensitive and involve all kinds of organizations and of course our countries at war. So being rash would be the worst possible situation. Don't you again Commander?"

Wang Chu and some other waiters had come back into the room with a platter of food. Mr. Chung began to chat to Chloe in Mandarin.

Fortunately, Derek did understand much of it. In the meantime, Chloe and her father were making up for some

192

lost time and he finally told her the whole story. Derek sat there amused a bit, ate and relaxed with his drink and waited for that big smile from Jack.

CHAPTER 16

By the time I had gotten to La Fonterra, Brad and Gary had
been waiting outside for me as the evening mist surrounded
the L.A. basin.

It was almost eerie as the light rain diffused the light from
the street lamps. The buildings on both sides of the street
looked like they were melting and the street itself looked
like it was a sheet of glass.

I got out of the car with my umbrella and went to the large
awning that covered the entrance to the club. The boys
were a little damp.

I said, "Good evening, any action yet?"

Brad responded, "Jack, a few minutes ago Carmine and
some of the top henchmen left, leaving the rest of the
Mancini's still inside."

Well I said, "Time's a wasting let's go in."

The club was swinging inside with the band playing away.
Cigarette and Cigar smoke filled the room with a very
prominent odor that floated through the air like a cloud.
The crowd was extremely loud and boisterous. After all,
most of the crooks of the city hung out there.

I stopped at hat check area and deposited my coat and
umbrella. Then we made to the reception host who looked
up at us as we came closer to the stand and said, "Good
evening. Name please."

I looked directly at him and responded with "Chung, Velvet
or should I say Chloe Chung!"

The host began to look at the register for my name and stopped dead cold and then looked back up at me and the boys.

The Guys held back their own surprise when I announced who I was.

The host then said, "Excuse me one moment, let me see what we have available."

Brad tugged at my sleeve and said, "What's that about?"

I answered, "I want to play out the game to see if anyone cares who I am or who will leave since Carmine isn't here."

The host returned and said to the maitre d', "Gino, please seat these customers at table 34."

Gino approached us and made the gesture to follow him to the middle of the room.

It was very crowded with many of the same faces that I had seen in the club in Palm Springs. I sensed that the members and festivities here were definitely in full swing.

After being seated the waiter came over and took our drink order.

I told the guys what I had uncovered and said that Uncle Mike and several squad cars would roll up shortly to interrupt this dinner party. They had to get the warrant to sweep the building and find what they could.

Both Brad and I kept looking around the room, to see who we had already come in contact with. Other than a nod or two from some minor thugs, no one seemed to mind who we were.

About 8:30 my Uncle showed up with several squad cars of police. As he and his police came through the entrance, none of us were aware that Francesco and Peter had been watching everything through a two-way mirror upstairs.

The cops sent the restaurant a spinning. We of course stopped eating, though I didn't want to, it was just too damn delicious.

Uncle Mike asked everyone to stay seated, as the police fanned out through the building.

Meanwhile on the second floor, in a room with the two-way mirror, Peter and Francesco had finished throwing money and documents into several bags and were now running out the back of the building through a secret hallway that had no stairs just a ramp, like a long spiral walk way that spilled out into the garage where their car was parked.

Unfortunately, by the time Brad and I had jolted out of our seats and managed to get upstairs, the only things we found were notes with Carmine's writing on them scheduling a trip to Boston via L.A.

As we were finishing our review of the room, Gary came running upstairs and said, "They've already gotten past our roadblock!"

"Who I asked, Peter and Francesco? How do you know?"

Gary answered, "The garage man told me who had left and who they were. "

"Crap" I said, "We had them by the short hairs of the neck and let them get away."

"What kind of car were they driving", my Uncle asked.

Gary said, "It was a Chrysler, black 4 door sedan. I wasn't able to get the license plate number."

"That's ok", Uncle Mike said. He then turned to his sergeant and said, "Charley, get an all-points bulletin out on that vehicle. Tell the dispatcher to have our men stop all vehicles like this and detain the passengers until we are able to confirm who they might be!"

I then asked Gary, "Did the garage man tell you where they were headed?"

He said, "No, but he did overhear Carmine tell his driver to go to the China Blossom."

I said damn, "That's Chung's club. Uncle Mike we must get there now! Chung and Carmine in the same room could lead to some real explosion in Chinatown, and I'm not just talking fireworks!"

Uncle Mike shook his head in agreement and then put his sergeant Charlie Kelly in charge and gave him instructions on who and what to do with what was found at the club.

The policemen were taking names and addresses of all the attendees as we ran past them to our cars to get across town to the Blossom.

Before leaving, Uncle Mike called dispatch again for additional police to back us up when we got there, since we were a little unsure what our reception was going to be like.

Sitting in the middle of Chinatown, The China Blossom was a beautiful club, not far from where I had met with Chung the other day. Its double doors were gold and red lacquer with a giant four-color dragon painted on it. The doors, standing ten feet tall, resembled a piece of art.

About 8:30, at the same time we were running through La Fonterra, Carmine and Tio Mancini were going through the doors at the China Blossom. As they entered the restaurant several of the Tong had surrounded them and escorted them to a table. One of the Tong went to the office down the hallway to tell Chung that they had arrived.

Derek and Chloe were talking with Chung, when the monk came in and whispered into his ear. Then without much fanfare Chung told Derek and Chloe to continue to eat and rest and that he would be back shortly. He never mentioned Carmine's name.

On the way out of the office, to meet Carmine and the Mancinis, Chung told Wang to make sure that no one went in or came out of the office. He then told another monk to send additional men to cover all the exits including the roof. He wanted to be prepared for the Italians in case they started something.

Carmine was getting impatient in the dining room. There was a revue that was dancing and singing on the stage but he wasn't paying any attention. His major concern was to make sure that Chung had secured the documents and everything else needed for him and the Mancinis he had requested, for them to get out of L.A. and head back to Boston. He was unaware that both Derek and Chloe were now under the same roof in the same building that he was in.

From the back entrance of the club Chung walked towards the table where the Italians sat. Carmine noticed him walking closer and stood up to greet him. "Good evening Mr. Chung!"

Chung responded, "Good evening Carmine. How may I assist you this evening? It is an unexpected surprise that you pay a visit to my humble establishment."

"Well", said Carmine, "I must ask you if you were able to take care of our arrangements and if you could possibly move up this request so that we could make our departure by midnight tonight."

Mr. Chung looked at him and said, "Tonight? That only gives me a little over two hours to arrange the shipments to your dock in time."

Carmine looking at Tio Mancini first then back to Chung said, "Certain problems have arisen that we must remedy. Hence we must leave earlier than expected."

Mr. Chung, wanting to bait Carmine, asked, "Does it have anything to do with certain kidnaps that I have been told about recently?"

Carmine looked surprised but responded. "I am not sure what you are referring too."

Mr. Chung responded, "Carmine, I am well informed of your recent encounters with the Navy, and with a certain private investigator. Many people seem to be very concerned over their lives and fortunes and the outcome of the War including me. But I must tell you that it appears you and Mr. Mancini have convoluted your interests to the point of insanity and that the U.S. Government is extremely upset over your dealings and are looking to put an end to it."

Carmine, the ever-sly Italian, retorted, "Mr. Chung, I am not fearful of my life. Nor am I fearful of the U.S. government. We have been merely misrepresented in our efforts to assist the Navy. Apparently now it appears that the Navy wants us to stop helping the U.S. government in their endeavor at winning the war."

"Not so", said Mr. Chung, as he looks at Tio and Carmine. "It is only the pure and simple truth that you and the Mancini family have gambled too high in regards to the lives of some people that have resulted in the government rethinking its position with you. No one at the top of the U.S. Government wants to be implicated with you. Both of you are now responsible and become the fall guys for your aggressive involvement. Taking a Military Officer from his own surroundings is a federal offense. The Navy won't stand for that!"

Still sitting down, Carmine snaps at Chung. "We only did what we thought was necessary to make sure that all of our clients were covered in their required needs and wants."

Mr. Chung then says, "Yes I understand, however kidnapping and death are not on the good side of the U.S. government, particularly during a time of war and because of this, I can no longer help you in your efforts."

Carmine then jumps up and said to Chung, "Why you dirty yellow belly chink! I trusted you and asked for your assistance. Now you are turning your back on me?"

Chung looked at Carmine and quietly responded to his insult, "Yes, particularly when it involves my daughter."

Carmine's mind froze as he realized what Chung had just said to him. He then tried to play down the situation and looking at Chung straight in the eyes said, "What?"

Chung says, "Carmine, you know damn well that Chloe is my daughter. You also know that if you did any harm to her that I would go to the ends of the earth to revenge any man who would harm her."

Carmine was about to respond, but Chung cut him off and said, "Chloe is my legacy. Make no demands except to excuse yourself to leave my establishment with your life. Do not attempt to retaliate against me, as you find that I am a very worthy adversary. You will have your shipment as requested by midnight, but nothing more ever again. And please make sure that you and your people stay on your side of the street. If you or they are ever spotted in Chinatown again you will never find them! Do you understand Carmine?"

Carmine stood there shaking. Tio being very silent was now standing and wondering how to appease both of these men, but decided otherwise.

Carmine looking at Chung then sees him holding the red silk scarf that he knew belonged to Chloe.

He asked Chung about it. "That's a nice scarf?"

Chung looking directly in Carmine's eyes says, "Yes and it goes around a very nice neck!"

Standing there, still in silence, Carmine is looking at Chung when Peter and Francesco hurriedly walk through the doors of the Blossom and up to Carmine.

Deafening silence was the only thing heard by all. The dancers and singers had stopped performing. The band had stopped playing and the other patrons were sitting with their mouths wide open.

Carmine shaking turns to look at Peter. Francesco who is between them leans in and whispers in his ear, "Jack and the cops are on their way here, I'm sure of it."

Carmine, fidgeting with his hands started to reach into his coat for his revolver wanting to shot Chung where he stood, but regains his control and some of his composure and then says, "OK, I understand. Thanks. Let's get out of here". Then Carmine turns starts to walk away as Peter, Francesco and Tio start to follow him at through the double doors. Chung then waves his arms and the band begins to play music again. For the moment everything returns to normal.

Chung then tells Wang to keep his eyes open for any problems and then walks back down the hallway and upstairs to check on Derek and Chloe.

Derek looked at Chung as he came through the door. Chung looked a bit tense. So, Derek asked, "What's wrong?"

Chung told Derek and Chloe, that Tio, Carmine, Peter and Francesco had been downstairs. He then told them, "I don't think that Carmine will come back here again. I don't believe that he is that stupid, but I will keep Wang on it just in case."

Both Chloe and Derek were feeling the anger filling up in their chest, when Derek replied, "Maybe not Carmine, but what about one of his henchmen?"

Chung waved the question off and started to speak to Chloe in Mandarin again to calm her down.

Outside, Carmine told Tio to get into the car. Tio objected and told Carmine to let it go, that there was more at stake than the girl.

Carmine replied, "It's not the girl it's Chung. He has turned against us and I feel we should take care of him for that?"

Tio responded, "Never mind that now, we need to get back to Boston and move our operation back to our homeland."

Carmine said "OK", but I need to take care of some things first."

Tio replies, "Carmine I forbid you to tangle with the Tong" and then gets into the car.

Carmine signals Peter to come over to him. He says to Peter, "Are you sure that Chloe and that Commander are both secure?"

Peter said, "Yea, I tied them both up together – why?"

"Well" Carmine replied, "I am positive that Chung was telling me that he now had Chloe in his possession by holding that scarf. Even if it's only business, he gets really protective about her."

Peter said, "Well tell the Chink to jam it. He's getting what he needs from us."

"I know", said Carmine, "But family is always family. The circle of life is always about family Peter. My dear friend, I want you to go back to the storage office and check on them. Make sure that they are both tied together. In the meantime, I am going to send a little parting gift to Chung and his famous hot spot. I don't care what Tio is telling me, nor do I care about the supplies from Chung. We'll live without it if we have too. Then I want you to bring our guests to the dock. We'll put them on board early. I'll get the rest of the goods and family to the ship tonight. We will leave at dawn."

Peter nodded and walked over to his car and got into it and drove off, as Carmine got into the car with Tio. They then drove back to the La Fonterra where Carmine was to put his parting gift together for Chung.

When we all had pulled up in front of the China Blossom with the seven squad cars, it was about 9:30 or so. The Chinese on the street were already on the lookout for anything weird or suspicious and looked surprised when all of us arrived.

Inside, Mr. Chung was notified that the cops had surrounded the building as we walked to the entrance of the restaurant. Chung told his guards not to worry and then met us in the hallway to the stairs to the office. He looked at me and smiled, "Jack I have a surprise for you."

I looked at him and he motioned for us to follow him upstairs to the office. He opened the door and there in the center of the room sat Derek and Chloe.

I couldn't believe my eyes. I smiled like a little girl and walked over to Derek. He stood up and we wrapped our arms around each other. He winched a bit from me holding him so tightly, so I let go of him just a little and kissed him on both cheeks and then on the mouth. For a moment I was the kid in the candy store.

After about an hour of getting everybody caught up, we realized that we only had a short amount of time to get to the docks to stop Carmine and the Mancini family from leaving the port.

Back in Hollywood, Peter had reached the storage office and found that his guests had flown the scene and the guard had been knocked out. He then phoned Carmine to tell him what had happened. Extremely upset Carmine demanded that Peter return as quickly as possible, before driving to the ship. He would have to first make a special stop at the China Blossom to drop off the parting gift to burn it down. Peter then drove back to the La Fonterra to pick up the gift for Chung.

Back at the Blossom, Uncle Mike had let all but one squad car leave the area. Mr. Chung had also relaxed his security from around the restaurant and just told Wang to stay close.

While Uncle Mike was making calls to the precinct, Mr. Chung got several of his men together. He then told them that they were to go to the docks, but to await further instructions from him.

A couple of hours had passed and somehow no one had noticed the two cars rolling down the street slowly with Peter and several of Carmine's men loaded to the gills with tommy guns and dynamite.

Inside the restaurant and upstairs, we continued our telephone calls and plans to seize the ship and the Mancinis.

Derek and Chloe needed to get some air, so both decided to go for a walk downstairs to stretch their legs. They both had had enough of the planning and needed a break from all of it.

No one was at the door or even heard Peter and his guys come into the restaurant. Unfortunately, Derek and Chloe were standing right in the middle of the hallway leading to the front doors and were grabbed and drug outside to the cars waiting. Both of them were wrestling and kicking and trying to scream when one of the gang hit Derek hard on the side of his face, which knocked him out. Peter smacked Chloe across the lips which also shut her up and unconscious.

Peter then walked casually inside the restaurant and planted a couple of sticks of dynamite before dashing out to the cars parked across the street.

At the same time, they were piling in the vehicles across the street, I had walked over to the window and saw one of the goons forcing Derek in the car. I turned in shock to tell everyone what I saw, when 'bang', the dynamite went off. The building shook and swayed and a fire started someplace below. Smoke was consuming us all when Wang came through the door with some sort of masks for us to put on, telling us to follow him. He had been in the kitchen when Peter and company had come into the restaurant and then the whole place exploded. By the time he ran out into the restaurant to see what had happened, he knew there was a huge fire already spreading, so he ran upstairs as quickly as possible to get us out of there.

We all followed Wang down the stairs and out through the back doors to the alley. We then ran around the corner so we could get to the front of the building. By the time we reached the front, the whole building was on fire. We stood there motionless, as we watched it destroy itself. Five minutes into the fire, the fire department arrived and started to put out the blaze. It took them nearly two hours to completely put it out. The restaurant had nearly burned to the ground.

Meanwhile, Jimmy Woo's Market doors opened with Jimmy looking in awe of what was happening at the restaurant. Jimmy had been awakened by the sounds of the explosions going off and was at the door as quickly as he could run. He opened them at the same time as we arrived from running around the building. He motioned for us all to come inside.

Jimmy looked at Mr. Chung and asked, "What happened? Where's Chloe?"

In an unlikely response, Mr. Chung stared at Jimmy and answered, "Those bastards took my daughter again!"

Uncle Mike asked if he could use the phone, having come in after speaking with the Fire Marshall.

Jimmy pointed to the phone on the wall.

Uncle Mike made several calls, including one to the Sergeant in charge at the precinct to inform him of what had just happened. Then he called the Sergeant at the docks. There was no answer. I heard Uncle Mike say, "What the hell?"

I said, "What is it Uncle?" He told us that he wasn't getting any answer from the police at the dock. He then called back to his precinct and asked if they had heard anything. The answer was no.

Uncle Mike then said, "I think the Mancinis have taken out my men. We need to get to the docks as fast as we can, because it's almost midnight and that ship is scheduled to sail at 1 AM sharp.

With that we all headed to our cars. Brad jumped in mine and Jimmy, Mr. Chung and my uncle in another, while Wang drove with Gary in his car.

It was now or never!

CHAPTER 17

Sirens blaring, Uncle Mike called for backup. We raced across town to Terminal Island where the ship was docked.

Uncle Mike must have been in contact with his back up, because I could see the squad cars following us through the streets of L.A.

In the meantime, Chloe and Derek were gagged and hand tied once again, only this time in a stateroom abroad the "Isadora" flying the Italian flag.

Peter, Francesca and Commander Martin were in another stateroom, planning on what to do with their captives. They argued that keeping them was more dangerous than letting them go. Peter wanted to kill them and leave them on the dock as a parting gift. Francesca just wanted to leave them behind.

When Carmine walked into the stateroom, he overheard the conversation and told them of his conversation with Tio that they would be kept as insurance against any interference by the cops or military.

Tio Mancini was now on a private plane back to Boston. He told Carmine that he did not want anything to happen to his captors. He wanted no part of it, stating that his family was on the line and to keep Derek and Chloe would only slow down their own operations, let alone trying to keep the Tong, the Navy and other authorities at bay.

Carmine said, "It doesn't matter now, they all will be looking for us, you can bank on that!"

Tio then told Carmine that he should arrange for a plane to Boston to catch the other ship from there that was bound for Sardinia. He would permit Carmine to bring Derek and Chloe and his other members with him, but he told him to leave as many people behind on the ship in L.A., in case the cops tried to seize the guns.

Carmine then told Peter, Francesca and Commander Martin that the decision was made to hold Chloe and Derek, at least till they got to Italy, and then they would decide on what to do with them. "The problem", he said, "was that the ship would be steaming for about four weeks and the Navy would no doubt be on the lookout for the Isadora".

Peter then begun to speak but Carmine waved him off as if it was of no consequence. Carmine had decided to leave Commander Martin in charge on the ship. Carmine felt that since Martin was a Navy Officer, that he had a better chance of getting the ship underway and to Italy than the rest of them. Besides Martin was not blood, so if he got caught it wouldn't matter in the long run – the rest of the Italians would be on Italian soil away from the U.S. Navy and American police.

With that Carmine made some calls from the ship's phone and made arrangements for the chartered flight to Boston. Peter and Francesca then gathered their captives and belongings and headed off the ship bound for a private airfield in Long Beach. Carmine told Martin to call him if there were any problems and that he would arrange help or an escape route.

Once at the airport, Peter marched Chloe and Derek over to the plane. He untied Derek from Chloe and Francesca took Chloe up the stairs into the plane first. Peter then forced Derek into the belly of the DC3. By 1 AM through the mist and fog, the plane had lifted off the ground with Chloe sitting there with her hands tied together as Carmine, Peter and Francesca enjoyed a glass of whiskey for their success.

When Gary, myself and the rest of us approached the docks, darkness was filled with lights and reflected shadows between containers, the pier and the ship. It was 12:35AM when we all got out of our cars and started to run towards the ship as the stevedores were untying the Isadora. Uncle Mike started shouting at the dock boss to stop, but the Captain of the ship saw the commotion and told his chief engineer to rev the engines and pull away from the pier.

The engineer moved the lever to full ahead and just as the last line was being tossed over the cleat at the pier the ship lurched forward and inched from the pier, leaving all of us out of breath standing there watching her pull away. Uncle Mike was first to speak and asked who was in charge of the stevedores.

An Italian looking dock hand stepped forward and said, "Si, I am in charge! My name is Giancarlo and I am in charge of my men who work on the docks."

My Uncle known for his no-nonsense chit chat, said, "Who do you work for?"

Giancarlo, responded proudly, like it was a sign of respect, "The Mancinis".

Uncle Mike, told his sergeant, "Round up these guys and hold them for aiding and abetting."

Giancarlo started to say something and Uncle Mike, yelled back at him "to shut up."

Brad, Chung, and I were standing there motionless, as Uncle Mike seemed to take charge of the situation.

Somewhere in the darkness, we heard footsteps. It was Wang and Gary.

I turned to hear them running towards us. I didn't know that they had taken off towards the dock shack down the pier when we had gotten out of our cars. Both of them were now out of breath, but were able to tell us that they had gotten a copy of the final manifest out of the shack about fifty yards down the pier. It looked like the names of Carmine, Peter, Francesca and two others were blocked out on the document. There was a scribbled note next to their names that stated that they had gotten off the ship just before it was scheduled to sail. However, it did say that Commander Martin was onboard and listed him as Officer in Charge.

Gary went on to say that the stowage was listed as clothes and food for Sardinia. Wang spoke up and said, "Distributed by the Unions of America." None of us were surprised, since this was where we had found the weapons at the warehouse.

Uncle Mike asked where the shack was and they pointed down the pier. So, he headed in the direction they gave. We all followed him with Gary by my side. Behind me, Brad, Chung and Wang walked together.

I told my Uncle that we had to call the Navy to see if they could seize the ship, and arrest Commander Martin for desertion. We also needed Martin to confess and tell us anything about where Carmine and the rest of them were headed.

My Uncle said, "Alright, but do it now girl!"

Once in the shack, I called Captain Stark because I thought that he would be the best one within the Navy to contact to stop the ship in its journey. He would also instruct some of us people to go to the pier to arrest Commander Martin to stand trial not just for desertion, but also for treason.

It was now almost 1:15 in the morning when I awoke him. He didn't mind it after I told him all about what had just occurred. He told me that he would call me back after he spoke with the Admiral.

Meanwhile, we all waited and watched the ship peacefully sail into the darkness of the night. Soon, lights from the ship disappeared into the horizon.

Gary and I tried to figure out where Carmine might have gone and Uncle Mike called the precinct and put out an APB for anyone who looked like him.

Chung told us that he would not be any good just hanging around and opted to go back to Jimmy Woo's and see what help he could contribute. He requested that I contact him, once I found out what Commander Martin knew. He and Wang started walking back down the pier towards Wang's car.

Brad said he'd had enough for one night and said that he was going to his apartment to sleep. He asked that I call him if something broke. He could call us from his newspaper in the morning. We said, "Goodnight" and he headed out the door and yelled to Chung and Wang for a lift back to his place.

About 2 AM, Captain Stark returned my call. He said that after convincing the Admiral of the dire nature of the situation and pulling some strings, the Navy agreed to search the waters for the ship and if it were to be found, that it would return it to Terminal Island. Stark said that they didn't know how long it would take but more than likely it couldn't be done until around the morning, since the Isadora had gotten a jump on where the Navy ships might be patrolling, but may have also past into the international waters area.

Stark told me that the Navy had two ships off the coast, the cruiser USS San Diego CL-53 and the gunboat USS Sacramento PG-19 in an area that patrolled the Mexican and American waters for subs and or terrorism threats. They were now being diverted to find and bring back the Isadora to Terminal Island.

I thanked Captain Stark. He said that Commander Bain and his team would arrive around 8AM to ready themselves to take custody of Commander Martin, once the ship was returned. I told him great, but that I really would need his confession so that we could find Commander Kent. He said that Bain was well aware of situation and that he would work with me to complete the desired results.

I relayed my conversation with the Captain to Uncle Mike and Gary, as one of the sergeants came through the door. He waited till I was done, then Uncle Mike said to him. "Sergeant Wilson, try to get any information from the dock hands that we might use. With any luck, the ship should be back here in the morning, if all goes according to plans. Keep them in another building under guard. We may still need to tie the Isadora back up."

The sergeant nodded and left us to complete his task, as we discussed our own plans.

Both Gary and my Uncle agreed that Carmine would have left the area by now. But to where they were not sure. Was it New York, Boston or Italy?

I told them that we'd have to wait to find out since we needed to interrogate Commander Martin. That he was our ticket to Carmine and the Mancinis.

It was nearly 3AM when we looked at the two couches and decided that we had better get some sleep and wait to see if the Navy was able to find the Isadora and bring her back.

I settled into one of the couches and my Uncle in another, Gary found some extra cushions and blankets and cleared off a table to lie on.

It was around 8:15 when the sergeant came back to wake us. He said that he couldn't get anything more from the crew during the night interrogation, except that before the gangplank was raised, Carmine, Peter, Francesca and two other people came down from the ship and walked to a car that was waiting for them. The two unknowns were a woman and another man. Giancarlo had told the sergeant that he remembers Carmine calling the woman Chloe and that Peter had held a gun on the other man and called him Commander.

I was still waking up and stretching when the sergeant said "Commander. Alive", I said out loud. "Derek and Chloe are still alive."

My Uncle told the sergeant, "Good work, now we just have to sit tight and wait to see if the Navy has been able to find that ship."

About a quarter of 10, Commander Bain, Chief Boatswains' Mate Watkins and two other sailors arrived at the pier. The Commander had told us that they had stopped by the Long Beach Naval Station to ready the brig for Commander Martin.

He then called Captain Stark and asked about the ship but the Captain had no news.

It was nearly 11 AM, when Captain Stark called back. He told me that the ship had slipped by the Navy blockade during the fog and apparently used a Navy oiler as a shadow and followed her out to sea. However, the Sacramento and San Diego assigned to the task had made their way out into the open waters to track down the Isadora.

We sat there like hungry children waiting for the meal to arrive.

Disappointed, I said to the Commander and to my Uncle, "We have to do something. I can't take just sitting around waiting for something more to happen. I've got to locate Carmine and Derek!"

Commander Bain said, "Look Jack, go about what you think you can do. As soon as we get Martin in our hands, I am sure that he will tell us what we need to know."

I said "Thanks, but I am kind of stuck in that I do not know what direction to go in first."

Gary was listening to us and chimed in, "Jack, we need to head to Boston. The Mancinis are there and no matter what, Carmine is bound to want to hook up with them. We should go there and quickly may I add."

I looked at Gary. I knew that he was probably right. Boston was the only answer.

Uncle Mike listening said, "Look, we know where they are in Boston, though it won't do us any good to call the PD there and tell them to round them up. I am sure that we would run into a road block. But Jack, you can go and basically fly under their radar and find out as much as possible, so that you can relay that to me and I can pass that onto the Boston police. In fact, I may be able to arrange for you to just go through them!"

I turned to Gary. He nodded his head. I turned back to Bain and then to my Uncle and said, "Alright, but you need to let me know as soon as you have Martin in your possession."

Uncle Mike said, "I'll call the BPD and tell them you guys are coming. They will assist you however they can. You are to contact Lt. Billy Mulligan. He's a good guy and will see that you all are taken care of."

Bain touched my arm and said, "Jack, I will contact the Navy office in Boston as well. When you call later, I'll tell you who the contact is. In the meantime, let me call Long Beach and see if they have any planes flying to the East Coast and where they are headed."

I looked at Gary and he smiled back at me and I said, "OK, Gary and I are ready to go."

Bain told the Chief to call Long Beach. After talking a few minutes to the person on the other end of the phone, the Chief said, "Commander you need to tell them what this is all about."

Bain grabbed the phone and asked, "Who am I speaking with?"

Bain made the sound hmmm hmmm and then said, "Yes that's right, I work for Captain Stark, NIS and we are sending two undercover members down now and should be there within two hours. Yes, that's great. Boston by 0800 tomorrow. Thanks. Tell Commander McBride I owe him one. Goodbye."

Bain then told Gary and me the flight information, as we began picking up our stuff. Bain told the Chief to go ahead and take us to the base to pick up the hop.

Bain looked at us and said, "Good luck and stay out of the line of fire, I know that Commander Kent would want you to be alive when he sees you again."

I said, "Roger that."

My Uncle said, "Jack, Gary, take care, we'll be in touch."

As we headed out the door, I said to the Chief, "You know Boats, neither Gary nor I have anything clean to wear, having been here all night."

The Chief chuckled and said, "Ms. Riley, I will take both of you to the clothing shop and mart to get you some clothes and toiletries. It will be a long night for you both. That's the least that I can do. I am sure that Uncle Sam is willing to contribute to your morale and welfare. After all you two are still Navy property…"

The three of us got into the Chief's car and headed to Long Beach.

CHAPTER 18

The Chief told us some funny jokes and stories to keep us in good spirits as we headed south on route 1 to the base.

He was very informed about the mob and the involvement of the Navy. He told us that during the first three months following the bombing at Pearl Harbor, the U.S. and its allies had lost over 100 ships to the German subs that were off our coasts. Because of this the Navy negotiated with the mobsters in New York and Boston who controlled the docks on much of the East Coast to help the Navy in the protection of the wharf and harbor areas, since the Navy was short of ships and personnel.

The Chief also told us that the Navy had first used an immigrant from Palermo, racketeer Joseph 'Socks' Lanza who controlled the Fulton Fish Market in Lower Manhattan to help control the waterfront areas. But after he was convicted of extortion, the Navy had to create 'Operation Underworld,' that linked itself to another mobster, Lucky Luciano. Even though he was in prison with a sentence of twenty-four years to serve, the Navy needed his help, so through negotiations, they contacted Meyer Lansky via some intermediaries to ask for Lucky's help. Hence the Navy had Lucky transferred to another prison that was kind of a hotel, The Great Meadow. It was located close to Albany NY. Here Lucky could live a pretty good lifestyle while assisting the Navy.

According to the Chief, "Lucky gave the word to keep an eye and ear out for saboteurs." The Navy was delighted in the response that Lansky and Luciano were able to achieve. However, when this branched out to L.A. and the West Coast the families tried to exceed their assistance by charging more and demanding certain agreements with the authorities. This didn't go over very well, so the Navy and other agencies started to work different angles to divorce themselves from the mob. This of course had now caused lots of problems on both sides of the war.

Another side note that the Chief told us was that somehow or at least this is what was reported, Lansky knew of the sexual preferences of someone way up in the government or at least that's here say and used it against him as proof of the matter. This helped keep the authorities out of the way of the Navy and the mob members working to protect the docks and the shorelines.

I said to the Chief that "I am not too surprised by what you have told us, though I must admit that it is strange to hear about things that you would think otherwise particularly when you read about a person or hear him speak and you would think that he was holier than thou."

The Chief laughed and said, "That's the beauty of it all, Ms. Riley. No one would have suspected any of this! I just know that everyone has a little closet they keep for themselves, but enough, I shouldn't be giving my opinion while I am dressed in uniform."

Both Gary and I laughed. It's true I thought. We all have some things to hide away for a rainy day that we don't like anyone to know about, including me.

It took us about an hour and fifteen minutes to get to the base. We made a mad dash to the mart and to the uniform shop and then headed over to the tarmac. An Army Air Force C-47 was waiting for us as we hopped out of the car and said thanks to the Chief.

We ran across the tarmac to the plane, where one of the crew members waved for us to hurry. We climbed the stairs to get inside and quickly were told to grab a seat. The plane, which was a "Skytrain" had a primary mission to transport troops and cargo. However, it was also used by the paratroopers sometimes to drop them behind enemy lines.

Once inside the cabin, we found that the plane was full except for two seats all the way aft in the plane.

Walking down the aisle we noticed the plane was full of young fresh scrubbed faces of paratroopers waiting to get to their next location. During the flight we found out that most of them were headed to England. We surmised where they would go from there but we didn't dare pry.

The C-47 was nicknamed "Gooney Bird" and had an air speed of almost 230 mph, with a range of over 1500 miles. Giving these calculations Gary and I figured that we would be in Boston around 8AM on Sunday morning if all went well.

After we had been in the air for about an hour, the navigator came back to speak with us. He was Major Dodds and he told us our route would take us to Denver, Chicago and then into Boston. We thanked him for the information. He also offered us some fruit and some sandwiches and said to get some rest, because it was going to be a long flight, about 17 hours plus the change of time.

I figured that each leg would be about five hours long, so after the first two hours of staring into the night and talking with Gary, I drifted off to sleep from the drone of the two props that continued to spin their mesmerizing tuneful noise. I thought about Derek, if he was alright and how could we, Gary and myself spring him from Carmine's grasp. Slowly it passed and I drifted further into the clouds along with the plane.

Close to 5:30PM in Long Beach the Isadora was tying back up on pier 3. She had been stopped by the U.S. gun boat, after being located some 7 hours, off the coast of Mexico near San Carlos. She had been sailing close to the shoreline of Mexico, following the oiler. Unfortunately, she was spotted and radioed to the authorities who in turn contacted the U.S. Embassy in Mexico, who then contacted the Navy at Commander Seventh Fleet, Command and Control in San Diego.

Commander Bain boarded her gang plank as the last rope was thrown on the bollard. Chief Watkins was right behind him with his sidearm out of his holster and in a ready position.

As they reached the top of the stairs to the deck, the captain of the ship stood there to greet them. Bain grabbed the captain by the arm and asked, "Where's Martin, Commander Martin?"

The captain pointed towards the nearest hatch door.

Bain let go of the captain and bolted to the door and opened it slowly.

Behind Bain and the Chief was Uncle Mike, along with five of his police officers. He told his men to take the captain into custody. He then followed Bain and the Chief into the hatch.

In the middle of the stateroom nearest the door, Martin was sitting there with a gun in his hand. Bain, the Chief and

Uncle Mike entered the room. Martin looked at them and held up the gun as to say stop!

Bain began to speak to him. "Commander Martin, you need to put that gun down. It will be better if you do so and come along with us."

Martin looked at Bain and the others and said, "Do you really think that I can be excused for my actions? For turning against the country that gave me a good life? What kind of life would I have if I let you take me back to the Navy? No doubt I'd be hung for espionage."

Bain tried to reason with him. "Martin, you can help us and your country and still come out alright. It's really up to you, you know?"

Martin snapped, "Look, Carmine's got Derek in Boston and they all are headed to Italy. What else can I tell you or do? I am just one of the middle guys. I don't know the plans of anything except that the Isadora was to go to Italy and drop off the weapons and merchandise. Me, I would have had to stay there, since I had already turned my back against the Navy and America."

Bain again tried to console and reassure Martin. "Martin, we can work this out, I know we can."

But with that Martin stood up. Everyone in the cabin moved back a foot, or so, not knowing what Martin was up to. But Martin swiftly put the gun to his temple and pulled the trigger. It was over.

Bain, Uncle Mike and the Chief had dropped down on one knee in a firing position, as Martin moved promptly to kill himself. Martin's body quickly slumped to the floor. In a split second his life expired. He had shot himself right through his head with the .45 caliber.

The three stood up and Bain went over to check Martin's pulse. There was none. He was definitively dead.

Uncle Mike and one of the police officers wasted no time going to the pilot house and looked around for the ships phone. "Hopefully" he told the officer "It's already connected." As he placed it next to his ear, he heard a dial tone. "Must be my lucky day", he told the officer. He then dialed the precinct and heard Sergeant Daly's voice.

Uncle Mike told him the story and then said, "You need to contact the BPD and let them know that Jack & Gary are on their way. Get a hold of Lt. Billy Mulligan and tell him to give this information to them when they arrive. They will know where to find the Mancinis, Carmine and the rest of the members of this Italian family."

The sergeant replied, "He would" and hung up.

Uncle Mike told the police officer who was with him to look around for any additional evidence and then to meet him in the stateroom. As he walked back to where Bain and the Chief were, he remembered that he needed to call Mr. Chung to let him know what all had taken place. So, he turned around and made the call and had a brief conversation with Wang, since Mr. Chung was not available. But Wang told Uncle Mike that he would relay the information and that the Tong would stand by and await if they could provide any other assistance.

Returning to the stateroom and following a brief conversation, it was determined that the Navy had jurisdiction because of the circumstances that included

Commander Martin and the weapons cache. Uncle Mike told Commander Bain that this was fine and that the LAPD were just there to assist.

Commander Bain thanked Uncle Mike and said "Though both the Navy and the LAPD were tied together in this, it was a Navy issue since the ship was transporting ammunition and cargo that was tied to the war efforts. However, Washington DC will no doubt give merit warranted to the LAPD for their assistance."

Bain told Uncle Mike that they would arrange for the body to be brought to San Diego for an autopsy and burial. Uncle Mike said that he was OK with that, since he didn't need to get involved in anything extra. He told Bain that he had enough on his plate without any more from the Navy and the Commander's death. Besides he was still concerned about Jack!

That said, Uncle Mike left one of his officers behind to assist the Navy as he left the ship and went back to the precinct.

CHAPTER 19

It was almost 9PM when the navigator shook us to wake up. We hadn't even felt the Gooney land. It must have been smooth as glass or we were just plain tired. He told us that we'd be in Denver for about an hour as they had to refuel and suggested that we get off and stretch our legs.

I asked him if there was a phone we could use and he replied, "In the office."

Getting out of our seats, Gary and I started stretching then walked to the stairs leading off the plane. It was just turning dusk as we walked over to the office. Once inside we asked the corporal at the reception desk where the phone was and if we could borrow it.

He said we could, as he had been told who we were earlier from the Colonel in charge. Word travels fast I thought. We also saw that coffee was available and helped ourselves to this treat, while we contacted the police and the Navy.

First, I called Uncle Mike to see if he was still at the precinct. He was. He relayed the events surrounding Commander Martin. I was a little shocked, but understood "his way out of the mess" that he had gotten himself into. I was also pleased to know that we were on the right trail following Derek, based on the Commanders chit chat before he took his own life.

I finished up by telling my Uncle that I would call him at the next stop in Chicago and he said, "Jack it will be around midnight. If I have anything new to add, I will pass it on to the Boston PD, if that's alright with you. You do know that I haven't had any good sleep lately since you've gotten yourself involved in all this Navy mess?"

I laughed and said smugly, "I'm sorry Uncle, it's just that I didn't want you to miss any of the good times!"

Uncle Mike laughed as well and said, "Well Jack, take care and I will speak with you sometime tomorrow."

I told him, "Goodnight Uncle Mike, I do love you and Aunt Dorothy, you know?"

He said, "Ditto!"

I hung up the phone and told Gary about Martin.

Gary responded in kind of the Marine Corps way, "In a way it was the honorable thing to do, even if he was a traitor. He saved us a lot of time and trouble as well as disclosing Commander Kent's whereabouts. And he saved the government money in his prosecution!"

I replied "Yes, but unfortunately we still have many hours to go before getting to Boston."

Gary nodded and then called Lieutenant Colonel Murphy to get updated.

The hour flew by when the corporal in the terminal announced over a PA system that the plane was about ready to depart and that everyone needed to be back onboard, so Gary and I ran back outside and up the stairs into our seats.

Once the plane took off we just nodded our way to Chicago. I was still going over the fact of Martin's demise. We are all "victims of life" in one way or another. Some not in a good way while others might be the lucky bastards!

I wondered, in his own death was my fiancé James one of the lucky ones? A question I would never be able to answer.

In Manchester New Hampshire, at another airport, sometime after 8PM, a private DC3 was landing on the secluded side, with the traitors and their captives on board that was unbeknown to the airport employees.

The airport was primarily a staging base for the heavy bombers routed to Germany. Headquartered not far away was The North Atlantic Wing of the Air Transport Command, who ran the massive operation. Unfortunately, the Navy and Army Air Force weren't cross talking and didn't realize who was getting off the plane.

Carmine and Francesca (aka Elizabeth), were first to walk down the stairs, as Peter pushed and prodded Chloe from behind down to the tarmac. Peter then went to the right side of the plane to open the belly.

Peter pulled Derek out. He was dazed and a bit confused after being in the hold area for so long. Fortunately for him it was heated, so he hadn't frozen throughout the long journey, but was very sleepy from the long flight. Gaining his sense of balance, he saw Chloe standing about 20 yards away. Her hands were tied in front of her. Derek thought that he heard heavy planes revving up somewhere close by.

Carmine was looking directly at Derek with a devious grin. Derek's stomach started to churn as he looked back. "If he could only get his hands on that guy", he thought.

Carmine then looked at Peter and they nodded at each other. Carmine and company then headed for the doors to the terminal.

Peter then pushed Derek towards a different door off to the right that looked like the cargo area. Inside there was an oriental worker who worked nights and watched as Chloe and Derek were marched and pushed along to the different areas. It was odd to see an oriental girl, especially being handled in the manner she was. No one from the plane had seen him watching their every move.

The worker was curious and walked back to the office to see where the plane had originated from and what the manifest said. No one was in the office when he found the clipboard with the information on it.

Only recently being granted a work visa by Henry Kong, the sponsor and honorary mayor of Chinatown[5] and a member of the Tong, Deng Dian felt obligated to report anything suspicious back to Mr. Kong. So, he picked up the phone and called the secret telephone number that he was given the day he arrived from Manchuria.

Deng did not know that during the day, Mr. Kong had received a phone call from his old mentor, Mr. Chung in California, who asked if he would not mind keeping a lookout for his daughter.

Henry told Lien that he would and if there was anything else that he could do, to just ask him.

Henry and Lien were very close as the story goes. It was reported that Chung and Henry were either related by blood or through boyhood in their native China. As it turned out, Chung had sponsored Kong to enter the United States and because of this friendship assisted him in establishing his

---

[5] Laundry and garment manufacturing plants, were controlled by the Tong in Boston

own family run business. And so, they looked out for each other.

Mr. Kong was thankful and intrigued by what Deng had told him. He asked Deng if he thought he could follow Chloe and to report back to him as soon as they arrived at their final destination. Deng said, "I can".

Back at the airport and outside the cargo area, Derek was being pushed inside a trunk of a black Zephyr. He had overheard Peter speaking with the chauffeur that it would take about an hour to go south and get them into Boston at the Mancinis warehouses.

In the front of the airport, Carmine and company were stepping into another vehicle, a shiny dark green 1940 Super Eight 180 Packard Limo waiting to take them in another direction to Boston.

Deng punched out his time card and left a note for his supervisor that he was sick, but that he finished all his jobs for the night. He then got into his gray Ford and waited for Carmine to leave. He was sure that no one had seen him, so it would be easy to follow the Packard to wherever it was headed.

Inside the Zephyr, lying still in the trunk, Derek began to listen for his whereabouts in case he could contact anyone. He figured that they had to have landed in New Hampshire or Vermont, but couldn't remember the airports and how close they were to Boston. However, he could hear Peter and the driver chatting away and when there was a break in their conversation he overheard the radio station give out its call letters, 1370 WFEA-AM Manchester New Hampshire.

So, this is where they landed, Derek thought. That's a starting point. Now he just needs to know where they are taking him.

While Derek was being taken elsewhere, Chloe asked Carmine, "Where are we going?"

Carmine staring Chloe down said, "I bet you want to know. It doesn't matter though China Doll, because as soon we can we will be on our way to Italy with the Mancinis and there is nothing you or your father or anyone else can do about it. And your friend is going to the docks right now!"

"Shush", Francesco scolded Carmine. "You don't have to be so arrogant around this woman. She will do as she is told or else."

Chloe looked at both Carmine and Francesco with disdain. Chloe knew that she had to find help somewhere and somehow, otherwise she might end up dead or in Italy with Carmine. She began thinking about how to get free. She didn't know where the Mancinis were located so she kept an eye out during the ride for markers or signs even though it was dark, just in case she was able to break free and had to relate this information to someone.

About an hour after they had landed the Zephyr stopped and the trunk was opened by Peter.

From the lights on the pier and the blackened shadows, Derek could almost make out the other person standing behind Peter holding a rifle. Derek was trying to adjust his eyes to the night, when Peter told him, "Get out and don't try and pull anything."

The "shadow person" was a goon as Derek found out who helped him out of the trunk to stand up. While Derek tried to surmise where he was and what was around him, Peter had begun talking to the goon with the rifle.

The pier was like any other pier, military or civilian. The office shack and other working buildings dotted the wharf. A lone ship was tied up about 30 yards down the left side of the pier. Cargo loading was taking place from the trucks under the crane and lights were ablaze on the ship and all along the pier. Derek thought that the only way he could get free was to run into a darken area so that he could get the ropes off his hands and be ready to fight his way out. The problem was how could he cut the rope from his wrists? Deciding that he would have to risk it, he opted for the right opportunity and waited for his move.

Peter completed his discussion with the goon and turned back to Derek grabbing his shoulder and said to him, "This way, Commander!", as the three of them began to walk towards the ship.

Over on the pier side Derek noticed that there were three stacks of pallets close to the edge. Derek decided to try and make a run for it. But first he had to make it look like he tripped so that they would stop and bend over to help pick him up.

As he crossed over a set of railroad tracks that went all along to the end of the pier, Derek took three steps and faked tripping.

Peter was the first to realize that Derek had fallen, so he went back to help him up onto his feet. The goon with the gun also stopped and walked up behind Peter.

When Derek saw this, he quickly jumped up in a forward motion with all his force, knocking Peter into the goon. Both of them fell backwards as Derek took off in the direction of the pallets.

It took him all of 30 seconds to reach the other side of the pallets. Standing there in a moment of silence while his heart pounded he found a wire band holding the bottom half of the pallets, so he started rubbing the band against the rope between his hands as he heard Peter and the goon yelling at him and coming closer.

Just as Peter yelled out, "Come out with your hands up", Derek cut through the rope. He peered through the stack. Peter and the goon were just standing there waiting for Derek to come out of either side. Because the three stacks formed an alcove where Derek stood, it hid him from their view. It was not a perfect triangle with more of a stack of pallets on one side than the other, but for now it worked.

Peter nodded to the goon as they separated and walked around each side to circle the pallets.

As Peter came around first from the right Derek pushed on the pallets toppling them onto Peter. He fell and hit his head on the side of the pier and tumbled into the water.

The goon with the rifle saw this as he came around the other side, and just as Derek turned around to fight him, the goon smacked Derek across the back of his head with the butt of the rifle. Accidentally a shot rang out from the rifle, as the goon had held his finger on the trigger when he slammed Derek in the head. From the blow, Derek passed out. He didn't know if he'd also been shot, but based on his head spinning he didn't care.

Then the goon started yelling for Peter, but in the dark he couldn't see anything or anyone move.

A couple of the dock hands ran to where the goon was standing. He told the two hands to pick up Derek and take him onboard to stateroom 3 on the port side.

In the meantime, the goon looked down at the water to see if Peter somehow survived. Nothing stirred. Apparently, Peter's luck had run out.

The goon all of sudden felt nauseous. He realized that his own life might now be on the line because of Peter's death. He needed to call the Mancinis. So he walked up the pier to the gang plank and into the stateroom where the two hands had taken Derek. He then called the Mancinis to let them know what had just happened.

Meanwhile the other car carrying Chloe was heading along route 28 to 38 when it came to Medford, Massachusetts. The driver told Carmine that he heard something funny from the left tire and that he'd like to pull over at the next service station that was open. Carmine said it was OK. About a half a mile or so down the road there was a Texaco service station. The chauffeur pulled into it around 9:25PM. The station was right across the street from the Tufts University entrance on Main Street. There were college students walking about everywhere since it was Saturday night. The station however was closed, but at least it had some light and enough room to change the tire if it needed.

When the chauffeur got out of the car and looked at the left front tire, he saw the gash on the side where the white and black rubber met. The tire was almost flat. He walked back to the left rear window and Carmine rolled it down to see what was going on.

The chauffeur said, "Mr. Carmine, we have a flat and I have to change the tire, before we can travel any further."

Carmine was amused, yet upset and said, "Alright but hurry."

The chauffeur said, "Thank you, I will."

Carmine then said, "Ladies we need to get out and stretch our legs a bit. It seems we have a flat."

Francesca looked at Carmine and asked, "Should we take the cuffs off Chloe?"

Carmine snapped with a grin, "Yeah OK, she knows what's good for her if she tries anything!"

Exiting the vehicle first was Francesca, then Chloe and then Carmine.

Francesca lit a cigarette and offered it to Carmine. He took it and walked around to where the chauffer was now engaged in changing the tire.

Carmine asked the chauffeur, "How long?"

The chauffeur replied, "About 20 minutes tops."

Carmine nodded and took a long drag from his cigarette and looked over at the college. He said out loud, "I could have been a great history professor!" And then laughed. Francesca looked at Carmine and laughed, "In your dreams!"

Chloe stood there in the dark looking over at the school and the kids walking in and out of the entrance. She decided this was the time to make her escape. She knew that this is where she needed to run into, since it would be the safest place to hide and get help and away from Carmine.

Francesca started to light another cigarette as a gust of wind blew out the lighter. Then she turned her back to Chloe and Chloe sensing that this was the right moment took off running towards the entrance.

Even though she was dressed in a Chinese dress and Chinese slippers she was able to dash so fast across the street that it wasn't until she was at the entrance that both Francesca and Carmine reacted.

Carmine was the first one to the entrance, but by the time he stopped at the archway and looked up into the grounds of the school, there was no sign of Chloe. All that he could see were the kids walking on the walkway in both directions. It would have been a miracle to locate her amongst the activity of the campus.

Francesca arrived only seconds later and said, "That bitch!" Carmine didn't look at her, but merely stared expressionlessly into the darkness of the campus and said,

"Yeah, but we're not going to find her now and way too much trouble. I will just have to lie to Chung if he comes looking for her."

They walked back to the car where the chauffeur was just throwing the old tire and tools into the trunk.
The chauffeur asked, "Any trouble Mr. Carmine?"

"Yes", Carmine responded. "What school is this?"

The chauffeur said, "Tufts University. I hear it's a good school. The Mancinis send their kids here!"

"Ah", Carmine replied. "I'll deal with Chloe when I see Tio! Let's go, we are already late." With that, all three got back in the car and headed for Boston.

Little did Carmine know that he had been followed by an unknown Chinaman.

Following the Packard at a safe distance Deng had noticed that the car was having some sort of trouble, so he slowed down to be three car lengths behind it. When it pulled into the service station, Deng pulled the car into a parking spot alongside a dry cleaner's store on the same side of the street but before the station. Then in the shadows of the night he walked across the street to the side of the campus and up a grass embankment that preceded the fence that connected to the huge arch. He then moved to the edge of the fence from the ridge and watched the exchange taking place near the Packard. He noticed that the girl's hands were now untied.

He watched as Chloe ran across the street. So, he darted to where she would enter and grabbed her as she came running through the gate entry into the college. He took hold of her left hand with his right and silenced her with his left hand.

She panicked but saw that he was Chinese and immediately relaxed a bit as he strained to pull her along as they ran back to the embankment.

She followed closely as they both knelt down in a corner of complete darkness. They could hear Francesca and

Carmine talking as they kept out of sight. Deng put his hand over his own mouth to convey to Chloe "to be quiet".

When Carmine and Francesca began to cross the street to return to the car, Deng stood up tugging Chloe to follow him closely down the bank and over to his car. By the time they had gotten into the Ford, the Packard had already pulled out and was out of sight in the traffic.

Deng said to Chloe, "Now that I have rescued you, I need to follow whoever had kidnapped you and report to Mr. Kong."

Chloe was still a bit stunned at being rescued and said "I don't understand! Who is Mr. Kong?"

Deng responded with, "I just do as I am told. I will tell you later who he is."

With that, Deng pulled the Ford out into the road. He knew he had some ways to go before he could catch up to the Packard.

Meanwhile, Carmine was now in a rush to get to the Mancinis. The Packard was driving fast through the towns and neighborhoods. However, Deng began to see its lights in the horizon and every time it crossed a street with a lighted corner, he confirmed to himself that he was indeed getting closer. He would stay on it till he found out where they were headed.

Chloe smiling to herself that she was free again, sat there as this Chinaman drove like a crazy man to catch the Packard. She knew that her Dad had had something to do with it, she just didn't know how. So for now, she would have to trust Deng and what he was doing.

CHAPTER 20

A little after 3AM Chicago time, the "Goonie" was once again landing.

Bored, yet anxious, both Gary and I looked forward to finally getting to Boston. It seemed like this trip was taking forever. Of course, I just wanted to find Derek.

At one point Gary was kidding me about the clothes that I had purchased from the Mart and uniform shops. I had on Navy pilot boots, fatigue pants, tan shirt and a green half jacket.

He told me that if he hadn't known any better that I would have passed for some "flyboys" wife.

We both chuckled but I said, "Yeah, I just can't wait to put on some "civvies" when we get back to California.

Off the plane into the terminal once again Gary called the Lieutenant Colonel for an update. Nothing much had changed. But per a conversation with the Tong in LA, we were to meet up with a Chinese gentleman by the name of Mr. Kong, once we arrived in Boston. He was contacted by Mr. Chung and would assist us during our stay in "Beantown." Either he or someone representing him would meet us at the airport.

After an hour walking around the terminal and getting some coffee, we headed back into our seats one more time. We were finally on the last leg of this journey.

In Boston, Deng and Chloe had been following the Packard. When they entered the area of Charlestown they continued over to Chelsea, making a left on 5th St then they followed the Zephyr and made a right. Deng knew that he was close to the Navy docks, as he could see the tops of two ships jutting above the brick and wood buildings. Deng never had been in this area before so he slowed down as much as he could in the traffic and drove the car into a parking space short of the corner next to a closed tattoo shop. That way he could get out and look around the corner to see where the Lincoln had gone.

He told Chloe to stay put while he went over to investigate. When he peaked around the corner, there it was parked about ten or so yards on the right hand. As his eyes got used to the night, Deng could see the lights from the pier shine past the shore patrol with rifles and guns standing at the Navy gate. He couldn't tell where Carmine and Francesca had gone, but he surmised that it was through one of the doorways that he could just make out as he looked down the side of the wall. He didn't want to stick his head out too far, in case someone was standing in the doorway and guarding it.

Deng walked back to the car and told Chloe that he needed to find a phone to call someone. After peering down the street, he spotted one across the street close to an alley.

Deng told Chloe, "Stay put!" But this time she said, "No".

So Deng opened the door so Chloe could get out. He told her to stay close as they ran across the street to the phone to make his call.

Carmine and Francesca having gone into the building had walked upstairs to the second floor to see Tio. When Carmine opened the door, he knew that there had been some trouble, as Tio was sitting there with two of his bodyguards not looking very happy.

241

Unbeknownst to Carmine, Tio had just confirmed again with the goon at the pier that Peter was dead or lost, but that they still had Derek.

Tio looked at Carmine and said, "Peter is dead!" Both Francesca and Carmine went into shock as they looked at each other aghast by the news.

For the first time Carmine felt vulnerable. He had lost Chloe again and now Peter. Gaining his composure, he said, "What about Commander Kent?"

Tio responded, "We still have him and we will now keep him under lock and key. Apparently, Peter and Kent got into a scuffle and Peter fell over into the water. Not sure why he never resurfaced, but our guard thought that he had seen Peter hit his head against the side of the pier as he fell. The guard quickly cracked his rifle over the Commander's head to knock him out."

Carmine feeling sad for his friend and associate told Tio the other bad news. After explaining what exactly had happened with Chloe, silence surrounded the room.

Tio then spoke, "Carmine, we can't be bothered by either loss. We still have the Commander for insurance, though I am concerned that Chloe might find her way to Chinatown where I am not at all friends with the Tong leader, Mr. Kong. He and I seem to battle over everything, so I must say that we need to speed up our shipping time, as there is no doubt that the Navy and the Tong along with other authorities might be after us at this point.

Carmine still in a stupor over Peter agreed.

Francesca in the meantime had called back to the coast to find out about the Isadora. She went white as the pilot master in Long Beach told her that the ship had been returned to the docks and had not set sail again. He also told her that the LAPD and the Navy had seized the ship.

Francesca looking grim turned to the others and informed them of the situation. A bad night all around it seemed had followed them to Boston.

Immediately, Tio made a call to Lewis Wharf to make sure that the ship "Angelina" would be ready to sail by Monday.

He was told it would, so he and Carmine began their process of cleaning out the offices.

At around 1:20 AM, Deng placed a call to the Tong office of Mr. Kong. The person who answered the phone told Deng to hold on.

Five minutes later, Mr. Kong spoke into the phone and said, "Hello Deng. What may I do for you at this hour of the morning?" Deng told Mr. Kong that he had Chloe and where they were. Then he said, "This is where I followed the others including Chloe's capturers, Carmine and Francesca!"

Mr. Kong said, "Fine, you must leave there immediately and bring Chloe directly to me. I will deal with the Mancinis in due time."

Deng answered "Yes" and hung up. He turned to Chloe and said, "We need to go to Mr. Kong's house now. He will take care of your friends here."

Chloe and Deng both ran across the street and jumped into the car and began to drive away when the chauffeur from the Packard came around the corner and saw them both in the Ford. Deng looked at the chauffeur and made a U-turn across the median and swiftly drove away.

A fear in the chauffeur's stomach spread from his stomach to his face as he ran back into the building to report what he had just seen.

Anxiety overtook Carmine as the chauffeur told them about the Ford and Chloe.

Tio said to them, "We can't worry about that woman and whoever was driving the car. We need to get things done here and head out to the ship. We can't stay here any longer, particularly since I am warring with the families in New York and Chicago. We have no other option now."

Back on the ship, Derek was awoken by a banging sound. He also realized that he had a headache and it felt like the size of the baseball on his head where he had been butt rifled by the goon. He looked around and realized that he was in a stateroom aboard the ship that he no doubt saw on the pier.

With his head pounding, he looked around to see if there was anything that could help him at that moment. There wasn't, so he would have to wait to plan out his next move. In the meantime, Derek figured that a little more sleep would prove to be most beneficial, if he could get through the pain in his head. At last he drifted off and saw Jack in his dreams. All was well with life.

It was almost 2:30 in the morning, when Deng and Chloe arrived at Mr. Kong's home. It was located in the downtown area on Beach Street. Here he could control his enterprises throughout the Chinese neighborhoods, which included the brothels of the red-light district and his restaurant, "The Garden Ling", across from his house on Beach.

After meeting Mr. Kong, both Chloe and Deng were led to separate bedrooms for the remainder of the night.

At 3 AM, East Coast time, Mr. Kong called Mr. Chung and provided Lien with the information about Chloe and where the Mancinis were.

Lien and Henry then decided on the approach to reprimand the Mancinis for their involvement in Chinese affairs. Mr. Kong and his Tong members were to assist Jack and Gary rescue Commander Kent. Thereafter, Mr. Kong would take over the property and operations that the Mancinis were involved with, provided that the Chinese in the U.S. and on Mainland China would receive the benefits from such a bold move. Lien agreed and said that he would assist in this transition with the U.S. government and the Italian families.

Lien asked Henry to keep Chloe in Boston for the moment, until such a time that it was safe for her to return to Los Angeles.

Deng would receive compensation for his brave acts in rescuing her and assisting the Tong families.

At almost 8 AM East Coast time, the Goonie was touching down at the Boston Airport. As the troops placed their bags over their shoulders and headed down the stairs to the tarmac, you could feel the tension mount in the cabin, not only for the soldiers but for Jack and Gary too. Once they

245

all departed the plane, Jack and Gary knew that soon their own adrenaline would be knee deep in a dangerous operation of rescuing Chloe and Derek.

Down the stairs and into the terminal everyone walked in unison and as they stepped inside Jack saw a rather large Chinaman standing with a sign that said, "Jack Riley". When they approached the man, Jack said, "I'm Jack Riley."

The Chinaman looked at Jack and pointed to the outside of the terminal. Thinking that the cops would have met them instead, Gary and Jack looked at each other and walked outside anyway to where a white Buick limo was parked. With just their carryon bags, they looked at the Chinaman and he just waived at them to get in.

Not saying a word, the Chinaman got into the car and drove out of the airport area. We had no idea where we were going or who had sent the car, but decided to play along to see where this was going.

It took about 45 minutes to arrive at a driveway with red faced dragons and golden bodies on both sides of closed gates that led up to a house.

Jack looked at her watch, it was almost 9 AM.

The Chinese man pressed a remote button inside the car. The gate swung open and the car then drove up the driveway. Gary could see the house which was another 50 yards up the pavement. A golden Buddha sat in the middle of the grounds with flowers all around. As the car came to a stop the twin doors to the house opened and out walked another Chinese man in a deep purple two-piece Chinese silk suit. Two girls followed the man, each wearing a different Chinese colored dress, one in blue and one in red.

The Chinese man walked to the bottom of the stairs. He opened the door to the car before the chauffeur could get out of the car to open it for us.

As I got out of the car and looked about I noticed how pristine it appeared. How non-American.

The Chinese man spoke after bowing, "Ms. Jack and Mr. Gary, it is with great pleasure and honor that you both have arrived safely. I am Mr. Kong. We are grateful for your assistance in these troubling times. Please let me show you inside, we have much to discuss."

I bowed and said, "Thank you." Gary on the other hand just stood there and stuck out his hand. Mr. Kong, smiled, reached out and reluctantly but cordially shook Gary's hand. I felt a little tension between them but I was hoping that it wouldn't hold back Mr. Kong's assistance.

We followed Mr. Kong through the entry way into a very large sitting room on the right-hand side of the house. The two Chinese girls disappeared once we entered the house and then reappeared with tea, cucumber sandwiches and chicken noodle soup, placing them on two specific tables alongside of where Gary and I had been instructed to sit down.

Mr. Kong said, "Please relax and enjoy. We will speak together very shortly." With that he and the two girls disappeared from the room.

Exhausted but hungry, we both devoured the food. Thirty minutes later we were asleep in the sitting room, when four monks came in and took us to our sleeping rooms.

When I awoke, I was alone and in a feather bed. I remembered eating and then nothing. Somehow, I had been dressed in a sleeping gown and I smelled like I had been bathed. I looked at the clock. It read 4:45. I walked over to the window and realized it was still daylight. Hopefully it was still Sunday?

Looking about the room, I heard the door opened. I turned and there was Chloe looking at me. She started crying and ran towards me, as I myself got choked up. We held on to each other for several minutes. Then she started telling me everything that had happened. I was happy that she was safe, but knew that Derek was probably not and that Gary and I needed to go find him as quickly as possible.

After Chloe explained everything, I said, "How did I get from the sitting room to here?"

Chloe said that Mr. Kong had placed a small sedative in our tea so that we would sleep. With the time difference and the number of hours that you had traveled, he knew that you both would need some rest before mounting the search for Commander Kent.

I asked Chloe where Gary was.

She said, "Next room over. And he is already up and shaved."

I said, "What, how do you know?"

Chloe shyly laughed and said, "I went in to check up on him first. He is a nice man, not like Carmine."

I looked at her and asked, "Do you like him!"

Chloe just nodded and giggled.

I asked her where Mr. Kong was and she said that he would like for all of us to join him at 5:30 for dinner.

I said, "And my clothes?"

Chloe responded to me by pointing to the closet. "I didn't know what size you were, so the girls and I just guessed and placed some things for you to try."

I said "Thanks, now go, so I can get dressed for dinner."

Finding a pair of silk black trousers, a white chemise and a red and black mandarin collar jacket, I slipped these on. It was a perfect fit and comfortable. No wonder the Chinese liked this type of clothing. At the bottom of the closet were soft low shoes. Chinese of course. I picked the red pair to match the jacket. At 5:25 I was closing my door when I overheard Chloe and Gary coming out of his room. I just smiled at them as we walked downstairs.

Mr. Kong was already waiting for us in the dining hall. It was across from the sitting room that we had been in when we arrived. It was decorated in red dragons and white swans with a large table that could easily seat 20 people.

As we all sat at our appointed seats around the table, Mr. Kong introduced Hu Kong. Hu had been the very large Chinese man who was our driver from the airport. As it turned out Hu was Mr. Kong's number one son.

We all chatted socially throughout our meal of won ton soup, vegetable sweet and sour, rice, chicken lo Mein and of course tea.

When the dessert (mandarin orange pudding) arrived, Mr. Kong looked at me and said, "Jack, it is time that we make our plans to rescue your Commander, as I have been told to assist you by Mr. Chung."

He continued, "We believe that the Mancinis will be leaving sometime in the morning from the docks at Lewis Wharf, which is not too far from here. It's the ship called Angelina. We are however now, securing their warehouses by the Navy shipyard. We believe they were one of the primary sources for the Navy, in ammunition and surplus items that unfortunately proved to be for both good and bad. Therefore, they had as much information as they seem to have had."

"Gary", Mr. Kong said looking directly at him, "I have been in touch with your service CO, again thanks to Mr. Chung. I am sending my son, Hu and some of my family members along with you to the Lewis Wharf. You must get onboard before it sails and retrieve Commander Kent. It would be more difficult to rescue him at sea, so we must try and complete this before the Angelina sails."

I looked at Mr. Kong and said, "What about me? I am also going with Gary. This is my job as well!"

Mr. Kong started to reply, "Jack, this is a…"

I stopped him from completing his sentence by jumping out of my chair.

I said to him, "A man's job! I know how to handle myself and will be all right particularly since Gary will be there."

Mr. Kong started to protest, but Gary stepped in and responded.

"Mr. Kong, Jack has gotten us this far. I think she can go the extra distance and help all of us in this rescue attempt."

"Very well all", Mr. Kong responded. "I will pass this information back to Mr. Chung. But before we plan our rescue mission, I must also inform you that yesterday, April 18, your Col. James Doolittle took off from the USS Carrier Hornet in a B-25 and bombed Tokyo. Other cities Yokohama, Yokosuka and Nagoya were also attacked by the American bomber pilots. It finally looks like we are changing the course of the war. I am not sure where the Mancinis fit in this picture but they can't be too happy about this new news."

I looked at Gary and he smiled at me. Finally, I thought a change for the good.

CHAPTER 21

While we made our plans, and had been resting and readying ourselves for the rescue of Derek, the Mancinis were on their way to the Angelina. About a quarter past one, they arrived. They proceeded up the gangplank almost running to the top of the stairs where they were greeted by the captain.

"Mr. Mancini", the captain spoke, "We will be ready to leave at 4 AM. The harbor pilot will be here around 3:15."

Tio nodded his head, "Good, now where is the Commander?"

The captain answered, "He is being taken good care of in the stateroom down the hall way", as he pointed to the port side of the ship.

Carmine, Francesca and Tio walked towards the stateroom where they found Derek tied up to a chair with a gag in his mouth. His head was pretty bloody from the rifle butt and he was in a daze.

Carmine was the first to speak, "I'd like to kill this SOB, but not yet. We need to take good care of him in case we need him for safe passage."

Tio responded, "Francesca get some bandages and medicine from the captain and fix this bastard up. No sense in killing him just yet."

Francesca did as she was told and soon Derek was coming around.

She had taken the gag out of his mouth as she cleaned up his wound and when he was able to open his eyes, he just looked at her and said, "Why?" He then dropped his head and went back to sleep.

Two cabins down the hall, Tio and Carmine were plotting their way to Italy and going over each detail of the path and days it would take them to get there. They would have to call their German contacts to ask for assistance across the seas, in case the Navy made a run for them. The U-boats were just sitting off the horizon and waiting for orders to blow up ships.

Back on Beach Street, Mr. Kong had been informed that his team that went to the Mancini warehouses found practically nothing except an empty building. It seems that they took everything that was not secured to load it on the ship and to leave no trace.

Gary, Hu and Jack, made ready to leave in the automobiles that Mr. Kong had supplied.

Jack in the meantime, had to change back into the fatigues that she flew out in. Besides she thought she'd save the Chinese outfit for another time and place, like walking around Palm Springs, when she got back home.

Mr. Kong supplied the semi-automatic .45 caliber Colt hand guns and holsters. Neither Gary nor I knew where he had gotten them since they were being used only by the armed services, but we knew better then to ask. Our job right now was to get Derek free no matter what.

On our way to the wharf area, Hu told us that another three cars were going the long way to the wharf and would be our back up on the other side of where the ship was docked.

And since it was night it would be easy for them to hide in the shadows.

It was almost 3:10 when we arrived at Lewis wharf. We parked the car about 50 or so yards from the pier entrance along the sea wall of Atlantic Ave. We then walked across the street where there were no lights. This way we could stay in the darkness of the night.

Much activity was in place as we reached the entrance. In the dark, Hu undid the binoculars from the case and looked down at the ship. He then handed it to Gary who in turn had handed it to me.

As it was, I was the only person who had ever seen Carmine. Gary had met Francesca but as LT Yardley once or twice but couldn't remember what she looked like, so it was up to me to point them out once on board or if I saw them on the deck of the ship.

Focusing the binoculars, I slowly moved them down the pier and then up to the deck of the ship. When I looked at the bridge, I saw Francesca standing with the captain. Moments later another man came out and started talking to the captain. He appeared to be dressed in some sort of uniform, but I couldn't make out who it was till he leaned over the side and said something. There next to the hull of the ship was a tug and apparently, they were getting ready to leave.

I handed the binoculars back to Gary and said, "There's Francesca with the captain and the pilot.

Gary peered through the binoculars and said, "Got it!" and then handed them to Hu, who then looked as well.

I said to the guys, "Let's wait to storm the ship as I want to see who else might appear on deck. Let's confirm that Carmine and Tio are on board, before we call out the army, no pun intended Gary!"

Gary just looked at me and chuckled.

Hu looking through the binoculars again said, "Jack, they are getting ready to leave and even if we haven't seen Carmine or Tio we need to go aboard now!"

I answered with, "I guess you are right, I just didn't want to chase after them if Derek was not on board!"

Hu replied, "He'll be on board, the Italians would not have left him behind!"

I thought for a moment and said, "You're right, I guess I am just playing it too cautiously."

Looking down the pier empty containers and pallets were stacked up across from the ship. It was nearly 3:45 AM when all the loading and movement on the pier stopped. The only people standing around were two lone stevedores, one aft and one forward by the bollards. They were waiting for the orders to cast off the remaining lines.

Smoke was billowing from the ship's stacks and the tug was grunting as well. Hu using his walkie talkie called the other cars and told them that we were ready to go aboard and to back us up.

I gave the signal to Hu. We began running to the sides of the containers. Everyone on the bridge had gone inside except for the pilot. He motioned to the two guys on the dock to throw off the lines. Busy with that he didn't see us running up the gang plank to the top of the ship. We had just made it when the electric wench began lifting the plank and bringing it into the ship's side to be tied down.

The ship shifted a bit as the tug nudged her from the pier. Gary and Hu went in one direction and I headed for the bridge house.

I looked down at the pier as I moved closer to the shack. Hu's men had already taken the two stevedores into custody and moved them off the pier.

Unknown to me, another two men from Hu's army had jumped into the tug and held the tug master at gun point as they took control of the boat. They swung the boat in reverse and were now moving to the other side. When the ship bumped into the tug the pilot started screaming at the tug master, but it was to no avail, as a Chinese man now controlled the ship and began pushing it back towards the pier.

Two of Hu's men ran back to the bollards and waited for the lines to be dropped back over the sides so that could tie the Angelina back up.

The ship had been pushed back to the pier by the tug as Hu had reached the bridge on the other side of where I was and held a gun on the captain and the pilot as he shut off all engines. He tied them up and waved to his guys on the pier to tie up the ship once more as he went racing to where the lines were to heave them back over to the pier. He then raced off to find Gary.

During those first few minutes, both the captain and Francesca ran out of the shack to see what was happening and as she turned to look down at the pier she saw me moving towards her. I saw the captain and the pilot run back into the shack as Francesca drew her knife out and came directly at me.

We began tussling with each other as both of us felt the side and bulkhead of the ship sharply stop us in our wrestling. At one point during the fight she swiped the knife at me and it caught me right under my ribs. The pain from the slice hurt but not as much as the uppercut to my chin as I was dodging another swipe from her knife.

I knew that the only way to get that knife from her was to get in close and take it from her.

Francesca started to come at me once again with her right arm pulled back ready to swing her arm forward to try and slice me. So I grabbed her right arm with my right hand and used my left hand to punch her in the face. Because it went across my body under in a diagonal direction it hit her directly under her nose. She immediately fell on the deck in pain as I continued to hold her right arm.

Francesca let go of the knife in the fall and I just stood there looking down at her. I reached down and picked up the knife. Her face was bloody, very bloody, but she wasn't unconscious as I found out.

She grabbed my left hand where I had the knife and she tried to pull the knife from me. Accidentally she pulled me down on top of her. As I lost my balance I crushed her with my weight while the knife was in my hand. She died almost immediately as I tried to roll off of her. When I finally untangled myself, I looked at where the knife had pierced. It was directly in her heart.

I staggered to stand up. I was all alone. I could hear yelling and screaming, but I couldn't figure out where it was coming from. It took me a few minutes to regain my composure. Even if this was an accident and even though she tried to take my life, this was the first person I had ever killed. I didn't like it a bit. All kinds of feelings and emotions were running through my head and stomach. I felt nauseous. I wanted to throw up. I stood there grabbing the side of the ship, letting my senses return to normal. I had not been aware, nor did I care at that very moment of what else was happening throughout the ship. I just wanted to feel better.

I hadn't realized till later that when we had initially gotten on board, Gary had gone looking for Derek. Not knowing what Tio or Carmine looked like in the flesh, he just figured that he would take anyone down if they didn't cooperate. On a freighter like this, he figured that the staterooms would all be up on the top two decks, so he spent most of his time opening up and finding no one inside them.

Hu had met up with Gary when Gary was almost done checking out all the staterooms.

Gary said to Hu, "We are going to have to go below, as I haven't found any sign of anyone in these rooms."

Hu responded, "Maybe they know what is going on and are hiding in the bowels of this old tub?"

Gary laughed and said, "We need to split up, it's too big for us to look together. Have your men secured the ship back to the pier?"

Hu answered, "Yes and they are standing guard at the bottom. I let the gangplank back down, so they are ready for whoever tries to flee."

Gary replied, "Good, maybe they know and have seen what has happened, so we need to be careful."

Hu asked Gary, "Should I bring up more of my men?"

Gary replied, "No, let's try and do this ourselves. You take the Port side and I'll take the Starboard. Do you have an extra walkie talkie?"

"Yeah", Hu answered. "Here you go, but just use it if you run into trouble. We don't want them to know where we are!"

"Right", Gary responded. "I know the drill."

Both Gary and Hu then split up and started looking below on the 2nd and 3rd decks of the ship. Neither one of them found anything except the freezers, refrigerators and dining rooms. However, Gary did find some cigarettes still burning in an ashtray in one of the rooms.

Neither Gary or Hu had known that Tio and Carmine had gone below to the bilge areas when all hell broke loose. They dragged Derek with them. The rest of the deck hands had gone to the armory and pulled out all the weapons and passed them around. Several of them were on the 4th deck of the ship when Hu caught up with them. This deck had several storage rooms, otherwise called the holds of the ship. Most of the rooms had containers or were filled with pallets. Hu walked slowly between them to stay out of sight and out of any gun range.

259

Hu was rounding a corner of pallets when one of the deck hands jumped him from behind. As they scuffled they slammed each other against the pallets and Hu's gun got loose on the floor. The deck hand tried to smash Hu with his own rifle, but Hu grabbed it and took it from him in the fight. Then the deck hand grabbed the ax from the emergency box, after breaking the window with his elbow. Because of the tight space neither Hu nor the deck hand could effectively use their weapons. The ax was thrown over hand and split the rifle in two. Hu tossed it aside and went after the deck hand with both fists swinging at his face. When the deck hand again tried to swing the ax, Hu was able to grab it with both hands and use the handle to abruptly smack the deck hand in the face and forehead knocking him backwards and out cold. Another deck hand heard the commotion and charged Hu only to find himself knocked out as well by the sheer force of the handle from the ax.

Hu then reached down and collected his weapon and ran off to continue looking for others. Walking along a hallway running the length of the ship on the 6th deck, gunshots rang out loud and clear. He stopped and dropped to the floor to see where they were coming from. It came from another passageway about 30 feet from him. He crept over the hatch comb to reach the area where the shots were being fired from and he saw Gary.

Gary couldn't see him from his position, but Hu saw that he was pinned down by three or four of the deck hands firing across the open storage space.

Hu took out his gun from its holster and raised it at shoulder length, aimed and pulled the trigger.

One down as Gary looked his way to see his comrade in this fire fight. Gary smiled and gave him the OK hand signal.

Hu smiled back and continued to fire at another deck hand that now turned to gain some protection against one of the bulkheads.

It was now a standoff. No one could move in any direction, so Gary decided to bring this to a close and signaled Hu to watch what he did and to cover him in his moves.

Hu signaled OK and reloaded his gun.

Then Gary started to move out from behind his cover and Hu began shooting in the direction of two of the deck hands, while Gary concentrated on the third.

As Gary continued his move across the open spaces, the deck hand that was focusing on Gary stood up from the cartons that protected him and Hu shoot him square in the chest. The other two deck hands also stood up and began shooting at Hu, which allowed Gary to take out both of them in two shots. In a matter of minutes, it was over.

Gary stood up and walked over to look up at Hu and said, "Thanks partner!"

Hu responded, "No problem, but we have more to find."

Gary patted him on his shoulder and said, "See you around" and took off running down the passageway.

Hu started running again in the opposite direction.

Close to the bilges Tio, Carmine and Derek were hiding. They had also brought along a few other deck hands for protection.

Tio said, "I think we should split up and go topside and get off of the ship!"

Carmine disagreed and told Tio, "You do anything you want to do, but I am staying put with the Commander as protection."

Tio said, "I am taking two of these guys with me. If you get out alive, call me back at the warehouse. I am going there to round up some more men."

Carmine said, "OK" and then told the other two guys that he wanted them to board up the passageway into the bilge area, so that they could hear or see anyone trying to come into it.

Tio and the two guys started down the passageway from the bilge to the starboard side of the ship. Through the open space areas to the 4th deck they started up the passageway to the stairs leading to the 3rd. Little did they know that they had someone following them.

Hu had doubled back after meeting up with Gary on the starboard side near the bilge area.

Hu and Gary had overheard the conversation taking place between Carmine and Tio. Hu signaled Gary that he would go after Tio and company.

Tio and his two men then went out through the Port side entrance before locking it back up.

Hu called his men outside on his walkie talkie. He told them to station themselves at the bottom of the stairs of the gangplank. He wanted to make sure that no one left the pier without some sort of escort.

By the time Tio and his men reached the top of the 3rd deck Hu realized that they would be back in the open holds of the ship which leant little protection in a gun fight. So he stepped up his pace to try and catch up with them.

Back up on the bridge, I was finally gaining my composure. I had overheard the Chinese men at the bottom of the gangplank talking on their walkie talkies. This was great I thought, though I had no idea what was going on down below.

Curious like any other woman, I decide to investigate, so I pulled open the hatch door that ran down the passageway to the stairs leading down to the next deck. As I was running across the open 2nd deck I heard a single shot from a gun whiz by me. I stopped in mid tracks and dodged to the left of a pile of cylinders. Bad idea I thought as I looked at them and realized that they said, CO_2 on the bottles.

I then rolled out from behind the canisters and started firing in the direction of the hatch comb where I thought the shots were being fired from. It allowed me to run over to another pile of empty pallets and stopped.

I heard some noise but no shots, then suddenly, I heard shots again, but they weren't coming my way. So I decided to stay where I was as the shooting continued. Then stepping out of the hatch comb a deck hand came firing his tommy gun.

It was no match for my .45, as the guy ran past me through the hatch comb to the top deck. Behind him was Tio and I leaned out and shot at him just as he shot back at me.

I only grazed him, as I felt two other bullets pass closely by me as the next guy came out of the hatch comb firing behind him.

I ducked down behind the pallets again and pointed my gun and pulled the trigger. The second deck hand fell face down which silenced the Tommy gun. He was dead.

A few seconds followed and Hu came running through the hatch comb towards me. Not knowing who it was initially, I had to pull back my hand so I would not shoot him. Likewise, Hu pulled back his hand.

I told Hu, "I only grazed Tio, sorry. Where's Gary?"

Hu stopped for a moment and replied, "Down in the bilges."

I said, "Great, you go and get Tio!"

Hu answered, "No problem, got men at the bottom of the stairs."

With that I headed down to the 3rd and 4th decks. There was no sign of resistance. However, when I reached the 5th deck, I slowed up my movements, walking cat like through the open space, alongside the bulkhead. When I got to the stairs to the 6th deck I sensed an eerie feeling that something was about to happen.

Taking slow and quiet steps forward I finally saw Gary.

Gary could feel the little hairs on the back of his neck stand up and he quickly swung around to pull the trigger, when he realized it was me.

Gary then put his left pointer finger to his lips and I stopped. He motioned for me to go back up and around.

I motioned back OK and slowly walked back up to the 5th deck.

I looked around for another hatch comb and saw it on the other side of the ship. I ran over and was wondering how I was going to open it quietly when there was a round of shots being fired.

I quickly grabbed the handle with both hands and moved the arm upwards. The hatch comb was now open and I could see Carmine hiding, but more importantly I could see Derek.

He was tied up and had tape over his mouth. He looked like hell, but he was alive. No one heard me open the door with the noise from the guns that were being fired.

Gary in the meantime had been firing at the two deck hands. He couldn't get through the pile of desks and other furniture that was stacked up in front of the doorway. So, he kept pushing against it in between the fire fights until he was able to knock one of the desks off the top. This allowed him to see the inside of the bilge area. But he couldn't see where Carmine and Derek were hiding because every time he went to take a look, one of the deck hands blasted out a round from a machine gun.

Looking down at this I realized that Gary was pinned down. I knew that I had to divert Carmine and the two deck hands so that Gary could get off a good shot at them.

Quietly, I looked around the area and found a chair close by. It was up against the bulkhead. I pulled it in front of me to use as a shield.

Time was right. As the shooting had stopped for the moment, I leaned forward and saw Carmine squatting between two file cabinets, and even though I didn't have a shot on him, I could at least divert the guns from Gary for a moment.

I fired two shots at the cabinets. Gary picked up on it as he fired a round into one of the deck hands standing up and looking my way.

Carmine now panicked, started shooting in my direction too. He then grabbed a hold of Derek and placed him directly in front of him standing up and started yelling obscenities at me and Gary.

Gary was then able to move the rest of the desks away from the hatch and climbed through it to stand in the room looking at both the deck hand and Carmine.

I leaned forward and said, "Carmine, it's over now. Lay down your gun and let Derek free! "

Carmine responded in a very nasty way, "What kind of guy do you think I am bitch? Why would I let your boyfriend live if I can't?"

I tried to reason with Carmine, "Listen, you think that you are making a major change here, then by all means, but what if you aren't?"

Derek's eyes opened wide. He couldn't believe what he was hearing. His feelings for Jack were quite extraordinary, especially after her coming to rescue him, but he felt himself getting upset over her using him for bait. Then Derek moved a little but Carmine grabbed him tighter.

Carmine then said, "I don't think your boyfriend liked that response from you. Maybe I should just kill him now, that way we won't have to deal with him later?"

I nodded and said "Hey whatever Carmine, you seem to have all the cards. What do you want to do?"

Carmine was about to answer when Derek decided that he wasn't going to go down without a fight and pushed himself against Carmine. As this was happening the guard aimed at me and I moved to the right with the chair as my cover. A shot tore through the chair as I aimed and pulled the trigger and the deck hand went down. I had just shot him in the face.

Carmine staggered backwards from Derek's push but regained his step and reached his arm out to shoot Jack, but Gary pointed his gun at him and shot Carmine directly in the forehead.

Carmine dropped to the floor almost on top of Derek.

I ran down the steps and over to pull the now deceased Carmine off Derek.

I turned Derek over and looked into his eyes as I quickly took off the tape from his mouth.

I immediately said to him, "I am sorry Derek for saying all that. I needed to buy time and figure out how to get you out of this mess."

Derek answered, "God, I'm glad. I was wondering why you would have come so far to free me if you didn't at least care a little!"

I smiled and answered, "Maybe just a wee bit!" I kissed him on the side of his face that wasn't swollen. All Derek could do was smile.

Gary came over and helped me pick Derek up off the floor. He said, "Good to have you back Commander. Now I can get back to standing those watches in an office building, instead of traipsing all over the place with this damn P.I.!"

We all laughed and untied Derek. Then we started walking back to the top deck to see what happened to Hu.

When we finally had gotten back up to the bridge we peered down at the pier. Hu was standing there with two squad cars from Boston's finest and he was talking to one of the officers.

After getting back down on the pier we walked over to Hu and the officer.

Hu said, "Tio and his men gave up as soon as they figured they had no place to go unless they picked death." I then called Mr. Kong who phoned the police.

Officer O'Connor said, "Jack, I spoke to your uncle. Tio and his men will more than likely spend a great deal of time in the slammer for kidnapping and attempted murder."

I answered, "I hope you are alright?"

O'Connor nodded his head with that Irish grin asked me, "What about Mr. Ialucci?"

I looked at Hu and then to the Officer and said, "You can find him in the bilge, but he's dead. He didn't opt to live any longer."

With that O'Connor replied, "Thanks, I'll let your Uncle know that you are A-OK."

I nodded and walked to one of the cars waiting for us.

I saw the Officer and his men fan out going onboard the Angelina to retrieve Carmine and the bodies of the other deck hands.

Hu and Gary got back into Hu's car and drove off back to the Mr. Kong's.

Derek and I wandered over to another vehicle, got in and gazed at each other and smiled. Then we looked through the glass of the Ford and watched the light from the morning sun come up over the bay. Today, it was finally going to be a good day, no doubt about it.

CHAPTER 22

After living like kings at Mr. Kong's, Derek and I realized that we needed to get back home.

Captain Stark had given Derek some time off to recoup from his injuries and I didn't have anything too pressing to get to, except maybe missing dogs, so we decided to take the train back to San Diego. It was a glorious trip, one that I would remember my entire life.

Derek and I shared those moments when no words could express how we both felt. We just did not dare try and put pressure on each other. The war was still very real and he had a job to do, just like I had. So, we agreed to be honest about how we felt but also agreed that it was not the best time to be engaged or married, so we enjoyed the days that we had together and for now hoped that in the future we would have more of them.

Back in Los Angeles, Uncle Mike and Aunt Dottie were happy to see me after I returned. We had our regular Sunday dinners, but now I had Derek join me for those wonderful meals.

Chloe was now with her Father in Chinatown. Brad was back at his newspaper desk, writing the local stories of the day. Life was getting back to normal, as much as it could with the War and its news every day.

I wasn't running around involved with the Navy and the War anymore, but Derek and I spent many occasions together and we talked about the war and the efforts of our boys both overseas and here on the home front.

Sometimes I saw some of the "family" members around town and especially at my favorite restaurant, Pasquale's. But I stayed out of their turf and they didn't bother me. I guess somehow they all came to respect me.

On most days now, I spend keeping the Palm Springs crowd happy with finding their missing purses, dogs, boyfriends or whatever. However, in the back of my mind I also realized that the "Circle of Chance" was always in the shadows lurking. I just never knew when it might involve me again.

But for today, well it was another beautiful day in Palm Springs, 83 degrees...